Campaign Trail

J.A. Armstrong

Chapter One

May 2018

"Mom?" Michelle Fletcher poked her head into the governor's office.

Candace Reid lifted her eyes from the screen in front of her and smiled. "Shell," she greeted her daughter. "Come in."

"I didn't want to disturb you."

Candace closed her laptop and made her way around her desk. "You're not disturbing me. What's going on?"

Michelle sighed. "I…"

"Close the door," Candace directed her daughter.

Michelle complied and turned back to her mother. Candace had already taken a seat on the sofa in her office.

"Sit," Candace said.

"If it's a bad time."

"Shell?"

"I don't want to disappoint you. I want to be with you next week…"

Candace smiled. Her campaign for the Democratic nomination was kicking into high gear. She was slated to travel to Iowa on Monday for three days that would include a campaign speech, a town hall meeting, and visits to several local businesses. Michelle had left her position working under Candace's Chief of Staff to help coordinate her mother's campaign.

"Let's have it," Candace urged her daughter.

"Mel managed to get an appointment with the fertility specialist that your friend recommended. It's Tuesday morning. I really don't want her to…"

Candace held up her hand. "Family first, Shell."

"I know, Mom, but this is family too, and it's an important trip. It's laying the groundwork and face it; Senator Keyes is revving up support."

"George Keyes is a personable politician, Shell. He's also experienced and capable. That's not surprising at all."

"Maybe so, but he might present a bigger challenge to you in the primaries than people expect."

"Which people?" Candace grinned.

"Mom…"

"This is part of how the game is played, Shell. George is a friend. He'll test my resolve, and I will test his patience," Candace chuckled. "In the end, one of us will step up to support the other. For now, we will press each other on the issues that we don't completely agree on."

"You don't seem concerned," Michelle observed.

"Concerned? No. I'm aware; aware that George is a formidable candidate. I'm not the only game in town, Shell, nor should I be. There's a reason we have primaries."

"I should be with you."

"You should be with your wife," Candace disagreed. She watched as Michelle shook her head despondently. "Shell," Candace called for her daughter's attention. "Campaigns come and go," she continued. "Lots of things happen in life, and unfortunately many things and people come and then go. You need to stay focused on the one who stays."

Michelle sighed. She felt torn—torn between supporting the woman who had supported her for a lifetime and being present for the woman she hoped to spend the rest of her life with.

Candace smiled. "It's just a campaign stop."

"No, it isn't," Michelle replied.

"It is. And, there will be many more. Trust me, Shell there will be a time when I need you there."

Michelle chuckled. "So, you don't need me, huh?"

"I'd love to have you with me."

"Um-hum, so that someone can keep the press away from JD?"

"That is helpful," Candace winked. "Believe it or not, I value your insights," she admitted. "You look surprised."

"Maybe I am."

"I would never have brought you into this world if I didn't believe you had the talent for it."

"I know."

"I've told you before; you need to trust me. This time, not just as your mother, but as your boss."

Michelle laughed. "I could fly in for Tuesday night."

"You could. You don't need to. Go with Mel," Candace said.

"You just want another grandbaby."

Candace winked. She would never deny the truth in Michelle's statement. She patted her daughter's knee and made her way back to her feet.

"Mom?"

"Hum?"

"Is everything else okay?"

Candace smiled. "Everything is fine, Shell—insane, but fine; I promise."

Michelle nodded. She had worked in her mother's administration long enough to have developed a sense of when Governor Reid's mind was preoccupied.

"Mom?"

"There are always twenty irons in the fire, Shell. And, most of the time it isn't any one of them that end up commanding my time. You know that."

"Anything I can help with?"

"Not this time," Candace replied.

"If I can...."

"You'll be the first to know."

"JD?" Jonah called to his step-mother.

"Hey, Jonah."

"Got a minute?"

Jameson nodded and beckoned Jonah to enter her office. "What's up?"

"It's the Mason Medical account," he began.

Jameson gestured for Jonah to have a seat. "What about it?"

"JD, I don't see any way that we can meet their deadlines."

"Did they push up the timeline?"

"If Don McGillis had his way it would've been ready a week ago."

Jameson considered the information silently for a moment. She had handed the majority of her architectural firm's business over to her step-son and daughter-in-law's care. Jameson had not once regretted the decision. Jonah and Melanie McKenna were both intelligent and talented. Melanie was a gifted architect with a strong command of engineering principles that complimented her artistic ability. Jonah was a civil engineer with a head for business and a feel for people that made him a natural leader. While she consulted on most of the projects the firm undertook, it had been a couple of years since she had immersed herself in any one project fully. She accepted a folder from Jonah and opened it.

Jameson laid out the copies of the initial architectural sketches and studied them thoughtfully. Sensing that Jonah was both concerned and frustrated, Jameson took considerable time in her study of the drawings. She toyed with her bottom lip between her teeth and reached for a pencil. Jameson shook her head, made a few notes on the papers in front of her, tapped her pencil against her forehead, and jotted down a few more notes. She placed the papers back in the folder and handed it to Jonah.

Jonah opened the folder and scanned Jameson's notes. He smiled and looked across the desk at Jameson. "JD, we need you on this one."

"No, you don't," JD disagreed.

"Yeah, we do. Look at this. In less than ten minutes you've reset three issues that we've been haggling over for a week."

Jameson shrugged. "I've been at this a while," she reminded him.

Jonah shook his head. Jameson's statement was true. Jameson's humility was not false, but Jonah wondered if his stepmother realized just how talented she was. Jameson Reid was an exceptional architect. She was also a savvy business-woman; something that Jameson rarely gave herself credit for. Jonah ran his hand over his face in frustration.

"Jonah," Jameson called for his attention. "You don't need me on this."

"Yeah, JD; I do," he looked at her.

Jameson took a deep breath and exhaled slowly. "Talk to me," she implored him.

"It's not the plans."

"Okay?"

"It's McGillis. No matter what we throw at him he's not satisfied, but he still wants it fixed yesterday."

Jameson smiled. "He's testing you."

"I'm failing."

"Let me see everything you have," Jameson said. Jonah looked up hopefully. "All of it. I'll look it over this weekend and see what I can come up with."

"JD, I..."

"Just get it to me before I leave at four."

Jonah nodded and made his way to the door.

"And, Jonah?"

"Yeah?"

"I'm not doing this because I think you need me."

Jonah nodded and left Jameson's office.

Jameson groaned. "Shit."

———————

Marianne laughed the moment she walked into the living room. Spencer and Cooper had constructed a fort of some type. Marianne could not imagine what the rickety display was meant to resemble. She was confident that they would explain their creation soon enough.

"Aaaheeem," Marianne cleared her throat, determined to keep a straight face. Her determination was immediately tested when Cooper emerged wearing a hard hat that was too big for him.

"Hi, Marianne!" Cooper greeted his big sister.

Marianne lifted a pale eyebrow at the youngster. "Coop," she addressed him. "I see you and Spencer have been hard at work." She covered her mouth to keep from laughing when her son emerged from behind his friend. "Spencer?"

"Hi, Mom!"

"Hi, Mom?" Marianne raised her brow a tad higher. "Just what are you two up to in here?"

Cooper looked at his feet. Spencer stepped out in front of his mother and held her gaze. "We is building a hospital."

"You are building a hospital?" she asked.

"Yep," Cooper answered.

Spencer held up a finger, dove into the mess of blankets, pillows, and bed sheets that were precariously secured to the corners of the couch, a chair, a loveseat, and two end tables. Marianne waited for him to appear again. He peered out from under a dinosaur bed sheet and handed his mother some papers.

Marianne accepted them and grinned.

"What on earth is going on in here?" a voice carried into the room.

Cooper's face immediately lit up and he ran toward the sound. "Mommy!" he yelled.

Candace was glad she had managed to set down her bag before Cooper landed against her with a thud. She leaned over and kissed the curls atop his head. "Hello, sweetie."

"Nana!" Spencer slid in his socks toward his grandmother.

Candace chuckled. "I thought I was in the wrong house for a minute," she teased them, referencing their creation.

"It appears we have a hospital taking shape in our living room," Marianne explained.

Candace nodded. "I see."

Cooper and Spencer looked at Candace proudly. "Yep, Nana," Spencer said. "Me and Coop built it."

"All by yourself?"

"Nope," Cooper replied.

"No? Did Marianne help you?" Candace guessed.

"Nope," Cooper shook his head. "Momma did."

"Momma did?" Candace was surprised. She had just spoken to Jameson on the phone. As far as she knew, Jameson was at least a few minutes behind her.

Marianne held up the papers the boys had given her for Candace to inspect. Candace stifled a chuckle. Jameson had given Cooper and Spencer some of her old architectural drawings to play with. The boys loved to visit Jameson's office and sit at the drafting tables, pretending to design buildings like Jameson did. They had apparently decided to take their skills to a new level.

"My goodness," Candace said. She followed Cooper and Spencer to their makeshift hospital. "Look at this."

"See, Mommy?" Cooper pointed to an opening. He pointed to Jameson's drawing. "That's the door!"

"Come on, Nana!" Spencer pulled on Candace's hand lightly.

Marianne smiled as she watched her mother drop to her knees and follow the two boys inside their makeshift building. She was certain few people would imagine a candidate for President of the United States climbing through blankets and furniture on the living room floor—in a business suit no less. "No one would believe it," she muttered affectionately.

"Believe what?" Jameson asked as she walked in from the kitchen.

"Your wife," Marianne turned to Jameson.

"Where is my wife? She said she was almost here when I talked to her a few minutes ago."

Marianne had just started to point toward the fort on the floor when Candace's head poked out.

Jameson smirked.

"Hi, honey," Candace greeted her wife.

"Uh-huh," Jameson replied. "Do I want to know?"

Cooper crawled out beside Candace. "Hi, Momma."

"Hi, Coop."

"We built your hospital," he told her.

"You built my hospital?" Jameson asked. Marianne handed Jameson the drawings in her hand. Jameson nodded. "Wow. You followed these all on your own?"

"Yep!" Cooper said. "Me and Spen."

"I see. Is Mommy your patient?" she asked.

JA ARMSTRONG

"No," Cooper giggled.

"Nana is Gubenor, Jay Jay," Spencer emerged from the other side.

"Oh, then why is she in the hospital?" Jameson asked.

"Cause she has to in'pect it, Jay Jay," Spencer said with a roll of his eyes.

"Ah, I see," Jameson nodded. She held out her hand to Candace. "So, Governor?"

Candace made her way to her feet and smoothed her skirt. "Excellent job," she praised the construction team.

Cooper and Spencer offered each other a high five.

"In fact, I think we should celebrate and all go out for pizza," Candace suggested.

Jameson was genuinely surprised by Candace's overture. She tipped her head in questioning. Candace offered her a wink.

"Pizza!" Cooper jumped up.

"Okay," Marianne stepped in to calm the boys. "Let's go upstairs and get you two builders ready."

"Pizza?" Jameson asked Candace, taking a step closer. Candace shrugged. "What are you up to?"

"Well, we have to do something to ensure the demolition team is ready," Candace replied.

"Bribery?" Jameson shook her head playfully. "I thought you were above that, Governor Reid."

"Did you?" Candace asked, stepping into Jameson's arms. "You are the one with all the plans," Candace gestured to the boys' creation.

"What do you think of my plans?" Jameson flirted. "Are they up to snuff?"

10

Candace considered the question for a moment. "They did manage to get me down on my knees," she teased her wife. Jameson nearly choked. Candace laughed. "You are so easy sometimes."

Jameson pulled Candace closer. "Oh, yeah? We'll just see how easy I am."

Candace looked in Jameson's eyes and sighed. "I missed you."

"I missed you too," Jameson replied, placing a tender kiss on Candace's lips.

"Mmm. Have any other plans that need inspecting?" Candace asked.

"I'm certain I can come up with something."

Jameson walked into the bedroom and found Candace sitting on the bed perusing some papers. Candace was lost in contemplation, and Jameson was content to observe from a slight distance. She had enjoyed the evening with the family over pizza. Candace had only begun to travel for her campaign and Jameson already missed her. Between the obligations of being the governor and the structuring of a presidential campaign, it seemed that Candace's work schedule had gone from eighteen hour days and twenty-four hours on call to twenty-five hours each day. Jameson sighed.

"Worried that wall isn't secure?" Candace asked without looking up from the paper in her hand. She heard Jameson sigh again and looked up over her glasses. Candace smiled, placed the paper in her hand beside her and patted the bed.

Jameson made her way over and plopped down beside her wife.

"Want to talk about it?" Candace asked.

"Not really."

Candace moved the papers that sat on the bed to the table beside it, took off her glasses and placed them on top of her work. She turned and hovered over Jameson. "Is there anything I can do?"

Jameson's eyes twinkled with mischief. She reached up and brushed Candace's hair aside. It continually amazed her; the way that Candace could make her heart race with nothing more than an exchanged glance. She smiled. "Thank you."

"Thank me? What did I do?" Candace wondered.

"I think you know," Jameson answered. She guided Candace's lips to hers.

Jameson lost her breath instantly. She had intended to place an affectionate kiss on Candace's lips. The moment she felt Candace draw closer, Jameson lost herself. She lifter her hands to hold Candace's face as their kiss deepened gently. Jameson's hands moved from Candace's face to her back, pulling her closer with urgency.

Candace gentled the kiss and pulled back slowly. "I missed you too," she whispered. Jameson's eyes were still closed. Candace softly ran a fingertip over Jameson's eyelids. "Jameson."

Jameson opened her eyes and smiled up at Candace. "I love you."

Candace smiled back. "I love you."

Jameson touched Candace's cheek and her eyes closed again. Candace watched, overwhelmed by the love that coursed between them. There were many moments when Candace found herself wishing that life were less hectic—simpler. She studied Jameson's features as if looking at her wife for the first time. She leaned in and claimed Jameson's lips with a possessive kiss.

"I do," Candace whispered in Jameson's ear as her lips drifted to Jameson's neck. "I love you so much, Jameson."

Jameson's hands lifted Candace's shirt, seeking the softness of Candace's skin. She pushed Candace away gently. When she opened her eyes, she found Candace's brow raised playfully. Jameson lifted hers in challenge. Candace understood the silent request and removed her shirt. She looked down at Jameson and grinned. Her fingers set about the task of unbuttoning Jameson's blouse slowly.

Jameson's hands massaged Candace's sides, traveling sensually up and down the softness of Candace's ribs. She desperately wanted to touch Candace's breasts, to feel Candace pressed against her. More than that, Jameson desired to make love with Candace slowly. She often felt urgency build within her when Candace was close. Candace's touch—touching Candace aroused a myriad of intoxicating emotions and physical sensations in Jameson. The slightest brush of Candace's fingertips across Jameson's flesh could make Jameson crave release. Touches and kisses often grew insistent between them, but neither ever sought to rush their lovemaking.

Candace pushed open Jameson's blouse and let her hand glide across the swell of Jameson's breasts. She leaned in and brushed her lips over the hollow of Jameson's throat, allowing her kisses to fall sensually lower.

"Candace," Jameson exhaled slowly and let her eyes flutter closed.

Candace delighted in the way Jameson felt beneath her. Jameson's hands moved up and down Candace's back tenderly.

"Jameson," Candace whispered. She waited until Jameson's eyes opened to meet hers. She smiled lovingly at her wife. When—Candace wondered, would Jameson stop looking at her this way? She was positive that she could never tire of looking at Jameson, of touching Jameson. Candace sometimes wished that she and Jameson could disappear into one of these moments forever. Making love with Jameson had always been sublime. Jameson's arms were Candace's home. Here, Jameson looking up at her with so many unspoken thoughts and feelings glistening in her eyes, Candace felt both safety and exhilaration.

Candace placed a soft kiss on Jameson's lips. "I've missed you."

Jameson directed Candace's lips back to hers and kissed her reverently. "I need you," she confessed.

Candace's heart raced. She marveled at the way Jameson managed to make her feel like a teenager in love. For many years, Candace had resigned herself to the belief that heart racing, skin tingling anticipation was impossible to maintain in a relationship. Jameson had shattered that notion completely and forever. She directed Jameson to sit up, removed Jameson's blouse, and gently pushed Jameson back on the bed.

"You have me," Candace promised.

Jameson's fingertip traced the outline of Candace's lips. She lost her breath when Candace's tongue circled her finger sensually. Her eyes met Candace's darkened gaze and she sighed.

Candace smiled. She placed a light kiss on Jameson's forehead and then claimed Jameson's lips with hers. The moment Jameson's searching became desperate, Candace pulled back. "I'm right here," she promised Jameson. "Look at me."

Jameson took a deep breath and opened her eyes.

Candace's fingertip delicately traced over Jameson's brow. "Stay with me," she requested.

Jameson bit her lower lip gently as Candace's mouth tasted the flesh of her neck. In an instant, Candace's gaze returned to meet Jameson's. Jameson reached out to pull Candace to her and Candace resisted. Wordlessly, Candace removed the rest of her clothing, then Jameson's. She smiled, leaned in and kissed Jameson lovingly. "Stay with me," she repeated her request.

Jameson fought to steady her breathing as Candace pulled away slowly and began to move sensually against her. Her hands reached out seeking Candace's breasts. Candace took hold of them and kissed the palm of each of Jameson's hands.

"Easy," Candace said. "Just feel me."

Jameson groaned in frustration. "That's what I was trying to do."

Candace snickered and cocked her eyebrow. Jameson's frustration was palpable. Candace leaned down and placed her lips just above Jameson's. "What do you want?" she asked.

Jameson's breath hitched and her heart skipped erratically.

"Jameson?"

"I need to touch you," Jameson said.

Candace sat back and resumed her movement against Jameson. She lifted Jameson's hands and placed them over her breasts. She smiled when Jameson moaned appreciatively. Desire burned in her veins as Jameson's fingers danced over her body. Candace held Jameson's gaze. She felt Jameson's need as it began to swell. She was tempted to put an end to both their suffering immediately, but something deeper seemed to be calling her. She had missed Jameson. Life was chaotic for them both. Candace had a million fires to put out and a million more balls in the air to juggle. She had not meant to be distant, but exhaustion had plagued her the last few weeks. After a long day of dealing with state business, intermixed with the realities of heading a presidential campaign, Candace would return home to the excitement of a five-year-old boy who demanded her attention. Sleep had become irregular. Jameson had expressed some concern that Candace was not getting enough rest. There had been several nights when Jameson had taken the papers from Candace's lap, removed the glasses from her face, and ordered Candace to get some rest. Candace was tired, but what she wanted—what she needed now more than anything else was to lose herself in Jameson.

Jameson sighed when Candace's fingertips brushed across her nipples. "Jesus," Jameson moaned.

Candace's hips continued their slow pace. Her eyes closed and she gasped when Jameson sat up and covered her breasts with a flurry of kisses.

"God!" Candace cried out. She fell into Jameson, her hands barely able to support her weight.

Jameson's hands dropped to Candace's backside and pulled her impossibly closer. Without warning, she felt Candace's lips cover hers. Jameson lost herself in Candace's kiss as both their bodies began to shake. A wave of ecstasy thundered through Jameson's body. She felt her body rise to meet Candace's as their kiss deepened further, swallowing both their cries.

Candace's head fell onto Jameson's shoulder. She held onto Jameson as if her life depended on it.

"Candace," Jameson whispered. "Candace," she repeated when she felt the warmth of Candace's tears bathe her neck. "Hey," Jameson called. She pulled away slightly and took hold of Candace's face. "Why are you crying?"

"I don't know," Candace confessed.

Jameson wiped the tears from Candace's cheeks and smiled. It wasn't the first time that making love had broken an emotional dam for one of them. She kissed Candace's forehead. "You're exhausted."

"I missed you," Candace said again.

"I know. I missed you too."

"I'm sorry, Jameson."

"Sorry?" Jameson was puzzled. "What are you sorry for?"

"I haven't made enough time for you—for us."

"Not true," Jameson disagreed. "We both knew that this would be hard; that it would put greater demands on your time. It's okay," she promised.

"It's not okay."

"Candace..."

"It's not," Candace said. "I can't do this without you."

"I'm here."

"I know," Candace replied. "But, I need to make the time for us, Jameson."

"I don't want you to worry about me."

"I will always worry about you," Candace said. "And, it isn't just for you. I need you. I don't mean just like this, but this is part of it."

Jameson tucked a strand of hair behind Candace's ear and smiled. They endured a great deal of teasing from family about their obvious affection for one another. Michelle had dubbed their private life "Bible Study." Jameson often found it amusing that Candace's children seemed to have some idea that Jameson and Candace were writing their own erotica. The truth was, they spent far more nights sleeping in a quiet embrace than they ever had making passionate love. When they did come together, it was always intense. Making love with Candace had always been about communicating the connection Jameson felt to her wife. Desire and lust colored those moments, but what made their intimate life exhilarating was the emotion that coursed between them. There were moments when those feelings went so far beyond words that the only way they could be expressed was through touch.

"I understand," Jameson promised. "I missed you too." She pulled Candace into her arms and felt Candace release a long, deep breath. "Do you want to talk about it?"

"Yes," Candace said. "I want to talk about everything. Not now," she said. "I just want to be here with you without anyone or anything else creeping between us."

Jameson closed her eyes. "Nothing has ever crept between us," she said. "I know it feels that way some days, but it hasn't."

"Thank you."

Jameson kissed Candace's head. "Thank you."

"For what? Being absent?"

"You're never absent," Jameson put the thought to rest. "That's why you're so wiped out. I'm going to be here no matter what. So, don't worry if you need…"

"What I need is you." Candace nestled closer to Jameson.

"Are you regretting that you launched this campaign?"

Candace sighed. "No; are you?"

"No."

"Are you sure?"

"Positive. You know," Jameson began. "You know how you will tell me to stay with you when we are making love?"

"Yes?"

"You need to trust that I am with you. I'm always there, even if I'm not standing with you."

"Yes, you are. I love you, Jameson."

"I love you too. Get some sleep."

"I promise you; when things settle down a little, I will make this up to you."

Jameson chuckled.

"Why is that funny?"

"I love you. When things settle down?" Jameson laughed. "You do remember who is in our family; right?"

Candace chuckled. "Point taken."

"Stop worrying," Jameson said. "Get some sleep."

"Think I need it?" Candace teased.

"Yes."

Candace closed her eyes. Jameson's hands ran softly over her back. She sighed in contentment. "Love you."

Jameson let her eyes fall shut. "Thank God."

Chapter Two

"What are you doing?" Candace asked.

Jameson lifted her head from the plans she had spread across the kitchen table. "Jonah asked me to look at something."

Candace's gaze narrowed. She grabbed Jameson's empty mug from the table and moved to refill it. "What time did you get up?" she asked as she set the mug back in front of Jameson.

"Thanks," Jameson said. "About five."

"You've been up since five a.m.?"

Jameson shrugged and took a sip from her coffee. "God, I needed that."

Candace grinned.

"I look like I needed it, huh?"

"Why were you up so early?"

"I wanted to put this to bed so that I could have the rest of the weekend with you and Coop."

Candace poured herself a cup of coffee and took a seat across from Jameson. "Problems?"

Jameson shook her head. "No. I just wish Jonah would trust himself."

Candace nodded. "He's been on edge lately."

"You noticed it too?" Jameson asked.

"A little. I think that Laura's pregnancy has him a bit nervous."

"Why?" Jameson asked. "Is something wrong?"

"Not wrong," Candace said.

"Candace?"

Candace sighed heavily. "Her blood pressure is a little high."

"Yeah, I wonder why," Jameson drawled.

"I'm sure some of it has to do with her father," Candace said.

"Is she in danger of losing the baby?"

"No," Candace said.

"You're worried."

"Not worried," Candace replied. "Aware."

"Why didn't you say something?"

"To be honest, I thought Jonah would have told you, and with us passing each other…"

"I can't believe he didn't say anything."

"He doesn't want to worry you about it," Candace smiled. "She'll be okay, Jameson. I just think it's an added layer for Jonah. He worries about disappointing you."

"Me?"

"Yes, you," Candace laughed. "Come on, Jameson. You know that."

Jameson shook her head. "That's crazy."

"Why? You worry about disappointing your parents."

"Not the same."

"Why is that?"

"Candace… Geez… Jonah could never disappoint me."

Candace smiled. "Maybe remind him of that."

Jameson looked at the plans in front of her. "I need to cut them loose."

"What?" Candace asked.

Jameson shook her head. "Candace, I need to let them buy me out of the firm."

Candace set down her coffee mug and took a deep breath. "Jameson…"

"We both know that I'm right. My presence is only going to complicate things for Jonah and Mel."

Candace sighed. She knew Jameson was right, but she also felt a sense of guilt about Jameson's appraisal of the situation. Jameson's architectural firm had a history of receiving government contracts. She'd designed buildings for the State of Arkansas, Texas, Maryland, Massachusetts, and New York. She'd largely recused herself from the business when Candace assumed the role of governor. Now, with Candace running for the presidency, the situation had grown more complicated. It would be tricky negotiating contracts for Jonah and Melanie as it was. Jonah was Candace's son and Melanie her daughter-in-law. However, they had a right to conduct their business despite Candace's aspirations. Jameson differed. She was married to Candace. That was already a point of contention for many people. Jameson had hoped to keep her hands at least partially on the reins until the Democratic primaries had been wrapped up. That was still more than a year in the future. It was already evident to Jameson that the time had come.

"It's time, Candace."

"Jameson…"

Jameson smiled. "I'm okay with it if that's what you're worried about."

"I don't want you to give up…"

"We both know this was inevitable."

"It's still a long road. You can bide your time…"

"No," Jameson disagreed. "And, it's not just what is best for your campaign. It's what is best for Jonah."

"For Jonah?"

"Right. He doesn't need me, and neither does Mel. Don't look at me like that. They don't. They are ten times more capable than I was at their age. And, they have each other. They'll be fine."

"And, what about you?"

"I have plenty of things to fill my time," Jameson said.

"Is that so?"

"Yeah. I have some projects I've been wanting to do here."

"More projects?" Candace grinned.

Jameson shrugged. "Besides," she said. "I want to be able to be with you when your travel takes off."

Candace smiled. "Are you sure this is what you want to do?"

"Yeah, I'm sure."

"You know that Jonah will fight you on this?"

"Well, he doesn't have a choice. He can either buy me out of the business or I'll just sign the whole damn thing over to them. And, we both know he will never go for that."

"Sneaky architect," Candace teased.

"I thought I was a snarky architect?"

"Sometimes."

Jameson laughed.

"Mommy," Cooper walked into the kitchen rubbing the sleep from his eyes.

"Good morning, sweetheart," Candace greeted him.

Cooper sleepily made his way to Candace and crawled into her lap.

"Still tired?" Candace asked. Cooper nodded. "Do you want some breakfast?"

"Can we watch Aladdin?"

"Aladdin, huh?" Candace asked. She smiled. *He finally pronounced it correctly.* "Do you want to watch Aladdin and I will make some pancakes?" she asked him. He nodded.

"Come on, Coop," Jameson pushed out her chair and held out her hand.

Candace watched as Cooper made his way to Jameson. She shook her head affectionately. *How did I end up with one son ready to give me another grandchild, and one son still addicted to Disney movies?* She laughed at her reality. *Only you, Candace.*

—————————

Jonah walked into his mother's office to find Jameson sitting behind the desk. "Uh-oh, am I grounded?" he joked.

"Why? Did you forget to take out the garbage again?" she bantered.

"Ha-ha. I'll make sure Laura never tells you my dirty little secrets again."

Jameson winked. "Sit down." She handed Jonah a folder.

"What's this?"

Jameson took a deep breath. "Before you open that, I want you to listen to what I have to say."

"JD?"

"I talked to Mel earlier."

"Were the plans that bad?" he asked.

"Jonah," Jameson shook her head. "The plans were excellent. I told you; McGillis is testing you—not your talent, your balls—for lack of a better way to put it."

"JD, he's…"

Jameson held her hand up. "Save it. You don't need me for this account. And, that is a good thing because you are not going to have me in any official capacity soon."

"What are you talking about?"

"I'm leaving the firm completely."

"JD! It's your firm."

Jameson smiled. "Not anymore," she said.

"What are you talking about?"

"Jonah, listen to me; I can't stay involved in the firm. It's bad for the firm and it's not good for your mom."

"For Mom? You mean because of my asshole father-in-law?"

"Lawson Klein is not the only detractor your mom faces. And, no—it is not only because of the Lawson Kleins in the world." She sighed and shook her head. "I can't keep dividing my attention."

Jonah was puzzled.

"I miss her, Jonah," Jameson said. "I don't want to be apart from her for long periods if I don't have to. Sometimes, we will have to be. I just…"

Jonah smiled. He marveled at his mother's marriage to Jameson. He aspired to what they shared. He also knew that at times, being married to his mother had to be a challenge. Being related to his mother could be a challenge. "I think I understand. She needs you."

"No," Jameson said. "I need her. The truth is, Jonah, I built that firm as much as I could. My heart isn't in it anymore. I'd rather be building something."

"What are you going to do? I mean, JD, I love you, but I can't see you just following Mom all over creation for the next however many years."

Jameson chuckled. She would happily follow Candace all over creation for the rest of her life. Candace would never allow it. And, as much as she sincerely wanted more time with her wife, Jameson also knew that she needed to have something for herself. "I have some ideas," she said.

"So? You want us to buy you out?" he guessed.

"No," Jameson said. "I want to hand it over to you and Mel, but I know you won't accept that."

"No way," he said.

"So, then yes—I would like you to buy me out."

Jonah opened the folder and sighed. "You know, this isn't what me or Mel want?"

"I know. It's what you need as much as it's what I need," Jameson replied.

"Are you sure?" Jonah asked.

"I am."

"JD?"

"Yeah?"

"Do you think she'll win?"

"Your mom?"

He nodded.

Jameson smiled. "She wouldn't be running if she didn't think so."

He laughed. "I'm sorry about Laura's dad. I..."

"We've been over this a million times," Jameson said.

"Yeah, but he's bankrolling this crusade against Mom with Jed Ritchie."

Jameson shrugged. "Your mom can handle those buffoons."

"JD, they are…"

"Trust me, Jonah. Trust your mom."

He nodded. "So? When do you want to do this?"

"Yesterday," Jameson replied. "You go over the documents. Make sure that you think it's fair. You and Mel will be equal partners if you agree."

"And you?"

"Oh, I'm sure I can find some things to occupy my time."

"You look tired," Dana observed. "Are you up to this trip to Iowa?"

"I'm fine, Dana," Candace said. "Cooper was up with a nightmare."

"So much for a restful weekend, huh?"

Candace shrugged. "Actually, it was the most restful weekend I've had in a while. So? Let's get the group in here and cross our T's and dot our I's before I need to board a plane."

"You okay?" Michelle asked Melanie.

"Nervous."

Michelle clasped her wife's hand. "Nervous about spending a couple of days with me or about seeing this specialist?'

Melanie laughed, but then sighed.

"I know how badly you want this to work out," Michelle said.

"I do."

"I know. Let's just see what they say; okay? You know, there might be options we haven't thought of."

Melanie nodded. "I don't want to disappoint you."

"Me?" Michelle was genuinely surprised. "Mel, what on earth are you talking about? How would you disappoint me? I mean, hell—I would think I should be the one worried."

"Why?"

"You want to have kids with me? You live with me. Someone might say you need your head checked."

Melanie shook her head. She appreciated Michelle's attempt at levity. She also knew that Michelle's self-deprecating comment held a nugget of honest insecurity. "Stop," she said. "You will be a terrific mom, Shell."

"I hope so."

"I know so," Melanie said. She leaned in and kissed Michelle's cheek. "You are the only person who has any doubt at all."

Michelle smiled. She felt Melanie's grip tighten on her hand. She did have her doubts. She believed that she was a good sister. Michelle felt confident that she was a trustworthy friend and a loving daughter—a mother? Could she be someone's mother? She'd watched her mother and

Marianne. She'd spent hours observing Jameson with Cooper. Somebody's mother? What if she screwed that up?

"Ms. McKenna?" a voice called.

"That's us," Melanie said.

Michelle took a deep breath. *Me as somebody's mom? I think I need to talk to Marianne.*

———

Candace listened carefully to her staff as they ran down a list of issues that were likely to land on her plate. Some days the list seemed endless. A budget that needed to be passed pronto, a predicted heat wave rested on the horizon that was expected tp present danger for the elderly and the homeless, an infrastructure project that was running behind schedule, and of course, a serial killer on the loose. *Iowa?* Candace massaged her temple. *Oh, is that all?* The beep of her phone's intercom stifled the conversation in her office.

"Yes, Susan?"

"Sorry to disturb you, Governor. You have a call from Agent Toles."

Candace wasn't sure whether she should be grateful for the reprieve or apprehensive about the reason. She looked at her staff. "We are where we are. Keep me apprised. I mean it. I will be accessible unless I am on the stage," she told them, leaving no room for debate. She watched as her press secretary nodded and closed the door. "Put her through, Susan. Alex?"

"Governor."

"Why do I have the feeling this call is not an invitation for dinner?"

"Probably because in that case, it would be Cass calling you."

Candace chuckled. "Something I need to know?"

"Actually, no—something I need your help with."

"I'm listening."

"I'm not sure you are going to like it."

"Alex, I don't like ninety percent of the things I get told. You wouldn't be calling me unless it mattered. I told you; whatever you need to let me know. So? Let's have it."

"Okay. Here it is: I need to get something out to the press indiscreetly."

Candace took a deep breath. She'd known Agent Alex Toles for years, and she trusted Alex's judgment. If Alex was asking to leak something, she had a good reason.

"I'm listening," Candace said.

"Look, I am still not a hundred percent certain what is going on," Alex confessed. "You said that you didn't want to meet again to review a body count."

"I don't. And, this conversation is not instilling confidence."

"I know; I'm sorry. It's a possibility—a possibility, that there might be two killers."

Candace was stunned. "You're joking?"

"I wish I was."

"And, you want that leaked to the press? Why?"

"Because, if there aren't, he won't want to share any credit. That's his pattern."

Candace placed her glasses on her desk and rubbed her eyes. *Shit.* "You want to try and flush him out."

"Yes."

"Alex," Candace began cautiously. "Won't that make him more eager?"

"Maybe," Alex confessed. "He's already eager, Candace. Where his focus is—that's what I'm not sure of."

"Are you sure this is the only way?"

"No," Alex said. "It's a chance. That's all it is."

"But, you think it's a chance worth taking," Candace surmised.

"I think he's not done and I think he's been at this a long time."

"And if there are two?" Candace asked.

"I hope one is isolated."

"Hope? Are you telling me you honestly believe there could be two serial killers?" Candace asked.

"I'm telling you that it's possible. Look, that scenario's a stretch, but I can't rule it out. I need to rule it in or out. The clock is ticking for someone."

Candace sighed. "Tell me what you need."

"Candace, if this is too risky for you politically..."

"My political career doesn't trump anyone's life, Alex."

"Do you think you can do it without anyone knowing where it came from?" Alex asked.

Candace grinned. There were always risks when attempting to use the media. After years in politics, Candace had more than a few trusted allies within the press, particularly locally. Dana had been on Candace's staff for nearly fifteen years. Dana understood the ins and outs, which alliances to tap and when, and most importantly how to float a story without anyone divulging a source. "Send me what you have," she told Alex.

32

"Thanks."

"You can thank me by putting this to rest."

"Working on it," Alex promised.

"Work faster."

Alex chuckled. "Understood, Governor."

Candace disconnected the call and let her face fall into her hands. "What else can happen?"

———

"So, you're making the trip with Candy?" Pearl asked Jameson.

Jameson took a final sip from her coffee cup. "On my way to Albany in a few minutes. Assuming I can pry Coop from the TV that is."

Pearl regarded Jameson thoughtfully.

Jameson put her cup in the dishwasher and turned to find Pearl staring at her expectantly. "What?" Jameson asked. "Do I have egg on my face or something?"

"Or something."

Jameson sighed. "Since when do you not say what you're thinking?"

Pearl smiled. "Oh, you'd be surprised how often I keep my thoughts to myself."

Jameson leaned back against the counter. "But there is something you want to say. Let's hear it."

"What are you going to do?" Pearl asked.

"I'm not sure I understand the question."

"It's pretty simple, Jameson—what are you going to do? Are you planning to follow Candy around blindly for the next however many years?'

Jameson sighed. "Jonah talked to you."

"No."

"Candace..."

"Candy mentioned that you were planning on signing over your firm to Jonah and Melanie entirely."

"And that's surprising because?"

"I'm not surprised," Pearl replied. "Have you thought that all the way through?"

"I have," Jameson answered. "Pearl, you know better than most what Candace needs right now. This is what I signed up for."

"What's that again?" Pearl asked.

"Pearl..."

"Jameson, I want you to listen to me. I know that you want to support Candy." She saw Jameson mounting an argument and held up her hand. "Don't say anything until you have heard me out."

Jameson nodded.

"I also know that you will miss her. I do know that. But, you are a young woman. Politics are not your passion. We both know that. What are you going to do if she wins?" Pearl asked. "Play First Lady all day long? That is not you."

Jameson sighed. She'd given her decision more thought than anyone might imagine—anyone but Candace. Pearl's concerns made sense. In fact, Candace had expressed those same concerns before Jameson had asked Jonah to speak with her. She nodded again. "No," Jameson said. "Politics aren't my passion at all," she admitted. "Candace is."

"Jameson..."

"Listen," Jameson shook her head. "Candace is my wife, Pearl."

"Yes, I know."

"If she makes it through this campaign I will be the first lesbian married to the president. That's not lost on me," she said.

"I know that too," Pearl said. "I don't want you to lose yourself. Jameson, you are barely forty. Whether you think so or not, that is barely beginning in life; trust me on that."

Jameson smiled. "If we are all so lucky to have your health."

"My point is that you need to take care of you if you hope to take care of Candy."

Jameson chuckled.

"That's funny?"

"No. That's exactly what Candace said."

"She's right."

Jameson took a deep breath. "Pearl," she began and then stopped to take another deep breath. "I think you and Candace worry too much about me sometimes."

"Is that so?"

"Yeah, it is. The truth is, I haven't been taking much of a role back at the office in more than a year. Jonah and Mel are running it. Will I miss it? Probably. I probably will miss it at times. I never wanted that to be my entire life," she explained. "You know me. I'd rather be building what Mel draws than designing something for someone else to build."

"I hate to break this to you, but I don't think they're going to give you carte blanche at The White House."

Jameson shrugged. "I don't expect they will if we end up there."

"So? Then what do you expect?" Pearl challenged.

"I'm not sure what to expect. That's the truth. Not much in my life has ended up the way I expected it," she observed candidly. "I never thought I would get married. I certainly never expected to be somebody's mom. And, there is no way I thought my wife might be president one day. I'm not even sure which of those things surprise me the most. Leaving the firm? That doesn't surprise me in the slightest."

Pearl was intrigued. "You have something cooking up there; I can see it."

Jameson's eyes twinkled. "I do."

"Care to share?"

"Not just yet," Jameson said. "When I'm ready, you will be the first to know."

"Me?"

"Yeah," Jameson said. "You and Mom. I'm going to need your input and your help."

"Let me give you a piece of advice before you even begin."

"What's that?"

"Make sure it doesn't involve too many tall ladders."

Jameson laughed. "I'm not sure I can make that promise."

Pearl shook her head and laughed. "Why does that not surprise me? Well, if campaigning with Candy doesn't kill you first, she might do it herself when you share this idea of yours."

"Maybe," Jameson agreed.

Pearl laughed harder.

"What?" Jameson asked.

"I just wonder how the Secret Service will cope with you climbing in trees."

Jameson winked. She made her way over to Pearl and kissed her on the cheek. "Thanks for looking out for me," she whispered and then headed out of the kitchen.

Pearl shook her head. "Oh boy. Candy thinks she has her hands full now? God help us."

———

"JD?" Marianne called to Jameson just as Jameson was about to climb into her car.

"Hey. I wasn't sure we'd cross paths this morning."

"I wanted to catch you before you left."

"Everything okay?" Jameson asked.

Marianne smiled. "Everything is good. Have you talked to Shell?"

"No, why?"

"She left me a cryptic message saying she was in NYC and hoped she could come here tomorrow. I thought she was going to Iowa with Mom?"

Jameson nodded. "I'm sure she'll fill you in when she gets here."

"JD?"

"Aw, shit," Jameson groaned. "I figured she would have told you."

"Told me what?"

"She and Mel went to see a fertility specialist in the city."

Marianne needed no more information. "She's starting to panic."

"Probably a little," Jameson agreed.

"That's fast," Marianne said.

"I think they just want some advice."

"Shell will be a great mom," Marianne said.

Jameson nodded.

"JD? Something is wrong; I can tell."

Jameson glanced in the rear window of the car at Cooper. He was happily looking at a book. She turned her attention back to Marianne and offered her step-daughter a smile laced with sadness.

"JD?"

Jameson sighed. "I guess sometimes I just wonder how much I already missed."

"You mean not having a baby of your own?" Marianne tried to understand.

"No," Jameson chuckled. "I've never had any burning desire for that."

"Okay?"

"I just feel like I have all these holes to fill with everyone, I guess."

Marianne nodded. "You mean with us."

"Yeah, I do—and with Cooper."

"I think I can understand that."

"I don't really want to miss more than I have to with him," Jameson said.

Marianne smiled. She'd suspected that the major reason Jameson had wanted to leave her architectural firm was to be with Cooper and her mother more. It still surprised her at times—how close she had become to her step-mother. Jameson had become her best friend. Their relationship differed from the one Jameson shared with Michelle and Jonah. Jonah and Michelle saw Jameson in a parental role despite their closeness in age. Marianne considered Jameson the closest friend she'd ever had. It had taken time for them to cultivate their relationship. She also understood that the rocky road they had traveled was the reason they had come to understand each other so well.

"I know," Marianne replied. "Talk to Mom," she said.

Jameson looked at her feet.

"JD, talk to Mom. She'll understand."

"I know," Jameson admitted. "Your mom has so much on her plate right now, and…"

"There isn't anything on her plate that matters more to her than you and Cooper."

Jameson sighed.

"JD?"

"I know that too. That's why I don't…"

"Don't shut her out," Marianne said. "You think you are keeping this to yourself for her. That's not what Mom wants from you. She needs you to do the opposite. Talk to her."

"Thanks."

Marianne winked. "Call me if you need to."

Jameson nodded and moved to open her car door. Marianne started back toward the house. "Marianne?"

"Yeah?"

"That goes both ways, you know? Call me if you need to."

"I know."

Jameson climbed into the car and started the engine. She closed her eyes for a second and took a deep breath.

"Momma?"

"Yeah, Coop?"

"We're going with Mommy?"

Jameson looked in the rearview mirror at her son. "Yes, Coop. You and me—we're going with Mommy on her trip."

"We get to stay in a hotel?"

Jameson laughed. Cooper was fascinated by hotels. "We do."

"Cool!"

Jameson glanced back one more time at Cooper before pulling the car down the long driveway. *Nope, don't want to miss a minute if I can help it.*

Chapter Three

Candace shook her head as she watched the news. Nothing was ever easy. She'd expected resistance to her candidacy. She hadn't expected it would become this visceral this early in the game. She rubbed her brow thoughtfully. Politics was a game. She hated that reality, but it was reality.

"Candy?" Dana called over. Candace shook her head some more. "Candy, you know that Jed Ritchie…"

Candace turned to Dana and sighed. "Jed Ritchie is getting plenty of help from Lawson Klein. We both know it."

"They are fringe at best," Dana offered.

Candace grimaced. "Don't underestimate them, Dana."

"You don't honestly think this bullshit they're pedaling will stick?"

"Oh, it will stick," Candace replied. "That's not even a question. The question is how many corners it will fill up."

"What do you want me to do?" Dana asked.

"There's not much you can do right now." Candace clicked off the television.

"What are you thinking?"

"I think we need to bring Doug into the equation now."

"Doug Mills?"

Candace nodded. Doug Mills was a top strategist with the Democratic party. Candace had known him since he had started his career in the party. He was bright, energetic, and creative. More importantly, Doug Mills had been raised in the opposing party. His father had been a Republican congressman from Alabama for six terms. Doug had departed from his father's political ideology after college. He had interned in GOP Congressman Ron Dalton's office for three years before leaving the Republican party. Doug had made connections during that time. Some of those connections loathed him; others saw him as a folk hero of sorts. He had moderate fiscal views but progressive social ideologies. As the Republican party moved farther to the right, Mills had tried to speak to the center. When that had failed, he moved to the other side hoping he might be more successful in that endeavor.

"Mills is a risk," Dana said.

"Everything is a risk."

"Candy, I know that you like Doug, but you've got the far right giving you an enema already. You can't lose the left this soon."

Candace laughed. "An enema?"

"You know what I mean."

"I do," Candace conceded. "I don't just like Doug; I respect him."

"His fiscal views are more conservative than yours."

"He's not writing the platform."

"No, but he has been outspoken the last few years on budget cuts. And, I might remind you that he's been somewhat critical publicly of your spending plans as governor."

Candace smiled. "Yes, he has."

"Candy…"

"He's good for the campaign. He's also good for me."

"This is your call, but I would be remiss if I didn't tell you that I have concerns. I imagine Glenn and Michelle will express the same doubts."

"Don't imagine," Candace chuckled. "They will."

"You've already decided."

"I decided to bring Doug on long ago. I had hoped to do it when we reached the general. I don't think it can wait that long. We need him now. I need him now."

"Do you think he will do it?"

"He'll do it," Candace said.

"And, what happens when he tries to push you in a different direction?"

"I suppose that will depend on his argument."

"Candy…"

"Dana, this is not state politics, and it is not a senate race. Presidential campaigns—more importantly, presidential leadership requires considering a vast array of perspectives. You can't win on your party alone, and you can't govern successfully if you don't consider the other side. This isn't a one-size-fits-all country. You know that. Doug is fair-minded, even if I disagree with him on certain things. I've learned to anticipate a lot of obstacles. He will see things coming before any of us do. He has that ability, and he is adept at countering it."

"When are you going to tell Glenn?"

"When is she going to tell Glenn what?" Glenn Freeman entered the room.

"Glenn," Candace greeted her campaign manager.

"Oh, I don't like the sound of that," he said.

Candace grinned. "You don't like the sound of your name?"

"Candace…"

Candace took a deep breath and let it out slowly. "Sit down."

"Oh, God," he groaned.

"A bit dramatic?" Candace said. "I want to bring Doug on board."

"Mills? Now?"

"Yes."

"Candace, that might be premature," he replied.

"I don't think so."

Glenn regarded Candace silently for a moment. She held his gaze firmly, a clear indication that she was resolved to pursue her line of thinking. "Are you sure?"

"Positive."

"I'll make the call," he said.

"No," Candace held up her hand. "I'll call him in the morning."

"Do you think that's wise—you reaching out to him personally?" he asked.

"If I didn't, I wouldn't."

Glenn scratched his head. "I understand your reasoning, but it might be advisable to keep him at a slight personal distance. He's been critical of you over the last year."

"Lots of people have been critical of me, some of them are related to me," Candace quipped.

"You know what I mean."

"I do. You need to trust me on this one. Klein and Ritchie are on a crusade."

"I agree, but they don't carry the mantle of the majority in their party," he pointed out.

"No, but the majority potentially benefit from the crusade. They're unlikely to challenge much out of Ritchie's rhetoric until they are forced to. And, face it—they will wait to see how it plays in the public sphere first. They want this election, Glenn. No way do they want another four years of a Democrat in office. Their agenda is stalled. At the very least, should I be successful, they will want to stall mine. I can't have that either."

"You're worried about the down ballot races already?" he asked.

"You should be too," she said.

"Candace, if…"

"There are no ifs," Candace said. "Not in life. Politics is just like life, Glenn. There's when, how, and who. Don't deal in ifs. That's the surest road to nowhere."

"You're the boss."

"Glad you remember that. Maybe you could remind my children when you have the time."

Dana started laughing. The door to the suite blew open.

"Mommy!"

Candace looked over at Cooper and smiled. He ran to her. "Where have you been?" she asked him.

"Momma took me to da pool!"

"She did?"

"Yep."

"Did you play fish?" Candace asked.

"Nope."

"No?"

45

"Nope. We played shark."

Candace laughed. "Of course, you did," she said as she pulled him up to sit beside her. Cooper leaned into her happily. She kissed him on the head and looked back at Glenn. "I'll make the call in the morning before we head out."

"Dismissed?" he asked playfully.

"For now," Candace winked. "I have to handle a shark."

"I'm not a shark, Mommy," Cooper giggled.

"No?"

"No! Momma's da shark."

"Is that so?" Candace asked.

"Yep. Sharks are only in da water, Mommy. We're dry."

Candace chuckled and pulled Cooper close. *If only that were true, Cooper. If only that were true.*

"What've you got?"

Lawson Klein swiveled in his chair. "On Reid?"

"On any of them," Ritchie said.

"Still digging into the Stratton Foundation."

"Better dig deeper," Ritchie replied. "If you don't find something soon..."

"If we don't find something, we'll create it," Klein said.

Ritchie smiled. *I like the way you think, Lawson.*

"I'm surprised that you didn't hop on a plane to Iowa," Marianne commented. She handed her sister a cold bottle of beer and took a seat across from her at the table.

"I was tempted."

"But?"

Michelle shrugged. "I kind of think I needed to stick close to home today."

"Okay? You're not home, though—you're here."

"Yeah, I know."

"What's up, Shell?"

Michelle sighed heavily. "She wants to try."

"You might need to give me a little more than that. I will go out on a limb and assume we are talking about Mel and having a baby."

Michelle nodded while her fingertips drew patterns in the condensation on her beer bottle.

"And, you don't want to have a baby?"

"No."

"Shell, that's a big…"

Michelle chuckled nervously. "No," she said. "I do want to have a baby. I just don't think it's a great idea for her to try."

"Lost me."

Michelle looked at her sister helplessly. "The fertility specialist we saw thinks there is a chance that Mel might be able to conceive—with help."

"Isn't that a good thing?" Marianne asked. Michelle looked at her hands. "Shell?"

"I don't know," Michelle replied. "It's still an uphill climb," she explained.

"You're worried she'll be disappointed."

"That's part of it."

"What's the other part?"

Michelle took a deep breath and released it audibly.

"Shell?"

"You'll think it's nuts."

"I'm used to you being nuts," Marianne teased.

Michelle looked back at Marianne teary eyed.

"Shell," Marianne reached across the table and took her sister's hand.

"I sort of got used to the idea."

Marianne smiled. "To the idea that you would be the one to carry your baby."

Michelle nodded.

"Did you tell her that?"

Michelle shook her head.

"Why not?" Marianne asked.

"Because I don't want to disappoint her."

"I see."

"What?"

"Shell, don't you think that Mel should know how you feel?"

"I honestly don't know."

"So, if I am following this; you are worried that if Mel can't conceive, she'll be disappointed."

"Yeah…"

"And, at the same time, you are disappointed because you thought you'd be making plans now to try and conceive. Am I following this?"

"I…"

Marianne smiled. "You need to talk to Mel."

"I'd love her to be the one," Michelle said. "I just… I know how much this means to her and…."

"And, what about you?"

"I don't know," Michelle said. "I always kind of thought it would be her. When we got the news—well, I just…"

"I understand," Marianne said. "At least, I think that I do. Don't look at me like that," Marianne laughed. "I'm lucky."

"What do you mean?"

"I mean that I never had to worry about any of this," Marianne answered. "I loved Rick. When we decided that we wanted to have a family, we just started trying. It didn't take us that long—either time. So, I understand as much as I can understand. But, Shell? You need to talk to Melanie. This is something that you are an equal part of no matter who carries your baby."

"I know."

"So, talk to her."

Michelle smiled and took a sip from her beer. "What about you?"

"Me?"

"Yeah, you. You and Scott have been spending a lot of time together lately."

Marianne smiled. She was grateful to have someone in her life again. After Rick's death, Marianne had thought she might be alone the rest of her life. Scott had changed that line of thinking. She had fallen in love with him. Marianne also understood that she was a long way from being ready to share her life full-time with another person. Her focus remained on her children. She was hopeful that in time

she and Scott might find their way to creating a family together. That was not something she had shared with anyone—not even Scott.

"We have," Marianne said.

"And?"

"How did this become about me?"

"Why are you avoiding the subject?" Michelle coun-
tered.

"I'm not."

"You so are."

Marianne laughed. "Maybe I am."

"You're holding out so you can get married at the
White House."

Marianne rolled her eyes. "If I were you, I'd concentrate on your proposed progeny and give up your bridesmaid
delusions."

"Delusions? You getting married to Scott is delusional?"

"Me getting married to anyone is delusional."

"If you say so."

"I do," Marianne said bluntly.

Michelle tipped her head and regarded her older sister silently. Something was on Marianne's mind; she could
tell. "What gives?"

"What?"

"You. Delusions. Did he ask you already?"

"Did who ask me what?" Marianne took a sip from
her beer.

"Duh—Scott. Did he already propose?"

Marianne spewed the beer in her mouth across the table.

"Sexy. I can see why he's so enthralled," Michelle wiped some beer from her chest.

"The only thing Scott has proposed is me and the kids spending a few days with him at his house for a change."

"Are you going to?"

"Stay at Scott's?"

"Yeah."

Marianne smiled. "In a couple of weeks—yes."

"What if he does?"

"What if he does what?"

"Propose?"

Marianne shook her head. "He won't."

"I wouldn't be so sure."

"He won't," Marianne said. "He knows how I feel about everything."

"What does that mean?"

"It means that he knows that I love him and he understands that I am nowhere near prepared to get married again."

Michelle sighed. "Why not?"

"Because, Shell I am just learning how to let someone in again. And, because when I do, I want to be sure I can give it everything, not just pieces."

"You know, Rick would be okay with it."

Marianne smiled. "I know," she said. "I have to be okay with it."

"Hey, have you talked to JD lately?"

"Yeah, I saw her yesterday; why?"

"I don't know. She just seemed kind of quiet the last few times I was with her. Then she signed away the firm..."

"I think JD is just figuring out where she needs to be the most."

"You mean for Mom and Coop."

"No. Actually, I don't. I mean for her."

"She built that firm from the ground up."

Marianne shrugged. "I wouldn't worry about JD."

Michelle was concerned about Jameson. Jed Ritchie's mudslinging campaign had gotten personal already. In some corners, Candace was depicted as a hero. In others, she was being vilified as a monster. Jameson was fiercely protective of Candace. Michelle hoped that as the press became more invasive, Jameson wouldn't feel the need to defend her mother pointedly.

"Yeah, well... Mom has been balls to the wall lately with work, and you know the media is a bunch of ass munchers."

"Is that a technical term?" Marianne raised her brow.

"Nope. It's an accurate one, though."

"Don't worry about JD," Marianne repeated. "She's smarter and tougher than you think."

"That sounded like an endorsement," Michelle laughed. "Weird."

"What's that?"

"You and JD all chummy."

Marianne nodded. She still carried a sense of guilt for the way she had treated Jameson when they had first met. But she had grown to love Jameson, and she valued the friendship they shared as much as she did any in the family. "She's my best friend," Marianne said.

Michelle smiled. "Like I said—weird."

Marianne laughed. "Maybe so. Weird beats ass muncher." Marianne raised her glass.

Michelle choked. "Classy," she laughed.

Marianne took a swig from her beer. "To the end."

"Want to talk about it?" Candace asked Jameson as she climbed into the bed.

"Talk about what?"

"Whatever is bothering you."

"Nothing is bothering me."

"Jameson, you are the worst liar I know."

"I'm not lying."

"Okay, so what is on your mind that you are reluctant to share with me?" Candace changed her question.

Jameson sighed.

"Jameson?"

"I've just been thinking."

"About?"

"About what I should do next."

"You mean with your career?"

"No, I mean in general."

Candace sat up and leaned against the headboard. "I'm listening."

"It's just… You know where you are heading."

"And, you aren't sure where that leaves you."

"No. No, I'm saying this all wrong."

"Honey, you're not saying much of anything."

Jameson sighed again.

"Jameson, talk to me."

"I don't want you to…"

Candace leaned over, took hold of Jameson's hands and smiled. "I told you when I decided to launch this campaign never to forget that you are the most important person in my life."

"I know."

"Stop worrying about me."

"That's never going to happen," Jameson said.

"Okay, then stop letting your worries keep you from talking to me."

Jameson sucked in a deep breath. "What would you think if I offered to work with a couple of NGOs?"

Candace narrowed her gaze. "What kind of NGOs?" she asked.

"I was thinking Habitat for Humanity for one."

Candace nodded. "You want an excuse to get your hands dirty."

Jameson laughed. "I want to do something that matters."

"Jameson…"

"And, I want to be there for you as much as I can be, for the kids too."

Candace kissed Jameson tenderly.

"Does that mean you approve?" Jameson asked.

"You don't need my approval. You know that I'll support you."

"As long as I stay off ladders?"

"There is that," Candace chuckled. "I think there is more that you aren't telling me."

Jameson sighed. "I'm not sure how to explain this. And, I don't want you to think that I have second thoughts about this campaign."

"Go on."

"It's just—we both know that you will be away more. Even when you are home... Well, Candace, you're going to be preoccupied a lot more. The kids..."

Candace smiled. "They are all lucky to have you in their lives."

Jameson shook her head. "I hope so."

"Why would you question that?"

"It's not that I question it. It isn't. I just—sometimes I feel like I have all these holes that need to be filled in. Do you know what I mean? Like for instance, what was Shell like when she was ten or fifteen? Does Coop do any of the same things that Jonah did? I don't have anything to compare it to. I don't know..."

"I think I understand. I feel that way with Cooper sometimes."

"You do?"

Candace nodded. "Of course, I do. I can remember Jonah's first tumble and Marianne's first words. With Cooper, there are blank spaces that I can't fill in. So, yes; I think I understand what you mean. I'm not sure why you would be afraid to tell me that."

"I'm not."

"Really?" Candace challenged gently

Jameson searched for the right words to reply. She wasn't afraid to tell Candace anything. At times, Jameson still worried about her relationship with each of Candace's children. She did know that all of Candace's children and grandchildren looked to Candace for guidance consistently. And, Jameson was aware that Candace's accessibility on a moment's notice would be challenged in the coming months and years. In a way, that presented an opportunity for Jameson. She wanted to be the person that Candace's children could seek out in Candace's absence, and she didn't want Candace to take that the wrong way.

"Jameson?"

"I just want to be there—not just for you—for them."

Candace smiled. "You're always there for all of us."

"I hope so, but Candace, with you away it... Well, it might give me a chance to..."

Candace leaned over and placed a kiss on Jameson's lips.

"What was that for?" Jameson asked.

"For being you," Candace replied. "I think that sometimes you forget how often the kids go to you first."

"I don't think..."

"I don't think so either. I know so. But I understand why you feel the way you do. I don't ever want you to feel that you have to give up something because of my career."

Jameson shrugged. "Compromise is part of life," she said. "I don't see any of this as giving something up. It's more like trying something new."

Candace smiled.

"What?" Jameson asked.

Candace lifted her brow.

"What?" Jameson repeated. "Why are you grinning like that?"

"I just know how lucky I am."

"I should hope so with all those damn fortune cookies you eat."

Candace whacked Jameson playfully.

"So, what do you think about my idea? Me offering my experience to a couple of NGOs? Would that hurt your campaign or…"

"I can't see how my wife wanting to help people would hurt my campaign."

"But?"

"How many ladders do you expect will be involved?"

Jameson laughed. "How about I promise that if there are any animals in the vicinity, I will stay grounded?"

Candace laughed. "You're a lunatic."

"Well?"

"Just be careful."

"Are we talking about the ladders?"

"Partly," Candace confessed. "Be careful not to close yourself off, Jameson. If it feels right to you to go back to work in some capacity, I want you to do that. I mean it."

"I promise."

"And, don't ever underestimate the role you play with the Three Stooges. They'd be as lost without you as I would be."

"I don't know about that."

"I do."

"Thanks," Jameson said.

"For?"

"You already know."

Candace pulled Jameson into her arms and laid back on the bed. "I love you."

"I love you too," Jameson replied. "Don't forget to take your own advice."

"You think I might be inclined to want a second job?" Candace laughed.

"Ha-ha. I think you need to remember that we would all be lost without you. You are so busy trying to take care of all of us that you forget we all want to take care of you too."

Candace closed her eyes and held onto Jameson tightly. She did know that. It was a fact that often gave her pause. Her decision to climb onto the political roller coaster impacted everyone in her life. She hoped that she could protect them around the inevitable curves. "I'll remember."

"Good."

Candace was content to lie silently with Jameson in her embrace. She felt Jameson's breathing deepen and sighed. She kissed Jameson's head softly. "I promise, I will try."

"What is this?" Grant Hill asked.

"Open it," Bradley Wolfe instructed him.

Grant opened the envelope, took a deep breath and nodded. He closed it and looked back at the man standing in front of his desk. "What does that have to do with Governor Reid?"

"Nothing specifically—yet."

"What do you want from me?" Grant asked.

"Ammunition."

"I would've thought you'd be talking to Lawson."

Wolfe grinned. "You helm the largest family values group in America. Who better to talk about what kind of values make a family?"

Grant nodded. "I'll see what I can find out."

"You do that."

Grant watched as Wolfe left his office. "Shit." *We have a different idea about values and family.* He picked up his phone. *I hope she's busy.*

Chapter Four

Candace massaged her temples. It did little to relieve her tension or the throbbing in her head. She threw her glasses onto her desk in frustration. "Damnit!" With a deep breath, Candace picked up the phone.

"Hello?"

"I got your message."

"Not what you wanted to hear, I'll bet," Grant replied.

"Grant... I want you out of this before it gets any uglier."

"That's not going to happen."

"It's going to get uglier..."

"I'm not walking away. We've both come too far."

"Grant..."

"No," Grant put Candace's thought to rest. "I just need to know what you want me to do. Hold it up or..."

"No," Candace said. "Grant, if Wolfe brought you this, chances are he already knows."

"About me?" Grant asked.

"Yes."

"You think he's testing me."

"You don't?"

Grant sighed. "I don't know what to think. If you're right..."

"You are already compromised. Listen to me; it's time for you to pull back," Candace advised.

"What do we do now? I mean, if Wolfe knows, Klein and Ritchie know."

Candace rubbed her eyes in a vain attempt to gain some clarity. She did not doubt that Grant's identity had been discovered. The only question that lingered in her mind was what the end game was. How did Wolfe plan to exploit the information that Grant was Jessica's son? Candace imagined that her relationship with Grant had also come to light. She had feared that this might happen.

"Mom will..."

"Your mother will be fine, Grant."

"You think that they will come out with it; don't you?" he asked.

Candace closed her eyes. "I do." She heard Grant's sharp intake of breath.

"I need to tell my parents."

"I'm sorry."

"Don't be," Grant said. "I don't have any regrets. I would do the same thing all over again."

"I know."

"I should call Mom."

"Let me."

"I can't ask you to..."

"You didn't. Let me talk to your mother."

"Candy, I... You two have become friends again and I..."

Candace smiled. Being someone's child, being some-one's parent—age had little bearing on the need for acceptance a child felt nor a parent's inclination to protect. "Jessica and I will be fine too," she said. "Talk to your parents. I'm sure your mother will call you after I speak with her."

"Candy... I'm sorry... I..."

"Grant," Candace addressed him gently. "You have nothing to apologize for."

"I don't want this to cause your candidacy any harm."

"Stop worrying about me," Candace said. "I promise; we will talk later."

"Are you..."

"I'm fine. Let me handle this now," she told him. "I'll talk to you in a bit."

Candace hung up the call and let her face fall into her hands. "Deep breath, Candy."

"Shell?" Melanie looked at her wife with concern.

"Hey."

"What's going on?" Melanie wanted to know.

"I need to talk to you about something."

"Okay?"

"I... I'm not sure how to explain this."

"Babe, you can tell me anything," Melanie said.

"I know. It's crazy when I think about it. I mean, when we first talked about what our life would look like, I assumed that you would be the one to carry our children. I don't know why; I just did."

Melanie nodded. "And, now?"

Michelle shrugged. "I want that. I do."

"But?"

"No. I do want that. It's just that I kind of got used to the idea that I would... Well, you know; that I..."

"That you would be the one having our baby."

Michelle nodded.

Melanie leaned in and kissed Michelle's cheek. "You still can."

Michelle's eyes widened in surprise. "You were so excited that you might be able to..."

"I am," Melanie agreed. "But, Shell, that doesn't mean you can't. I mean, I always thought we would do this at least twice."

"At least twice?" Michelle laughed.

"You didn't?"

Michelle smiled. "I've been so caught up in how we would start our family, I really hadn't given it a lot of thought. But, yes; I would want our child to have a brother or sister if possible."

"Me too."

"I just... I'm a little worried about you too," Michelle admitted.

"I know you are. I will be okay if this doesn't work. I will," Melanie chuckled. "I know most people might find it hard to believe, but this is something I've always wanted since I was a kid. Some people dream about mansions and fairytale weddings. Me? I was the weirdo that dreamed about a minivan."

Michelle smiled. "It is a little weird," she teased.

Melanie laughed. "Why didn't you just say some-thing?"

"I don't know. It will sound crazy."

"If I couldn't handle crazy, we wouldn't be having this discussion at all."

"True," Michelle agreed. "I don't know. It's not like I never wanted kids. I mean, I love kids. I just never gave much thought to the idea that I might give birth to any."

Melanie nodded. "And now?"

"And, now? I think it's something I want to do."

"Then we will make that happen."

"You're not upset?"

"Upset? Shell, sometimes you really are a little crazy. Why would that upset me? Listen, we will be lucky if it works out for me. I know that. The odds are still not in my favor. I'd still like to try. It might take some time. To tell you the truth, this makes me feel a lot better."

"It does?"

"If I can't—I mean, I think that we should agree on a time-frame. How long do we try to get me pregnant before we try something else? I don't think I could handle years of disappointment."

"What are you thinking?" Michelle asked.

"We try for a year or so. If we don't have any luck, we move to our other options."

"Are you sure?"

Melanie nodded. "I can't go on and on in disappointment, Shell. What matters most to me is that we get to have a family together, not how we do that. I have something I need to tell you too."

"What?"

"I've been thinking that maybe someday we could look to adopt."

Michelle smiled.

"You don't look surprised," Melanie observed.

"I'm not. And, I would love to do that. I would do that even if everything works out."

"Trying to keep up with your mom?" Melanie teased.

"No," Michelle held up her hand. "Four? Hell no! Three's company. Four's insanity."

"Oh? So, you wish that she hadn't adopted Coop?"

"What? No! I love Coop. It's different, though. In a lot of ways, it's like Mom only has one now."

Melanie laughed out loud.

"What?"

"Somehow, I doubt your mom or JD would agree with that assessment."

"You don't think so?"

"No."

"Well, I mean she does have Marianne at home, but she's not always there so…"

Melanie smiled. "I don't think that's what it's about," she said. "Your mom is everybody's mom in a way. She's the matriarch."

Michelle smiled. "She is. Please tell me you aren't hoping to keep up with her," Michelle said.

"No," Melanie chuckled. "But, I would never rule anything out where you are concerned."

"Are we talking about kids?"

Melanie grinned.

"Oh." Michelle moved to wrap Melanie in her arms. "Let's see how many things I can get you to rule in."

"You look exhausted," Jameson commented when Candace walked into the room.

"Understatement. I need to talk to you."

Jameson put down the book she had been reading and gave Candace her full attention. "What's wrong?"

"Grant."

"Hill? What about him?"

Candace let out a long breath. "It seems that Ritchie and Lawson uncovered the truth."

"That he's Jessica's son?"

"Not just that."

Jameson nodded. "What does that mean?"

Candace flopped into a chair and sighed. "It means that we either wait for their next move or we take the ball and run with it."

Candace was not one to sit idly by while someone attempted to derail her. She would not tolerate anyone she cared for being harmed in the process if she could help it.

"What do you need from me?" Jameson asked.

"Jessica is talking to Grant now. It's up to him."

"What is up to him? You have a plan. You always have a plan."

Candace chuckled. *True.* "It depends on what he wants to do. I don't know how his conversation with his adoptive parents went."

"What is your best-case scenario?"

"I don't think there is a best-case scenario this time," Candace replied. "No matter what, Grant is going to get hurt. That's unavoidable. And, no matter what I say or do, this will become fuel for their cause."

"Fuel? How is it fuel? You accepted Grant as part of Jessica's life. How can they possibly make that into a negative?"

Candace raised her brow. Jameson saw the world through her heart. Candace cherished that. Not everyone's heart was the size of Jameson's. There were many ways that Grant's relationship with Candace could be leveraged against her. Right now, that was the least of her concern.

"Let me count the ways," Candace said. "That isn't the issue right now."

"You're worried about Grant or are you worried about Jessica?"

"Jess is fine," Candace said. "She never would have pressed Grant to be open about their relationship. To be honest, I think part of her is relieved. She wants to eviscerate Wolfe and company. I'm not sure I will be able to reel her in."

"And you?"

Candace shrugged. "It's up to Grant."

"If you have your way?"

"I'd like Grant to come out to the farmhouse with Jess and meet the family."

Jameson nodded.

"Does that bother you?"

"I don't know how to answer that."

"Honestly?" Candace suggested.

"A little," Jameson said.

"Why?"

"Candace, I like Jessica. I appreciate everything she has done for us and for Cooper—I do."

"But?"

Jameson sighed. "She's your former lover."

"And, you're my wife."

"This isn't about trusting us."

"What is it about?" Candace asked. Jameson shook her head. "Jameson?"

"I'm not sure," Jameson admitted. "Sometimes, it's hard."

"I'm listening."

"You are so many things to so many people," Jameson said. "It's like I told you; there are all these gaps that I can't fill—all these parts of you and your life that I wasn't a part of."

Candace made her way to sit beside Jameson. "Jameson," she smiled. "You are a part of all of it."

"Am I?"

"Yes," Candace said. "All of it led me to you."

"I know. I can't help how I feel sometimes."

"I understand."

"You do?"

"Of course, I do. Don't you think that I wonder about all the pieces of your life that I missed? I do, you know? Although, I try not to think about it often."

"Oh?"

"No offense, thinking about you twenty-five years ago is a bit unsettling."

Jameson laughed. "You know that I will support you no matter what."

"I know. I also sense that you still don't trust Grant."

"I don't know Grant. I trust you."

Candace nodded. "This is not going to be easy for him."

"I can't imagine that it would be."

"He's going to need to know that he has a place to land."

Jameson smiled. "And, of course, you are going to make sure he knows you are that place."

"Not just me."

Jameson sighed.

"Jameson," Candace implored her wife. "Grant is a good person; I promise you. I understand why you have your doubts. He's lived his entire life with doubt—about who he is, where he belongs, what he should do. He needs to know that his faith in Jessica and I was well-placed."

"Okay."

"Okay?"

"You're the best judge of character that I know. Besides, you love him; I can tell."

"I do."

"I know. What about the kids? Candace, they are going to want to know why you never told them about Grant— why Jessica never did."

Candace closed her eyes. Jameson was right and she knew it. It had taken years for her children to begin to heal the rift with Jessica that Jessica's betrayal of Candace had caused. It had taken time to rebuild trust. "I can only hope that they will understand that we both had to follow Grant's lead and wishes."

"So, you're going to tell them with Jessica?"

"I hope that you will be with me."

"It's not my place…"

"It most certainly is your place," Candace disagreed.

"I don't want you to worry about me."

"Don't be ridiculous—crazy I can handle, ridiculous is something else. I need you with me."

Jameson smiled. "Are you sure?"

"Jameson, honestly? I didn't force Grant into this. That doesn't change the fact that I feel partially responsible."

"It's not your fault."

"No, but my presence in his life is the main reason he finds himself in this position."

Jameson shook her head. "I'm sorry, but no—it isn't. It's not," Jameson said. She could see Candace mounting a protest and held up her hand. "Grant Hill is not a child, Candace. I get it. I understand that it's been hard for him, but he's an adult. He could've chosen to be honest with his parents. He could have chosen to do a lot of things."

"He wanted to…"

"I've heard it. I hear you. He wanted to try and change things. So? That's what you do every day," Jameson pointed out. "And, Candace? Sometimes that means that you get hurt. You choose to stand up for what you believe when people are screaming at you for doing it, and you compromise on many things when you'd rather not. You have never pretended to be someone else. That was his choice."

"It's not that simple."

"Yes, it is. I get that you and Jessica wanted to protect him. I understand that he loves you both and that he has another set of parents that he doesn't want to lose. It sucks. But you would normally be the first person to say that pretending leads no place good. I hate Lawson Klein. I think Jed Ritchie is a self-righteous asshole."

Candace smirked.

"The things they do—I can't pretend to understand the things they do. But this is as much on Grant as it is on them or you and Jessica or anyone else for that matter. He's not a child, Candace. Even if you feel like he is one of yours. He's not Cooper or Spencer. He was an adult when he found Jessica, and he's an adult now."

Candace nodded. Jameson wasn't wrong. Emotion often worked against rational reasoning. "Maybe so," Candace said. "What I know doesn't change how I feel or what I feel I need to do."

Jameson kissed Candace on the cheek.

"What was that for?"

"I wouldn't expect it to change anything. I just think you need to be reminded that you are not responsible for everything that happens to everyone you love."

"Thank you. Will you be okay with this?"

"I will be."

"Are you sure?"

"I can't help how I feel either. I can control what I do about it. That was my point."

"Give him a chance."

"I told you; I will support you any way that I can. Don't ask me not to be cautious. You're not the only one who feels protective of this family."

Candace smiled. "I know," she said. She held out her hand.

"Where are we going?"

"I was thinking for pizza?"

"Pizza again?"

"You love pizza."

Jameson smiled. "I do," she agreed. "But, I was thinking maybe some chicken wings tonight."

"Really?"

Jameson nodded. "My wife likes the fortune cookies."

"Is that so? What about what you like?"

"I like her fortune cookies too—in…"

Candace burst of laughing. "Lunatic."

"Should you add 'in bed' to that one?" Jameson joked.

"Play your cards right and I will."

Jameson laughed. "Which cards might those be?"

Candace swatted Jameson. "I'll tell Drew we are going out. You see if you can corral Aladdin upstairs."

"Yes, ma'am."

"Don't forget the cards," Candace teased.

Jameson snickered. *She should be careful what she asks for.*

"What do you think he'll do?" Jed Ritchie asked Bradley Wolfe.

"I suppose that depends on how close we are to the mark."

"He's definitely spoken to Reid, and we know he was looking for his birth mother years back. His college roommate gave that up easily."

Wolfe shrugged. "That doesn't mean the governor is his mother, Jed. I wouldn't go pinning your hopes on that donkey's ass."

"Excuse me?"

"Pin the tail on the… Never mind," Wolfe said. "It doesn't fit. We cast out the line. Now we wait and see what tugs at it."

"Why not just float the narrative and hope for the best?"

"Because if the narrative we float is wrong, we might just get our asses pinned to the wall."

Lawson Klein listened to the conversation as it unfolded. He took a sip from his glass of scotch and smiled at the pair arguing a few feet away. "Float it," he said.

Wolfe and Ritchie looked at him with disbelief.

"Float it. It doesn't matter if it's true. Some of it will stick with most people, and all of it will stick with some. Just float it. They don't have to know who it came from."

"Risky," Wolfe said.

"Not really," Klein disagreed. "Make something stick before she has a chance to stick it to you."

Wolfe took a deep breath and then nodded. "Fine. You're the expert, Lawson. Make it happen."

Chapter Five

Jameson's fist clenched tightly as the news played in front of her. Anger swelled within her. Her jaw tightened and her face flushed.

> *"That's quite the leap,"* the anchor said.
> *"My source is confident that the information is accurate."*
> *"If it's true, that would mean that Governor Reid's longtime adversary, Grant Hill is her biologica son."*

"I'm going to kill that son a bitch," Jameson muttered.

"JD," Pearl's hand gripped Jameson's shoulder.

"I mean it, Pearl. I am going to beat the hell out of Lawson Klein."

Pearl clicked off the television and took a seat beside Jameson on the couch. "No, you aren't."

Jameson glared. Pearl was sure that she had never seen Jameson as angry as she was now. Jameson's eyes glistened with fire. It was early on in Candace's campaign, and Lawson Klein and his crew had already chosen to cross a sacred line. Jameson had no desire to contain her temper, and Pearl could hardly fault the woman before her. She felt inclined to lash out as much as Jameson did. Pearl also understood that any emotional reaction to the current narrative would only serve to strengthen its intent.

"Jameson…"

Jameson hopped to her feet. She ran her hand through her hair and turned back to face Pearl. "What am I supposed to do? Take it lying down? Let them smear Candace? I won't do it, Pearl. It's not bad enough what that asshole has put Laura through, the crap he's spewed about Cooper—you expect me to sit quietly by while he trashes my wife?"

Pearl nodded. "No, I don't."

Jameson was genuinely surprised by Pearl's response.

"I expect you to take a deep breath," Pearl said. "We both know that this story is a bunch of hootenanny. You need to trust Candy. She can handle it."

"I know she can handle it!" Jameson snapped. "She shouldn't have to handle it!" Jameson took a deep breath and collapsed back onto the couch with a defeated thud. "What the hell is wrong with these people?"

"How much time do you have?" Pearl attempted to lighten the conversation.

Jameson shook her head. "Is this really worth it?" she asked.

"That depends, I suppose."

"Depends on what?"

Pearl smiled. "What do you hope to gain?" she asked Jameson.

Jameson shook her head.

"Jameson, listen to me; Candy expected this. You know that as well as I do."

"That doesn't make it okay."

"No, it doesn't. It's hurtful and it's vicious."

"So? So, what am I supposed to do?"

"Love her."

"Love her? I love her more than anything. That's not enough."

"For whom? For you or for Candy?"

Jameson groaned. "This is going to kill her."

Pearl sighed. "It's going to fuel her," she said. "Candy won't take this lying down, Jameson. You have to know that."

"Yeah, well, I wish she would come out swinging."

Pearl chuckled.

"That's funny?"

"No. I'm sure she wants to."

"I do want to," Candace's voice agreed from behind the pair.

"What are you doing home?" Jameson asked.

"Pearl, would you give me a minute with Jameson?"

Pearl patted Jameson's knee, made her way to Candy and kissed her on the cheek. "Be gentle with her," she whispered.

"Don't expect me not to be pissed off," Jameson told Candace when Pearl had left the room.

"I don't."

"Good. Because, Candace? If that asshole comes within a mile of me, I can promise you I will lay him out flat on his ass."

Candace smiled. She took a seat next to Jameson and held Jameson's hands. "Do you know one of the reasons I love baseball?"

"Please tell me this is going somewhere."

"Do you?" Candace asked. Jameson shrugged. "Baseball is a lot like politics, Jameson. When you step up to the plate, you know the pitcher is trying to strike you out. You want so badly to knock the ball over his head—to show him who is stronger, better, worthy—to hit a home run. You have to be careful not to let your eagerness make you swing wildly. If you want to win the game, you have to know how to wait for the right pitch. That's how you take control. That's how you win."

Jameson shook her head with disgust. She was in no mood for analogies and in no frame of mind to be taught anything. She wanted to deck Lawson Klein and Jed Ritchie. She wanted to step in the ring with them and show the world exactly how cowardly they both were. Even if she lost, Jameson felt sure that it would make her feel better.

Candace squeezed Jameson's hands. "I understand how you feel."

"No, you don't," Jameson replied.

Candace sighed.

This was not the first time Jameson had become frustrated with Candace's professional life. She hated feeling helpless. There were times when playing the dutiful spouse drove Jameson mad. She wanted to protect her family. Wasn't that part of loving them? Jameson shook her head again and pulled away from Candace. She stood up and placed a few feet between them.

"Do you know what Pearl's solution to this was—for me, I mean?" Jameson asked.

Candace silently waited for her to continue.

"To love you. That's it. Jesus, Candace! To love you? What the hell does that even mean if I can't take care of you?"

Candace felt Jameson's hurt hit her like a tidal wave. "I'm sorry."

"Sorry?" Jameson was confused. "What are you apologizing for?" Jameson rubbed her eyes vigorously. "Sorry? Candace…" Jameson took a deep breath. "Don't you understand?"

"I'm trying to."

"Part of loving you is taking care of you," Jameson said. "Protecting this family."

"You already do that."

"Really? This feels awfully familiar."

Candace closed her eyes and nodded. She had expected that the road to the future would be bumpy. Now, it felt much more like running off a steep cliff. "Jameson…"

"I know. I know what you are going to say. I do. Maybe it's enough for you. I don't know how to make it enough for me. Do you know what it's like to watch people take cheap shots at the person you love?"

"I'm sorry."

"Stop it," Jameson said. "Damnit, Candace; I won't take the swing at them, but don't ask me to feel differently. I can't."

Candace smiled. "I wouldn't have it any other way."

Jameson groaned. She could feel the fight evaporating from her rapidly. Anger had a way of depleting a person. "It's not fair for you to have to handle everything by yourself."

Candace laughed.

"I'm glad you're amused."

"No," Candace said. "Is that what you think—that I handle everything alone?"

"You do."

"I most certainly do not," Candace disagreed. "You know that better than anyone. Don't you think I would love to take to the airwaves and call those idiots every name in the book? I would; you know? I can't. I can't. You know that I'm right. What would that prove? I'd feel better for five minutes and then I'd regret it. This isn't a sprint, Jameson. This is the marathon. I told you that they would throw the kitchen sink at me."

"It's a lie."

"Yes, it is."

"People believe this shit."

"They do," Candace agreed. "And, the people that do? I'm never going to change their minds—neither are you."

"See, that's where we disagree."

Candace was taken back by Jameson's response.

"That surprises you? We disagree. Those people, Candace—they like drama and they see power differently from you. They like thuggery."

True. Candace nodded. "You're not wrong," she conceded. "I can't let that dictate what I do."

Jameson let out a heavy sigh. "I know."

"Jameson, if this is too much…"

Jameson shook her head. "Too much?" She laughed. "It's more than too much," she said. "Lying about you. Trying to paint you as a deceptive, immoral person. Candace…"

Jameson took a deep breath. "It pisses me off. You're my wife. I don't appreciate anyone hurting you."

"I know. We've been down this road before. You're the glue, Jameson. I need you to understand that. I need to know that you believe me. I can't do this without you. I don't want to."

"Without me? I just don't know what I'm doing that helps."

"This."

"This?"

"Right. Caring enough to want to fight, and loving me enough not to lash out."

Jameson groaned. "I hate it."

Candace chuckled. "You don't say."

"What are you going to do?" Jameson asked.

"Tell the truth—with a little bit of flair."

Jameson finally grinned. "I have no doubt. Care to share?"

"I do," Candace said. "But before I do, can I ask for a favor?"

"You know you can."

"Just hold me for a minute."

Jameson pulled Candace into her arms and held her close. She felt the warmth of Candace's tears against her neck. Sometimes, Jameson momentarily lost sight of how much Candace needed her. It often sounded hollow to Jameson—the notion that loving Candace was what Candace needed most from her. Moments like this served as a stark reminder. Candace seldom shed tears in front of her children or the public. She needed a place to let go. She needed a place where she could be Candace. Most of Candace's time was spent playing the role of mother, grandmother, mentor—leader. All those roles were a part of Candace, but they took up so much space that most people forgot there was a woman underneath it all.

"Candace," Jameson soothed. "I'm sorry."

"Just hold me for a while," Candace requested.

"For as long as you need," Jameson promised. She gently lowered them both on the couch and pulled Candace even closer. In a short time, Candace would take a deep breath, kiss Jameson tenderly, and gather herself to face the rest of the day. Jameson would hold her wife until that happened. That was her role to play now. Candace was everyone's rock. Jameson was Candace's anchor. "I love you," Jameson whispered.

"Thank God," Candace replied. "I love you too."

"How can you be so calm?" Michelle bit.

"It's not easy," Jameson said.

"It's a fucking lie!" Michelle yelled.

"Shell," Jameson directed Michelle to sit.

"It is a lie, JD."

"Yes, it is."

"So? Why the hell is she hold-up in that office and not screaming the truth on the news?"

"Because there are people to consider."

"What people? Lawson Klein people? Screw that..."

Jameson chuckled. "Pretty much what I said when I saw the news."

"Yeah? So? Why are we sitting here in a holding pattern? And, why is Jessica's car out front?"

Jameson took a deep breath. "Your mom is in a meeting with Glenn and Jessica right now."

"Oh? Who else? Doesn't she think maybe I should know what is going on?"

"Do you mean as someone helping with her campaign?"

"What else would I mean?"

"Maybe the reason you are out here is that you are her daughter first."

"I don't get it. What aren't you telling me?" Michelle asked.

"A lot," Jameson conceded. "It's not my story, Shell."

"Aren't you pissed?"

"Understatement."

"So? Can't you convince her to fight?"

Jameson smiled. "She is fighting."

"Really?"

"Your mom has to fight this her way."

"Oh, you mean with a smile on her face?"

"Trust me; she's not smiling."

"Is she even mad?"

"She's concerned," Jameson said.

"Concerned?!"

"She doesn't have the luxury of anger."

"Funny. It doesn't feel luxurious to me. A nice new BMW would be luxurious. A Riviera cruise—that's luxurious—a weekend at The Plaza, yes—Lawson Klein's bullshit? That's a lot of things. Luxurious is not one of them. That's more like being forced to bathe in a sewage plant."

Jameson laughed. "Interesting perspective."

"JD, I'm serious."

"I know. I get it. When the news broke this morning, I wanted to catch the next flight to wherever Klein is and kick his ass."

"Whoa, JD," Michelle chuckled. "Mom stopped you, huh?"

"More like she reminded me I had more important things to attend to."

"I don't want to know."

Jameson rolled her eyes. "Only you, Shell."

Shell's eyes lifted to the hallway when she heard her mother's voice approaching.

"I appreciate it, Glenn," Candace said.

"Are you sure this is what you want to do?" Glenn asked.

"We're sure," Jessica replied.

Glenn nodded. "I'll make the arrangements."

"Thank you," Candace said.

"It's what I do," he told her.

The threesome came into view, and Michelle's eyes met her mother's. Candace smiled at her and turned back to her campaign manager. "Call me when we are all set," she said.

"Of course."

"Jess, could you," Candace began.

Jameson spoke up. "I'll see Glenn out," she offered.

Candace nodded her thanks.

"Mom?" Michelle addressed her mother cautiously.

"Shell. Why don't you have a seat?" Candace suggested.

"What's going on?" Michelle wanted to know.

Candace smiled. "Your brother and sister will be here in half an hour."

"Family meeting? Mom? You're not dropping out; are you?"

"No," Candace put the thought to rest.

"Okay? No offense, but is Jessica representing you again?"

Jessica shook her head. "Nothing like that."

"What is it like?" Michelle asked.

"Shell," Candace warned. "We'll explain everything when Jonah and Marianne are here."

Michelle huffed and got up from her seat.

"Where are you going?" Candace asked.

"Well, if you aren't going to tell me anything, I might as well go raid Grandma's cookies with Coop."

Candace snickered. "At least, some things never change."

"Candy, I'm sorry this has all come down on you," Jessica said.

"I'm not."

"It's my fault for not…"

"No, it isn't," Candace cut off Jessica's train of thought. "This is where we are. We'll all get through it—all of us. How is Grant?"

"I think he's relieved," Jessica said. "I can't believe he was worried that I would be angry."

"He loves you," Candace said.

"He loves you too."

"I know. You're his mother, Jess. As much as he loves Mr. and Mrs. Hill, you're the mother he's needed."

"I hope I don't disappoint him."

Candace smiled. "Don't sell yourself short. You've been wonderful to him and with him. I know it hasn't been easy to hide that relationship."

"It's what he needed."

"Exactly," Candace said.

"How do you think the kids will react?" Jessica asked.

Candace shrugged. She honestly wasn't sure how her children would react. She suspected that Michelle would feel a modicum of betrayal when she learned about Grant. But she also guessed that Marianne and Jonah would understand and be supportive. That would inevitably help Michelle to come around. Candace's biggest concern was for Grant.

"They'll be fine," she said. "It's not about them."

"I wish that it could have been different."

"Me too," Candace said.

"Hey," Jameson stepped into the room. "Sorry if I'm intruding."

Candace smiled and patted the cushion next to her. "Not at all."

Jameson looked at Jessica. "How are you doing?" she asked.

"Nervous," Jessica said.

Jameson nodded. "I can imagine. For whatever it's worth, I'm sorry you have to go through this publicly."

"Thanks," Jessica said. "I appreciate you being so understanding. I'm not sure that I would be if I were in your position."

Jameson took a deep breath. "I remember when Klein paraded Cooper's grandmother on the morning shows. I was so angry. More than that, it hurt. Cooper's my son. All I want it to keep him safe."

"I understand," Jessica replied.

"I'm sure that you do," Jameson said.

"But Grant isn't four-years-old," Jessica pointed out the obvious.

"No," Jameson agreed. "It doesn't matter. If it had been Jonah or Shell or Marianne, I would have felt the same way." She exchanged a smile with Candace.

"I'm going to go talk to Shell," Candace said.

"I thought that you wanted to wait until Jonah and Marianne got here?" Jameson was confused.

"I do. But this is Shell. Honestly, I think it might be best if I didn't blindside her with her sister and brother in the room."

"Do you want me to go with you?" Jessica asked.

"No," Candace replied. "I think it's best if I talk to her first." She offered Jessica a smile, winked at Jameson and headed off to find Michelle.

"She doesn't expect that to go well," Jessica observed.

Jameson considered how she should respond. Jessica and Michelle had been close during Candace's relationship with the lawyer. Their split had hurt Michelle deeply, and it had taken Michelle a long time to allow Jessica to be a part of her life again. Jameson had spent enough time with Candace's former partner to know that Jessica Stearns still cared deeply for Candace and her children. She also felt sure that Jessica carried a great deal of regret.

"Shell will be okay," Jameson said.

"I don't know."

"I do. She loves you. She's Shell. You know her, she gets up in arms for a few minutes. Once she calms down, she'll be able to see things clearly. That's why Candace wants to talk to her first. Shell does love you, Jessica."

"She loves you, Jameson. I'm her friend."

Jameson shook her head. "I think she sees you as more than that. You were a second parent to her for seven years. I wouldn't underestimate what that means to her."

"I made a lot of mistakes."

"That you wish you hadn't?" Jameson asked.

Jessica sighed. Jameson had always treated her with kindness. This was an awkward discussion. It was unusual for Jessica to be alone with Jameson. There was no point in lying. She was sure Jameson would see right through her. "Yes. If I'm to be honest—yes. I wish I had made different choices."

"You still love her."

"Candy?"

Jameson nodded.

"In my own way."

"Can't say I blame you."

"The truth is I just wish I hadn't hurt them all so badly. I don't think Candy and I were meant for the long haul."

"Good thing for me."

Jessica laughed. "There is that," she agreed. "She didn't deserve what I put her through. I know that. You don't come across women like Candy every day."

Jameson smiled. *That's an understatement.* "Don't worry about the kids. I think they might surprise you."

"I let them down too," Jessica admitted. "

"And you think that means you will let Grant down; am I right?"

"I don't have a terrific parental track record."

Jameson shrugged. "Who does?"

"You do."

Jameson laughed. "Oh, no I don't. For a year, I thought Marianne was plotting my death."

Jessica chuckled. "She can be a tough nut to crack."

"I don't know what the hell I'm doing most of the time with any of them," Jameson confessed. "I just do the best I can to be there when they need me."

"Sounds simple."

"Not even a little bit," Jameson said with another laugh. "Sometimes, I can't believe the things that come out of their mouths, or their butts," she laughed harder. "Not the grown-up ones," she clarified.

Jessica smiled. "Thanks for clarifying that."

"You're welcome. The point is, you will be fine. Just be honest," Jameson suggested. "Listen. Be there. That's really all you can do."

"Thanks."

"Hey, I'm a novice. I just got lucky and married an expert who was raised by the chief herself. Good thing I'm graded on a curve or I'd be screwed."

Jessica laughed. *No wonder she loves you, Jameson.*

———————

"I thought you were raiding the cookies with Cooper," Candace said.

"Coop went upstairs to draw. Beer looked like a better option. Call it preparedness."

Candace took a seat at the kitchen table. "The sky is not falling, Shell."

"Really? Then why were you hiding in the office with Glenn and Jessica?"

"I wasn't hiding."

"Okay?"

Candace shook her head. "I'm going to tell you what we talked about."

"Now?"

"Yes, now."

"Really?"

"You know, Shell you are one of the most intelligent and thoughtful people I know. There is one thing that you need to work on a bit."

"What?"

"There are times when things happen in my life that aren't about you—any of you."

"You mean us kids."

"I do."

"And, this is one of those things? Because, Mom? Hearing we have a brother we never knew about on the news kind of feels like it might be about us too."

"You don't have a brother that you don't know about."

"So? What's the deal then?" Michelle asked. "What does Grant Hill have to do with you?"

"Grant is Jessica's son."

Michelle stared at her mother.

"She had him when she was seventeen," Candace explained. "Grant found her the year we got together."

"Jessica has a kid?"

Candace nodded.

"How come you never told us?"

"We wanted to," Candace said. "Grant's adopted family would not have been supportive of him having a relationship with Jessica. He's spent most of his adult life trying to reconcile his two families."

Michelle pondered the information. "That's who's been calling you all these months since Lawson Klein got canned from FVI."

Candace nodded.

"Holy shit. He's been helping you?"

Candace nodded again.

"Holy shit." Michelle remained silent for a few minutes.

"Shell?"

"Is Jessica okay?" Michelle asked.

Candace smiled. *Well, I'll be damned.* "She's worried about Grant. She's also worried about what you might say."

"Me?"

"Yes, you. Do I need to remind you that you and Jess have had a rather mucky path?"

"Yeah, but this isn't about me. I mean, I can't even imagine being pregnant at seventeen. Hell, I'm scared now! And, Grant Hill? Seriously? Of all people..."

"Grant isn't who you think he is."

"Obviously not. What about you, Mom?"

"Do you mean me or my campaign?"

"Both."

Candace sighed. "As a candidate, I will be fine."

"And you?"

"I'm worried about Grant. And, I'm concerned for Jess. She's hurting too. She feels like who she is has made his life more painful."

"Bullshit. She's not the bigot in the room."

"No," Candace agreed. "She is his mother, Shell. And, believe it or not, that means the world to her."

"I believe it."

"Maybe you should tell her that," Candace suggested.

"Me?"

"Yes—you. Jess loves you, Shell. I think it nearly killed her, knowing how much she hurt you kids—you most of all. I know she's worried you'll push her away again."

"I wish you had told us," Michelle said. "But I think I can understand why you didn't. Do you really think she's worried about me?"

"I don't think it. She is."

"I'll talk to her."

———

Candace appeared in the doorway and Jessica looked at her fearfully.

"Shell wants to talk to you. She's waiting for you."

"Is the kitchen really the best place for this talk?"

Candace smiled. "Worried about the knife block?" she teased.

"A little."

"Go on," Candace said.

Jessica nodded.

Candace chuckled as Jessica left the room.

"You're not worried about knives, I take it?" Jameson said

"Not at all."

———

"Hi."

"You look like the last victim in a horror film," Michelle said. "Want a beer?"

Jessica was genuinely confused.

"No offense, you look like you could use one," Michelle said. She moved to the refrigerator and retrieved a beer for Jessica. "I'll join you."

Jessica tipped her head slightly. "What did your mom tell you?"

Michelle passed Jessica a beer. "She told me that Grant Hill is not my long-lost brother. At least, not biologically. Are you okay?" she asked.

Jessica's eyes flew open and instantly began to water.

Michelle smiled. "I'm sorry, Jessica."

"Sorry?"

"That you were afraid to tell me. Sometimes, I can be an ass."

"I wouldn't say that."

"No? I would—so would my wife," Michelle joked. "I can't imagine how hard this has been for you. I mean, having to hide your relationship with your son. I can't even imagine what that must have felt like."

Tears slipped over Jessica's cheeks. "I wanted to tell you—your mom did too."

"I know."

"I don't want you to think that we were trying to keep secrets from you."

"You were. It wasn't your secret you were keeping this time," Michelle said.

"No, it wasn't."

"Can I ask you something?"

"Sure."

"How much of a toll did this take on you and mom?"

Jessica sighed. "It took a toll on me. That caused issues between us."

"I'm sorry."

"Me too. I have to admit I am surprised at your reaction."

Michelle nodded. "Mel and I are trying to have a baby."

"Wow."

"I know, right?" Michelle laughed. "It's kind of an uphill battle for us right now. We've talked about all kinds of options including adoption. I think Mom and JD adopting Cooper made me realize a lot of things. And then, Mel finding out how difficult it would be for her to conceive—I don't know, it gives you a different perspective. I guess thinking about becoming someone's mom makes you see things you can't see as someone's kid."

Jessica smiled. "That's true."

"You still love Mom; don't you?"

Jessica smirked.

"Is that a funny question?"

"No," Jessica replied. "Jameson asked me the same thing earlier."

"Oh."

"I will always love your mother, Shell; just like I will always love you. I'm not in love with her if that's what you mean. That took a long time for me to get past. I'm glad that I have her friendship. I feel like my baggage is hurting her again."

Michelle shook her head. "She doesn't feel that way."

"Maybe not, but it feels that way to me."

"This isn't your fault," Michelle said. "I think Mom is more worried about you and Grant than she is about her campaign." Michelle chuckled.

"Why is that amusing?"

"It's not. I was just thinking that we should all probably be more worried about Klein and Ritchie. Problem is, I look forward to watching her eat them for dinner."

Jessica laughed. "I hear you. Thank you."

"Don't thank me. I know how much you care about Mom."

"Not just your mom."

"Yeah, I know," Michelle said.

"What do you think Marianne will say?"

Michelle shrugged. "Marianne will understand."

"You think so?"

"She's the same but different."

"Uh-huh."

"She'll understand," Michelle repeated her opinion. Jessica sighed. "Look, I know that Marianne is still kind of distant where you are concerned."

"More like she's in another galaxy."

"Yeah, well… She's protective, and not just of Mom."

"She and Jameson have gotten close," Jessica surmised.

"I think JD is her best friend—weird, I know. I just know that JD tells Marianne things she wouldn't tell me or

Jonah. I think Marianne tells JD just about everything. After Rick died, they started to bond. At first, I thought that was because of Spencer. I think it's a lot more than that. Jameson is super protective of all of us too. Their relationship is different."

"I think I understand. I just wish she would forgive me."

Michelle shrugged. "She saw more than we did. I didn't know for a long time. She found Mom on the floor crying when you left. She remembers seeing Mom like that after an argument with Dad, and she is the only one who remembers anything about Mom after Lucas died—even if that is more like impressions for her. It's harder for her."

Jessica nodded. "Marianne is a lot like your mom."

Michelle smiled. A few years earlier, Michelle would have disagreed with that statement. As time passed, as the family changed, Michelle had come to realize that while Marianne's actions sometimes challenged everyone, Marianne's reasons resided in the same place as their mother's. Just like Candace, she was the protector. "She is." Michelle pushed her chair back and offered her hand to Jessica. "What do you say we go see what Mom and JD are up to?"

"Why? Think they will try to escape this family meeting your mother has called?"

"Nah. Not unless there is a Bible handy."

Jessica narrowed her gaze curiously. Michelle grinned.

"Never mind," Jessica said. "I'm pretty sure I don't want to know."

Candace watched her children's faces as recognition struck them. Jonah looked at Marianne.

"What do you need from us?" Marianne asked her mother.

"I would like to invite Grant up here next Sunday when I get back from New Hampshire," Candace replied.

Marianne smiled. "Barbecue?"

"I think that's a great idea," Jameson chimed.

"Let's keep it to the family," Candace said. She looked at Michelle.

"Why are you looking at me?" Michelle asked.

"Family, Shell," Candace said. "God knows, our family is big enough now to intimidate almost anyone. Grant is feeling insecure about all of this. No campaign ploys from anyone. This is about family."

"His parents didn't take it well?" Marianne guessed.

Jessica shook her head sadly. "Not at all. They told him to make a choice."

"Jesus," Jonah groaned. "What the hell is wrong with people?"

Jameson squeezed Jonah's shoulder. His father-in-law had been a thorn in the side of the entire family. Lawson Klein's crusade against Candace hadn't hurt anyone as much as it had Laura. Jonah dealt with the fallout daily.

"Is he behind all of this?" Jonah asked pointedly.

Candace took a deep breath. "Lawson Klein isn't the only player in the game, Jonah."

"Maybe not but is he the one behind this?" Jonah challenged.

"He is close to Jed Ritchie and Bradley Wolfe," Candace said.

"So, in other words—yes."

"Jonah," Jameson steadied her voice.

"What?" Jonah snapped. "I'm sorry, Jessica. I'm not upset with you at all. I'm sick of lying back while this son-of-a-bitch hurls accusation and lies at my family. When do we hit back?" He looked at his mother.

Candace's eyes closed. She understood Jonah's frustration. She felt it acutely. More than once, Candace had fantasized about taking to the airwaves and spewing all of Lawson Klein's dirty laundry. She had plenty of ammunition she could unleash. Now was not the time. If Candace could help it, she would avoid mud wrestling with the likes of Lawson Klein. What Jonah couldn't understand was that Candace's reasons for sticking to her script had more to do with protecting Jonah's family than with advancing her career. Regardless of Klein's actions, he was Laura's father. Candace didn't want to drag her daughter-in-law's father through the mud—even if he deserved it.

"Mom?" Jonah urged.

"We hit back when your mother wins this election," Jameson replied.

"If she wins," Jonah said. "I'm sorry, Mom. I want you to win. I do. But I'm sick of this asshole."

Candace smiled. "You don't have anything to apologize for, Jonah." She turned to the rest of the room and changed the subject. "If you are all comfortable with a barbecue to introduce Grant to this circus, I will…"

"I'll take care of it," Marianne said. She looked at Jessica. "Maybe you could help?"

Jessica nodded. "I'd love to."

"Good. Why don't we open a bottle of wine and sit out back for a bit?" Candace suggested. She let the room begin to empty and grabbed hold of Jonah's arm. "A minute?" she asked him.

Jonah shook his head. "Mom, I…"

Candace held up her hand. "I understand how you feel."

"Do you?"

"Yes."

"You have to have something on him."

Candace sighed.

"See? You do!"

"Jonah," Candace began cautiously. "Be careful what you wish for."

"What is that supposed to mean?"

"It means that Laura has already been hurt enough. That's what it means."

"Yeah, by him."

"Perhaps. That doesn't mean he can't hurt her any more than he has."

Jonah shook his head.

"I know you want to punch back—so, do I," Candace said.

"Why don't you? I know you. You won't make up some lie. If you have something, it's the truth."

"Just because something is true doesn't mean it can't hurt innocent people."

"I don't care," Jonah said.

"Really? Even if that person is your wife? Even if it's her mother? Jonah," Candace sighed again. "Sucker punching Lawson Klein might feel great for a few minutes. It won't knock him out of the ring, and the collateral damage is... It's not worth it. Jameson was right. It's best to wait for the knock-out punch."

"Mom... She was throwing up this morning and not because of morning sickness—because he came at you—again. She's so afraid that something he does will push me away, will make you hate her..."

"There is nothing Lawson Klein or anyone else could ever say or do that would make me hate Laura."

"Yeah, I know that. She knows that. She just... She feels responsible no matter what either of us say."

"I'll talk to her."

"What do you have on him?"

"Jonah..."

"Mom, come on."

"Let's just say that Lawson has both personal and business relationships that do not align with the values he espouses publicly."

"What? Like he had an affair or something? He stole? What?"

"Let it go, Jonah."

"Are you going to? Let it go?"

"I keep my cards close to the vest," Candace said. "You need to trust me—if and when the time comes that Lawson's deeds become public, it will hurt Laura and Mary."

Jonah sighed. "I just hate being helpless."

"You're not."

"I am! I can't even protect my family."

"You do protect them."

"Really? How exactly do I do that?"

"You love them."

"That's not enough, Mom."

Candace smiled. *So much like Jameson.* "It's everything, Jonah." She kissed him on the cheek. "Come on," she said as she took his hand.

"Planning on getting me drunk to calm me down?"

Candace laughed. "Will that work?"

"Maybe."

"I think Jameson has some beer in the fridge."

Jonah shook his head. "You call JD a lunatic?"

Candace shrugged. "Takes one to know one," she said with a wink.

Chapter Six

"Doesn't it make you angry?" a young girl asked. "I've seen lots of things on the internet about you that are mean. Doesn't that make you angry?"

Candace sat on her stool and listened. She lifted the microphone in her hand slowly. "What's your name?" she asked the girl.

"Jen."

"Well, Jen the truth is it does make me angry. It's hurtful."

The girl considered Candace's candid reply. "Why do they do that? The truth always comes out anyway. That's what my mother says."

Candace imagined that Jen was about thirteen. "Your mother sounds like a smart lady," she said. She took a deep breath. "What grade are you in?" she asked.

"Eighth."

"Oh, I remember when my daughters were in eighth grade." Candace chuckled along with most of the audience. She shrugged, got up from her stool and made her way to the girl in the audience. "Politics is a bit like middle school." She laughed. "There are groups of people who like the same things that sit together at lunch," she explained. "Every so often there's a bully in the cafeteria. A wise woman always told me to consider the source. I'm not sure I can answer why people do what they do. I suppose they think it will make people like them. Some people think the best way to be popular is to make someone else look foolish."

"Who do you tell?" the girl asked innocently. "I mean, my mom would tell me to tell my teacher or something."

Candace smiled broadly. She loved engaging with people—young people most of all. The innocence of youth kept her hopeful. "That's a good question. I guess I still believe that most people will see who I am no matter what someone else says. So, I just tell the truth and answer people's questions—like yours, and I hope they will accept that I am who I say I am."

The girl thought for a minute.

"Did you have another question?" Candace asked.

"Do you ever want to quit?"

Candace laughed. "Daily," she said. "But then I meet someone like you, and I remember why I ran for office in the first place. Maybe one day you will think about doing the same thing."

The moderator stepped in. "Thank you all so much for coming. Governor Reid is due at the State Capital shortly for a meeting with Governor Brandt. I wish we had more time."

Candace offered the room a wave. She held her finger up to the moderator and Michelle who stood off to the side. She stepped up to the young girl who had asked the last question and extended her hand to a woman she presumed was her mother. "You must be Jen's mother."

"Sheila," the woman said. "Thank you so much for answering her question. She's been so excited to see you."

"Thank you for bringing her," Candace replied. She looked back at the girl. "And thank you for speaking up." Candace held back a chuckle when the girl blushed. She waved Michelle over. "How about we have Shell take a picture for us?" she suggested. An excited nod served as her reply.

Michelle took Sheila's phone and snapped a few photos. Candace looked at the star-struck teenager. "Tell you what; why don't you give Shell your contact information? On one of my stops, you and your mom can be my guest. Sound good?"

"Really?"

Candace winked. "I have to run. Nice meeting you both," she said. "Shell."

Michelle nodded her understanding. "I'll catch up to you."

Candace nodded her thanks.

"Is she serious?" Jen asked.

"My mom never breaks a promise if she can help it," Michelle said.

"Your mom's her hero," Sheila said.

Michelle beamed. "Mine too," she told them. "Mine too."

"Momma?"

Jameson put down her pencil and swiveled her chair to greet her son. "There you are."

"Yep. Grandma took me for pizza."

"I heard."

"Whatya' doing?" Cooper asked.

"Me? I was just working on a project," Jameson told him.

"When's Mommy coming home?" he asked.

Jameson pulled Cooper onto her lap. "She'll be home in two days."

Cooper frowned. "Can we call her?"

Jameson looked up at the clock above her desk. "Aw, buddy, not right now," she told him. "Mommy is talking to a big group of people right now."

Cooper huffed.

Jameson pulled Cooper up onto her lap. "You miss Mommy, huh?" Cooper nodded. "Me too."

Jameson did miss Candace. Candace had been away for three days. Two more seemed like a lifetime to Jameson. Logic told her to roll with it and reassure Cooper. Inevitably, there would come a time when Candace would be away for longer than a few days. This trip was a chance to ease Cooper into that reality. Jameson felt Cooper nestle against her and she sighed. *Aw, screw it.*

"Tell you what," Jameson said. "Why don't you go see if Grandma is still in the kitchen? Tell her I said you could have a couple of cookies while I finish a couple of things here."

"But I just ate pizza."

Jameson chuckled. "That must have been hours ago now." Cooper giggled. "Go find Grandma and I will meet you in the kitchen."

"'Kay. Momma?"

"Yeah?"

"Then can we call Mommy?"

"Then we will call Mommy."

Cooper smiled and scurried off happily.

"Shit," Jameson groaned. "I have no willpower." She picked up her cell phone and dialed Michelle.

"JD?"

"Yep, that would be me."

"Everything okay?"

"Depends on how you define okay."

"Well, do I need to pull Mom away from the people she's talking to?"

"No. Nothing is wrong. Just... Shell, do you think you could get your mom's room upgraded?"

"Upgraded?" Michelle was confused. "She's got a suite, JD."

"Oh."

"What's going on? Oh, wait—you're coming here; aren't you?"

"Coop is missing his Mommy."

Michelle sniggered. *Yeah, I'm sure it's all about Cooper.* She was sure that Cooper was missing Candace. She was also certain that Jameson was worried about how Candace was holding up. "She's okay," Michelle said.

"I'm sure she is," Jameson replied.

"I'll make sure they bring in a rollaway for Coop."

"Thanks."

"Anything else?" Michelle asked.

"How is she—really?"

Michelle looked off into the distance to where her mother was standing with several of Governor Brandt's interns. "She's good, JD—honest. She should be at the hotel by around nine."

"That late?"

"Yeah. She has dinner with Governor Brandt and some of the DNC's larger local donors at six-thirty."

Jameson glanced back up at the clock. "Can you..."

"I'll make sure they know you are coming. Do you want me to tell her or..."

"No. Not unless you think..."

"She'll be happy to see you both," Michelle said.

"Shell?"

"Yeah?"

"Thanks." Jameson put her phone in her pocket and placed the plans she'd been drafting in her desk. *Well, it's a good way to practice packing.*

Candace heard the chatter at the dinner table. Little of it penetrated her consciousness. Her mind was on other things and other people.

"Governor?" a voice pulled her from her private musing.

"Sorry," Candace apologized.

"Dale was just asking about the story circulation that The Stratton Foundation is under federal investigation."

Candace pressed down her disgust and smiled. *More bullshit.* "It's an interesting story," she said.

"But is it true?"

"Not to my knowledge."

"You're not concerned?"

Candace took a sip from her wine glass and set the glass back down slowly. "Why should I be?"

"If there is any..."

"In the last month, I have been accused of having a long-lost child that I hid for over thirty-five years. I've heard the rumor that my wife is a drug addict and there was an elaborate cover-up to disguise her addiction therapy with a story that she was volunteering her services at the clinic her cousin directs. And, I have listened to the ridiculous assessment that my son is really my grandchild—another conspiracy afoot." Candace offered the table a sickly-sweet smile. "None of it is true."

"I understand, but the foundation is a different matter."

"Is it?" Candace asked. "My brother has released all The Stratton Foundation's financial records for the last thirty years. If there is something to find—anything to find—I am certain someone will uncover it," she said.

"You're not concerned."

"No."

"Governor Reid, we all respect you. You have to know that innuendo can sink a campaign—even one as formidable as yours."

"Yes, it can," she agreed.

"What's your plan to combat this?"

"Which this are you referring to?" Candace challenged the table. She took a deep breath before continuing. "You want me to strike back, make denials, hit Wolfe's surrogates below the belt."

"That's part of the game."

Candace nodded. "You think this is a game?"

"Candace," Governor Brandt decided to enter the conversation. "You know that everyone here supports you."

"Is that so?" she asked. She took another deep breath and exhaled slowly. "You all want to support a winner, and you want that winner to support your interests. That's the playbook." Candace sipped her wine again. "I've been at this longer than some of you have been able to vote," she said. "I've seen people climb the ladder only to be knocked off the last rung. I have no intention of letting that happen."

"So, you do have a plan."

"The plan is to campaign as I always have."

"Some of the dirt is going to stick," one of the older men said. "If there is something that might be damaging, we might be able to help quell it."

"Perhaps. Anything can be damaging, gentleman. My wife and I adopted a little boy who had lost his mother. He happens to be the light of our lives. Somehow, that became a weapon for the other side. My grandfather established a foundation to give back to the community that had always supported him. That is now under a microscope. That's how some people play this game. No good deed goes unpunished," she said. "I expected that when I chose to launch this campaign. I also know that the people out there supporting me expect certain things of me. Win or lose, there are people looking to me. I have more at stake than riding on Air Force One. I'm not going to compromise myself to win any election, and I am not going to betray the reasons I started in this life in the first place. That doesn't mean I won't fight."

"You know, if the establishment gets behind Wolfe, he could become a formidable opponent."

"If he wins the nomination, they will. They'll have no choice," Candace surmised.

"People like an outsider. Not to be... You know that being a woman and..."

Candace smiled. "And being a lesbian puts me at a disadvantage. That's what you were going to say. Maybe. I may not be an outsider," she admitted. "I'm hardly the status quo." She let her eyes meet with each person at the table. "You each have to decide what horse you want to back in this race. Look around you," she instructed them. She smiled. "No one looks quite like me; do they? That's never lost on me, gentlemen."

"We all understand that you have a legacy you want to create. You have to get elected to do that."

Candace shook her head. "That's where we part company." She pushed out her chair and stood. "Winning elections or losing elections is not what creates someone's legacy. The money you invest in my campaign or in my opponent's—that won't guarantee your legacy either. It might not even secure your interests. What I can promise you is that what you see is what you are buying. Period. I will listen to your concerns and ideas on policies that matter to your legacy. That's what I can guarantee." Candace smiled at the group. "Now, if you will excuse me, I have an early morning tomorrow. There is still that thing we call governing that requires my attention."

The table's occupants all stood as Candace took her leave.

"Why do I feel like we were just dismissed?"

Governor Brandt chuckled. "We were."

Candace closed her eyes and let her head fall back onto the seat behind her.

"Mom?"

"I don't want to know," Candace replied without opening her eyes.

"I thought you handled it well," Michelle said.

Candace pried one eye open.

Michelle laughed. "I'll bet you'll see an uptick in donations."

"Were we at the same dinner?" Candace sighed. "Why is it that I don't think you asked for my attention to comment on my bullshit meter?"

"Jonah called."

"Why do I think I am not going to like this?"

Michelle groaned. "Klein called Mary."

"What?"

"Apparently, he told her that she and Laura could come home. He thought now might be a good time—before things got ugly."

Candace rolled her eyes.

"Jonah's pissed, Mom. I'm not sure I have ever heard him sound that mad."

"I don't blame him."

"What are you going to do?" Michelle asked.

"There's not much I can do, Shell. There's not much Jonah can do either except support Laura."

"Isn't there something we can do to shut him up?"

Candace sighed. "I'm not sure anything will do that."

"There has to be something on him."

"There's plenty on him," Candace said. "People like Lawson Klein don't back down. That's why they're called zealots."

"So, we just ignore him?"

"There is nothing someone like Lawson Klein hates more than being ignored."

"Won't that just make him more vocal?"

Candace smiled. "That's what I'm hoping."

"You want him to go after you?"

"I want his loose lips to sink his ship."

Michelle remained confused.

"I'll call Laura tomorrow," Candace promised. "Trust me on this one, Shell."

"I do trust you. I just think there is something you're not telling me."

Candace smiled, closed her eyes and let her head fall back again.

What aren't you telling me, Mom?

Jameson heard the door to the hotel suite open. She leaned down into Cooper's ear. "Mommy's back."

Cooper looked up at her and Jameson gestured for him to meet Candace. Cooper flew off the bed and ran into the other room. "Mommy!"

Candace jumped slightly at the sight that greeted her. "Cooper? What are you doing here?" she asked as she bent down to accept his hug.

"I missed you."

"I missed you too. Where's your momma?"

"Hi," Jameson greeted her wife. Candace looked up gratefully. Jameson immediately noted the fatigue in Candace's eyes. "We missed you."

Candace let Cooper lead her to the sofa. "I can't believe you're here." Cooper climbed up beside her and cuddled up against her. "Tired?" she asked him. He nodded. Candace kissed his head and closed her eyes in contentment.

"He made me promise that he could wait up for you," Jameson explained. She looked at Cooper and chuckled. "Now that you're here, I guess he figured he could give in."

Candace jostled Cooper so that his head fell onto her lap.

"Bad day?" Jameson asked.

"Long day."

"I hope it's okay that we came."

"I can't begin to tell you how glad I am that you did."

"Want to talk about it?"

"Nope."

Jameson smiled. "Let me go put him down so you can get comfortable."

"No," Candace protested. "Leave him for a bit. Come sit with me."

Jameson complied. She leaned in and kissed Candace tenderly. "Are you okay?"

"Just tired."

Jameson placed Cooper's legs over hers. Candace's head fell onto her shoulder, and Jameson kissed her temple. "I can put him down."

"No," Candace said. "I just want to sit here for a while."

Jameson made no reply. Candace's breathing deepened immediately, and Jameson was certain that sleep would claim her wife in an instant. She managed to get an arm around Candace and hold her closer. "I wonder if I can carry them both," she chuckled softly.

"Don't even try," Candace's groggy reply came.

Jameson laughed. "The sofa it is."

Candace watched as Jameson climbed into the bed. "I can't believe you came. Why didn't you call?"

"I called Shell. You had a full plate."

"Is that what you call it?"

"It was a bad day," Jameson surmised.

Candace nestled into Jameson's arms. "No," she said. "It was just a day."

"I know that we agreed that Cooper needs to adjust to your travel, but I…"

Candace silenced Jameson with a kiss.

"What was that for?"

"Honestly, Jameson? I know he needs to learn to cope with my absences. I just don't have the desire to keep him from traveling with me when it's possible."

Candace had told Jameson that when Shell and Jonah were little, she had made a point of getting them acquainted with her travel schedule. Jameson sensed that when it came to Cooper, Candace's intentions differed. "Rethinking keeping Cooper home?"

Candace shifted so that she could look at Jameson. "Maybe it's selfish," she admitted. "I know that it's inevitable—separation for longer periods than I would like. Whenever possible, I'd like him close."

"I don't think it's selfish."

"It is. I don't want it to be harder for him than it has to be when I'm away. Common sense tells me I need to stick to my guns and let him get used to short separations."

"But?"

"I don't know. It's different with Cooper than it was with the other kids."

"How so?"

"For one thing, they had each other," Candace said. "And, for another? I'm different. My life is different, and I don't just mean this campaign or my career."

Jameson listened without comment.

"Pearl's not a young woman anymore."

"Don't tell her that," Jameson quipped.

Candace giggled. "I won't. You know what I mean. And, the kids? They are all dealing with their families. It's not fair to ask them to take on Cooper too."

"They don't feel that way."

"No, but that doesn't make it less true."

"And?" Jameson asked, sensing there was more.

"Jonathan is a good man, Jameson. He wasn't what I would call an enthusiastic father. He was content to take the kids to the movies once in a while or sit at a holiday dinner. If it hadn't been for Pearl, I'm not sure what I would have done."

"And now?"

"I miss being with you and Cooper. Don't misunderstand me; I missed my kids when I had to travel. Three kids on the road with me all by myself? There was no way I could make that work for them or for me. I wish I could have. With Cooper..."

"I get it."

"I know what I missed out on," Candace explained. "I hate that I missed so much. I want to be there for as much as I can be with Cooper. God knows, if I win this election that will become more challenging."

"So, you don't mind us meeting you when we can?"

Candace smiled. "I hope that you will."

"Do you want to tell me about your day now?"

Candace sighed. "There's not much to tell."

"I find that hard to believe."

"The serial killer case is still prominent in the news. My donors want to know what I am going to do to fight Wolfe's cronies. There's flooding in Plattsburg that is threatening multiple communities. The budget needs to pass without any major dissension. I need to be in five places at once," Candace said. "And this is the only place I have any desire to be."

"In a hotel?" Jameson teased.

Candace laughed. "With you, you lunatic."

Jameson stroked Candace's back. "Whatever you need, all you have to do is ask."

"This," Candace replied. "This is what I need."

"Tell me again why people say you are demanding?"

Candace laughed again. "Because I am."

"You'll figure it out."

"I'm glad you are so confident."

"You will," Jameson said. "It's what you do."

"Not according to some people. I wish I had the answers."

Jameson reached over to the bedside table and handed Candace a fortune cookie. Candace lifted her eyebrow. "Well? Open it. See what it says."

Candace cracked open the cookie and rolled her eyes.

"What does it say?" Jameson asked. Candace handed Jameson the slip of paper. Jameson read it aloud. "Some days you are pigeon, some days you are statue. Today, bring umbrella—in bed." She pursed her lips and shrugged. "Kinky."

Candace's laughter filled the room. "You are certifiable."

Jameson winked. "Beats the one I got."

"Oh?"

"Yeah, mine said You have no luck—in bed."

Candace chuckled. She climbed on top of Jameson and grinned. "Defective cookie." She kissed Jameson soundly.

"Should I get the umbrella now?"

Candace shook her head. She kissed Jameson again. "Do you have one?"

Jameson lost all hope of remaining serious and burst out laughing. "I love you," she said.

Candace winked. "I think your luck just changed."

Jameson closed her eyes as Candace's lips tasted hers. *Thank God for fortune cookies.*

Chapter Seven

Candace looked at the name of the caller on her phone and groaned inwardly. She had received a call from FBI Assistant Director Bower late the previous evening advising her that the task force had concerns for her safety. It was not in Candace's nature to overreact. The call had startled her more than she had let on to her staff.

"Alex," she accepted the call.

"I'm sure you are thrilled to hear my voice."

Candace laughed. "That depends on whether it's to tell me I need to head to a bunker or not."

Alex smiled. There was little doubt in her mind that Bower's call would have unsettled the governor. But, Alex had known Candace for many years. She was a seasoned politician who was often in the spotlight. Threats were a reality someone of Candace's notoriety had to deal with. "If it makes you feel any better, I think you're safe."

"But?" Candace questioned.

"I'm not one to take chances. You know that."

"I suppose, I do."

"Have there been any unusual threats lately?" Alex asked.

"Not that have been brought to my attention," Candace said. "Which means, if there have been, they were not deemed credible."

"No letters or anything?"

"There are always letters, Alex. I get thousands of letters," Candace replied. "It takes time for staff to pour through them."

"I'd like our team to take a look," Alex said. "Just to be certain."

"Out of an abundance of caution?" Candace asked.

"Something like that."

Candace laughed. "We both know this is a courtesy request."

Alex sighed. It was true. The FBI wouldn't meet with resistance if they asked to see Candace's fan mail. "It is," she admitted. "As an FBI agent, I want you to know that him coming after you does not fit the profile."

"And, as my friend?"

"I won't take any chances."

"Whatever you need, Alex. I told you that at the beginning."

"Candace, if you see anyone new around that doesn't fit, I want you to call me."

"Alex, there are new faces around me hourly."

"Everyday contractors, press, new security guards at the Capitol, volunteers at the campaign—those kinds of people."

"That's a daily occurrence."

"I know. You make a living reading people, just like I do. If someone doesn't fit, I want to know—me, not Bower, not anyone else—call me."

Candace closed her eyes and nodded—one more thing on her plate to deal with.

"Candace?"

"I'll keep my eyes open."

Alex debated with herself for less than a second before clarifying her reasons. "I don't think he's coming for you. I think he might want us to think that. He's delighting in the spotlight. Someone close, a campaign or staff member— that might be enough for him. Don't over think it, just pay attention."

Candace sighed. "You'll be the first to know."

"Good."

"Do me a favor?" Candace asked.

"Yeah?"

"Catch this son of a bitch?"

"Working on it."

Candace hung up the call, tossed the phone on her desk, and massaged her brow. "What the hell else can happen?" The phone on her desk beeped. "Really?" Candace looked at it. She pressed the intercom. "Yes, Susan?"

"Dan is here to review the flooding in Plattsburg."

"Give me two minutes," Candace requested.

"You've got it."

Candace let her face fall into her hands. She sucked in a deep breath, let it go forcefully and straightened her posture. She stretched her back, took another breath and readied herself for the next meeting. *Here we go.*

———◆———

"All due respect, it's not true," Deena Davis said.

Lawson Klein grinned. "According to?"

"According to everyone."

"We must have a different understanding of who everyone is."

Deena nodded. She was widely considered a fair-minded and even-handed TV journalist. While people understood that her personal leanings were more liberal, Deena Davis had made a name for herself as someone willing to take anyone to task when warranted. That made her show a hotbed for anyone hoping to validate a story.

"A different understanding?" she asked. "The sealed adoption records were released. Grant Hill has made a public statement. I'm not sure that I understand how you can maintain that Governor Reid is his biological mother."

"Records are only as good as the person who types them," he replied.

"Are you suggesting that Mr. Hill's adoption records were altered to protect Candace Reid?"

"I'm not suggesting anything other than the fact that records are only a reflection of the person who created them. Look at The Stratton Foundation. There's a mountain of evidence that the foundation engaged in funding the governor's campaigns when she was in the senate. We've seen it. Now, suddenly thirty years of records dispute that?"

Deena narrowed her gaze. "But, to your point, those records have existed for thirty years. Our team of analysts has poured over them. They've found a few instances where the foundation accepted money from well-known surrogates of Governor Reid's during election years. That's about it."

"I'd say that's a pretty big red flag."

"What do we do?" Michelle asked.

Glenn sighed. "Not much we can do. Once David released those documents, they became open to conjecture."

"Great."

"Relax, Shell," Glenn said. "It's a dead-end."

"Glenn, no offense, but it doesn't look great."

"It's typical. Your mother was not involved in the foundation other than to be its mouthpiece."

"That's our argument? Somehow, that sounds weak to me," Michelle observed.

"She's right," Candace said as she closed the door. Everyone hopped to their feet. "Sit," she instructed them.

"Mom, I..."

Candace held up her hand. "You're not wrong."

"Really?"

Candace chuckled. "Really." She looked at her campaign manager. "This is the one we need to worry about."

"Candy, once those documents made it into public..."

"I know. It's a potential long-term problem. Bring Doug in now."

"Candy," Glenn cautioned. "I know you have an affinity for Doug, and I know he agreed that he would..."

"Now, Glenn."

Glenn nodded.

Candace turned her attention to Michelle. "I need you to spend some time in the Albany campaign office."

"Why?" Michelle asked.

"I need eyes there that I can trust," Candace said.

"Is this about the campaign?"

"Yes and no," Candace replied.

"What's going on?" Glenn asked.

"The FBI wants us to keep our eyes open," Candace said.

"For?" Michelle asked.

"Anyone new that seems suspicious."

"Mom, the campaign office gets lots of people in an out."

"Yes, I know. That's why I need you there—one of the reasons."

"Okay? What are the other reasons?" Michelle asked.

"That's home base," Candace explained.

"Candy," Glenn interjected. "I still think it would be best to set up your main headquarters in the city. It's..."

"I know what it is. It's glitzy and central," Candace cut him off. "We're not running on glitz. We're running this campaign in grit. Albany it is."

"You're the boss," Glenn mumbled.

Candace sensed her campaign manager's frustration. She prided herself on listening to the advice of her staff. In the end, she was responsible for the success or failure of every decision made by her administration or her campaign. Sometimes, things that seemed simple to others carried greater weight with Candace. While it was true that she preferred to concentrate on the working pieces of her career, she did understand that optics mattered. Balancing the need to create excitement—even illusion in politics, and the gravity of managing policies was the crux of Candace's job both as governor and as a candidate.

"Listen," Candace began to address the room. "I know that you are frustrated with what you perceive as my opposition to your opinions. I've heard all of your arguments," she told the small group.

"Your poll numbers are holding," Glenn said. "But that isn't deterring Wolfe's team."

"No, I wouldn't expect it to."

"I just think that a higher profile office, maybe some advisers that play to your base right now is the best..."

Candace nodded. "You're not wrong," she told Glenn. "If the only thing to consider were this campaign, then I would be inclined to follow your advice. Maybe Manhattan would be a more attractive option for headquarters. Maybe we would wait to bring Doug on board until we are closer to the convention and the general. Maybe that would be the case. That is not where we sit. That's not where I sit. I still have a state to keep running," she reminded them. "A state whose legislature is held by the opposition party. I need to keep the moderates at the capital on board with this budget. I need the people in this state to know that they remain my priority and that I understand New York is more than the Big Apple. That has a direct implication for this campaign as well."

Glenn sighed.

"You know that I'm right. We might be able to seal the deal on my nomination without the suburbs. That will not work in a general election. If we hope to bring this home, we're going to need more than my base. That's not an opinion. That's a fact. The people we need live in places like Albany and Plattsburg—all over this country. Take a breath," she told them. "Don't get so tied up in this moment that you lose sight of the finish line."

Michelle listened to her mother and found herself smiling. She had little doubt that there were a host of reasons

Candace wanted her to take a role at Campaign Headquarters. She sometimes lost sight of how talented her mother was as a politician. Candace had glided to the governorship. As a senator, Candace had been an immensely popular figure in New York. Michelle was confident that her mother was correct. The east coast, cities across the country, and Candace's base would lock in their support for a Reid presidency early on. There might be some battles now, but the war was on the horizon.

"Whatever you need, Mom," Michelle said.

"What I need is for all of you to take a break," Candace said. She chuckled at the grateful collective sigh that followed. "See you later this afternoon," she said. "Shell?"

"Yeah?"

"Care to join me for a bite?"

"Is it leftovers in a carton?" Michelle asked.

"No. I thought that we could step out for lunch," Candace said.

"Seriously?"

"Why is that strange?"

"A month ago, it wouldn't have been," Michelle said. "I'm just surprised you want to go somewhere on the spur of the moment."

Candace nodded. It was becoming increasingly difficult for her to make impromptu visits to any public venue. It would only become a greater challenge as the months wore on. She had a few selfish reasons for headquartering her campaign in Albany. It was close to home and work. Candace enjoyed personal relationships with many local business owners. That would make last minute plans more feasible. The part of becoming president that Candace dreaded was seclusion. For as long as possible, she intended to enjoy some modicum of freedom. "I could use a little air—and maybe a fattening bowl of pasta loaded with cheese."

"Comfort food?" Michelle asked.

"Something like that. What do you say?"

"Are you paying?"

"I'll write it off as a business expense," Candace joked.

Michelle held up her hand. "I'll pay!"

"Why? Worried about an audit?"

"That and what they'll say when they see the receipt for artery clogging lunch. They'll probably have you on a gurney by dinner time. If anyone asks me, I'll say you ate my salad."

Candace laughed. "Always looking out for me."

"Hell yeah; I want to sleep in Lincoln's bedroom."

Candace rolled her eyes. "I'll bet you're the first lesbian to say that."

Michelle stopped in her tracks and looked at Candace in disbelief.

"What? Do you know another?" Candace asked.

"I'm betting there's more than one First Lady who would have taken Mary over Abe."

Candace fell into a fit of laughter. *Lunatics.*

"Hey, JD."

Jameson looked up from her plans at Jonah. "Hey. I didn't know you were coming by. Everything okay?"

Jonah shrugged. "What are you working on?"

"Oh, just this project I've been thinking about for a while—something for Coop and Spence."

Jonah nodded.

"What's up?" Jameson asked.

"JD, has Mom said anything to you about Laura's father?"

Jameson rolled up her plans and put them aside. "Let's take a walk."

"That doesn't sound good."

"It's nice out. A beer by the pool sounds like a good idea to me."

"Beer too?" Jonah shook his head. "It is bad." He followed Jameson into the kitchen.

Jameson laughed. "And here I thought Shell was the dramatic one." She handed Jonah a beer.

"What did she say?"

"Jonah, your mom doesn't have any use for Lawson Klein; you know that."

"Yeah, but she's not doing anything about it."

"I don't think that's true."

"Feels true to me."

"What do you want her to do?" Jameson asked.

"Take him out."

"Last I checked, your mom isn't Jimmy Hoffa."

"You know what I mean."

Jameson took a long pull from her beer. She could hardly blame Jonah for being angry and frustrated. She wanted to be sure that he placed that anger in the correct corner. No one was harder on Candace than Candace. If Candace had thought that she could stop Lawson Klein's ramblings and his hurtful overtures to his family, she would have already done something. Candace was an astute study of character. She may not have been able to understand what drove someone like Lawson Klein. She was adept at predicting what he would do next. And, Jameson was also positive that any action Candace took toward Lawson Klein would be carefully planned.

"I do," Jameson replied. "I think she's hoping he will be his own undoing."

"Hasn't worked yet."

"True, but this is a different ball game," Jameson reminded him. "He's got more people paying attention now."

"That's my point. How long is she going to let him keep going? Jesus, JD she's not even defending herself!"

"Probably because she doesn't need to."

"What?"

Jameson shrugged. "Nothing he's said is true."

"People still believe it."

"Yeah, I guess they do."

"Doesn't that piss you off?"

"Me? Yeah, it pisses me off. But your mom is right. People will believe what they want. Getting defensive will only make that worse."

"So, why not go on the offensive?"

"What makes you think she isn't?"

Jonah groaned. "She isn't. That's the point."

"Jonah," Jameson shook her head. "When your mom sat you all down to talk about starting this campaign, she told you that this was going to happen."

"Yeah, but I expected she'd fight it."

"She is. She just isn't fighting it the way you want her to."

"What am I supposed to do? Just sit here and be quiet while he rakes my mother over the coals, sends my wife into tears?"

"Drink your beer."

"What?"

Jameson took another long sip from her beer. *Can't blame him.* "Sometimes, a cold beer or three is the best way I know to cope with how you are feeling right now."

Jonah looked at Jameson curiously.

"You don't think I know how you feel?" Jameson asked. "You don't think I'd like to beat the shit out of Lawson Klein?"

"Did you ever tell Mom that?"

Jameson laughed. "More like I screamed about it."

"No way. What did she say?"

"Mostly, she listened. We've had more than one argument on this front."

"Seriously?"

Jameson nodded.

"I can't picture you and Mom fighting."

Jameson shrugged. "It doesn't happen often," she admitted. "It does happen."

"Mom told me that I should be there for Laura."

Jameson nodded again. *Familiar.* "She's not wrong."

"But?"

"That might be enough for them."

Jonah sipped his beer. "What about us?"

"I don't know," Jameson replied. "There've been days when I wanted to hop a plane, meet Klein outside his house and throttle his ass into next week."

Jonah chuckled. "I'd enjoy watching that."

Jameson clinked her beer against his. "Thing is, I know it would just make things worse for your mom—and for Laura."

"That's sort of what Laura said. I don't know. I think it might be worth it."

Jameson laughed. "I feel you."

"It really bugs you that much?"

Jameson looked at Jonah. "Jonah," she started and then stopped.

"What?"

"I love your mom."

"No way," he teased.

Jameson remained serious. "More than I can believe most days. When your mom and I first got together—well, to be honest, I hadn't considered all that it would mean."

"You mean living with a politician?"

"No, I mean taking on a family."

"Do you regret it?"

"What? No!" Jameson shook her head. "No, I just never imagined me being anyone's mom."

"And grandma."

"Yeah, and that," Jameson agreed. "I hate watching the way Klein's bullshit hurts this family. I'm supposed to take care of all of you. Sometimes I feel like the world's biggest failure on that front."

Jonah sobered. "JD, you're not a failure."

Jameson shrugged. "Maybe not. I can't help but feel that way sometimes."

Jonah sighed. He hadn't stopped to consider that Jameson was in a similar position. "Mom has never been happier; you know that; right? I mean, Mom can take care of herself."

"To a point," Jameson said. She looked at Jonah and smiled. "Your mom isn't made of steel, Jonah. That's how most of the world sees her—as someone larger than life. I think even Lawson Klein sees her that way."

"Seriously?"

"Yeah. I think that's part of what makes him so crazy where she is concerned. She never quits. She never folds."

Jonah smiled. "She doesn't waver at all."

"Oh, but she does," Jameson corrected him. "She's not indestructible. She's human. I have to stop and remember that too sometimes."

"You're worried about her."

"Yes and no. I always worry," Jameson said. "I know that she feels the same way we do a lot of the time."

"She's the one that...."

"She's your mother," Jameson stopped Jonah's thought in its tracks. "She's my wife. She wants to protect us. And, she feels responsible for how we feel."

"That's crazy. It's not her fault that Klein is an asshole."

"No, but listen to us sitting here. There's a target on her back, and that puts us all in the line of fire," Jameson said. "I have to remind myself that this hurts her, and no one is more frustrated or angry about all of this than your mother."

"I guess, I never thought about it that way."

"Imagine it was JJ he attacked."

Jonah shuddered. "I just want to help."

"You do help. You just have to accept that you can't make it all better."

"JD?"

"Yeah?"

"Do you hope she wins?"

Jameson sipped her beer. "I think we need more beer."

"You don't; do you?"

"I do," Jameson replied honestly. "She can do so much, and she wants to."

"But?"

"But, I hate watching people attack her. The rest I can handle," Jameson said. "I hate the separations. If you want to know the truth, I will miss working at the firm. I love this house. I love our life as it is."

"And?"

"All of that I can handle—moving, changing my career or putting it on hold, even the separations. I can handle all of that. When I hear someone call her vile names, accuse her of—Jonah, your mom is the best person I know—the strongest person I know. She may not be perfect, but she cares so much about so many people. I know it hurts her. She can handle it. She shouldn't have to. It's the one thing I struggle with."

"I get it."

"I know you do."

"So, we drink beer?"

Jameson raised her bottle as a toast. "We drink beer."

Chapter Eight

Sunday

Jameson walked into the kitchen to find Candace shucking corn. "What did that corn do to you?"

Candace turned and sighed.

"Are you more worried about Grant or the stooges?" Jameson asked Candace.

Candace shrugged. "Truthfully, I'm more worried about you and Jess."

"Me and Jessica? Why?"

"Because you have your reservations about Grant; reservations I'm quite sure the kids share. And, we both know Jess is afraid somehow this will cause a setback in her relationship with Shell."

"Candace, you can't blame us for being concerned about you, and honestly, neither can Jessica."

"I don't. But it isn't just concern about me; is it? You're skeptical of his motivations."

Jameson nodded. She was skeptical about Grant Hill. She didn't know Grant but she was familiar with his body of work and his history of taking shots at Candace publicly. Jameson was having a difficult time squaring the Grant Hill Candace described with the public image of the man.

"See what I mean?" Candace said. "Maybe this wasn't such a great idea."

"No, I think this is exactly what's needed."

"Really?"

"Look, you aren't wrong. I don't trust Grant Hill. I'm sorry; I don't. I do trust you. If he wants the trust of this family he will have to earn that, Candace. No one is going to make him feel unwelcome. No matter what happened in the past, the kids care about Jessica. Hell, I care about Jessica. I understand how hard this is for her. I can even understand that it has been painful for Grant. What's difficult for me to accept is that he's been on your side this whole time."

"Jameson, I know it sounds crazy but I'm telling you..."

Jameson held up her hand to stall Candace's thought. "I've heard you. I understand hiding the relationship he had with Jessica and you from his parents. I do get that. I don't understand how he could do and say so many things that hurt you when he says he loves you—or Jessica for that matter."

Candace sighed. "Hindsight is always 20/20, honey."

That's what worries me. "True enough," Jameson replied. "We'll all do our best to get to know Grant."

"But?"

"We'll also be watching your back—and Jessica's."

Candace smiled weakly. She could hardly blame her family. She also felt responsible for the current situation. She'd let Grant follow the course of feeding her information from inside Family Values International. She found herself wondering if she should have shut that down years ago. Maybe the results would have been less painful for Grant.

"I know," Candace said.

Jameson walked over and kissed Candace on the cheek. "There's another bag of corn in the pantry if you feel the need to eviscerate something else."

Candace chuckled. "Thanks, I think."

Jameson winked and headed out the back door.

"Where are you off too?"

"I think I'll avoid the corn massacre this morning," Jameson teased.

Candace laughed when the back door closed. *Lunatic.*

———

Jameson had wandered into the kitchen on the promise to deliver a few more cold beers to the cooler. She needed to take a breath. So far, the afternoon had been uneventful. Marianne had engaged Grant almost immediately, which had surprised Jameson. Michelle had followed suit. Jonah had kept his distance. Noting Jonah's discomfort, she had spent most of the afternoon close to him and Laura. It made sense. Grant Hill had spent years keeping close company with Lawson Klein. She replayed a brief exchange that she'd had with Jonah before making her way inside.

"I'm trying," Jonah whispered.

Jameson smiled. "You don't have to be his best friend."

"I don't trust him."

Jameson nodded.

"Come on, JD; you don't seriously trust him?"

"Let's just say that I'm keeping my eyes open."

Jameson sighed and attempted to shake off the thought. She heard the back door open and turned expecting to find Jonah.

"Thought maybe you could use a hand."

Jameson offered Grant a strained smile.

"You don't like me much," he observed candidly.

Jameson set down the two six packs of beer in her hand and looked at him. "I don't know you."

Grant nodded. "I wouldn't trust me either."

"I'm not sure what you expect me to say."

"I don't expect you to say anything. I can guess it's uncomfortable having your wife's ex-partner's kid brought around as family."

Jameson shook her head. *Not scoring points there, Grant.* "That doesn't bother me in the least."

"Really?" Grant sounded surprised.

"Why would it? Like you said, Candace is my wife. We have three kids that are from her first marriage. Why would you being Jessica's son be an issue for me?"

Grant studied Jameson without comment.

"Look, Candace loves you. That's how she is. Jessica was a big part of her life for a lot of years. They loved each other. You were a part of that in your own way. I wouldn't expect anything else from Candace."

"And you?"

Jameson took a deep breath. "Candace would say trust is given until someone breaks it. Maybe. I think there are exceptions."

"And I'm guessing this is one of those."

"It is."

Grant sighed. "Candace and my mother are the only two people who've ever let me be myself. I would never do anything to hurt them."

"Maybe not intentionally," Jameson said.

"Is that how Jonah feels?"

"I don't make it a habit to speak for the kids. Jonah and Laura have been through a lot thanks to FVI, so has Candace."

"I'm sorry about that. Lawson doesn't give an inch to most people. Believe it or not, I tried to get him to see reason. For the record, I know what it's like to have your father hate you."

Jameson sighed. There was genuine pain in Grant's voice. "Maybe that's your common ground with Laura and Jonah."

"And with you?"

"You want the truth?"

"Please."

Jameson looked Grant in the eye. "Most of the time, Candace can see people and situations for what they are—more clearly than most people, in fact. There's one exception. She's just a person, Grant. She's not the folk hero or the villain people make her out to be. She cares about you. She trusts you. I just hope her trust is well-placed. If you're asking how to gain my trust, the answer is simple; don't betray hers."

Grant nodded and then smiled at Jameson. "Fair enough. So, can I help carry that beer?"

Jameson reached into the refrigerator and grabbed a bottle of wine. "Carry that instead. I'm betting your mother and my wife are ready for another one by now."

Grant chuckled. "Safe bet."

Jameson followed Grant out the door. *Decent start, Grant. Decent start.*

"Hey," Jessica came up behind Jameson.

"How are you doing?" Jameson asked.

"I'm okay. I'm not so sure Jonah is."

Jameson glanced over at Jonah who was attempting to hold a conversation with Michelle and Grant. She sighed and looked back at Jessica. "You can't blame him."

Jessica nodded. "I wish we'd done things differently."

"Well, someone told me earlier that hindsight is always 20/20."

"Can't imagine who that would've been."

Jameson laughed. "Give it time," Jameson advised.

"He wants to work for Candy."

"Maybe that would be a good thing."

"She blames herself," Jessica said. "For this being so public."

"She cares about you," Jameson said.

"I know."

"And, she cares about Grant."

"It's not her fault. If anything, it's mine."

Jameson shook her head. "I know that Grant is your son. He's not a little kid," Jameson pointed out. "You and Candace followed his lead. He was an adult capable of making his own decisions. It's not anyone's fault. It's the consequence of the decisions. It wasn't your place—either of you to tell him what to do. You've stood beside him through all those decisions. I would guess some of them hurt you a little bit."

Jessica's head fell in defeat. Grant's choice to hide his relationship with her had hurt her deeply. She felt she deserved it on some level. After all, she'd chosen to give up her child.

"Jessica," Jameson gripped Jessica's arm. "Quit beating yourself up. You were a seventeen-year-old kid. You have the right to be hurt. You didn't walk away when he found you. Give yourself a break."

Jessica looked at Jameson with watery eyes. "Not an easy thing to do, JD."

"Now, what do you think those two are talking about?" Marianne asked her mother.

Candace looked over at Jameson and Jessica and smiled. "I'm not sure. I'd wager Jameson is telling Jessica to stop blaming herself about Grant."

"Why do you think that?"

"She told me the same thing."

"She's right; you know?" Marianne said.

Candace nodded. *She usually is.* "Yes." Candace smiled at Marianne. "But she forgets to take her own advice a lot."

"What do you mean?"

"Oh, she blames herself for every little thing that happens to Cooper. She worries about all of you—whether something she did or said hurt you. It goes with the territory. What you know and how you feel often don't agree, particularly when it comes to your kids."

Marianne chuckled. "Ain't that the truth. What do you think Grant's going to do?"

"Time will tell."

Three Weeks Later

"How's it going there?" Candace asked.

Michelle looked around the office. "Quiet."

"How are you doing?"

"I'm okay, Mom—honest."

Candace sighed. Michelle had shown up on the doorstep with Melanie the weekend before. Melanie had gotten the results back from a second round of tests. The results had not been as encouraging as they had hoped. Rather than risk a pregnancy not making it to term, Michelle and Melanie had opted to take a different route. Melanie would attempt to be the egg donor, and Michelle would carry their baby. Candace felt sure that Michelle was more disappointed for Melanie than Melanie was upset over the news. She was confident that when they finally conceived, all the turmoil of the past few months would fade in an instant.

"I know you're okay," Candace replied. "I was just wondering how the appointment went yesterday."

"Oh, I see," Michelle laughed. "It went well, Nosy Nana. Hopefully, sometime by the end of the year, you'll be expecting another addition."

Candace could hear the excitement in Michelle's voice. "I look forward to that."

"That's good because if it all times out there will be another seat required at your inauguration."

"Perhaps a crib in the Lincoln bedroom?"

"No way. You get to babysit that night."

Candace laughed. "I'm sure we can figure out something, Shell."

"Thanks for checking on me."

"You call if you need anything."

"Are we talking about my womb or this office?"

"Either."

"I will," Michelle promised. She chuckled as she placed her phone in her pocket. "She really is nosy." The sound of the front door to the office opening drew her attention

"Hi," a man peeked in through the door.

"Welcome," Michelle greeted him.

"I heard you were looking for some help," he said.

"Oh, you have no idea how much help we need." Michelle winked and ushered him in. "Have you ever worked on a campaign before?"

"No. Is that a problem?"

"Not at all. I used to be a teacher," she said.

"You're the governor's daughter," he observed.

"Guilty as charged," Michelle held out her hand. "Shell."

"Brad," he said.

"Nice to meet you, Brad."

"I hope I can help with something."

"Well, can you man a phone?"

"Sure."

"Can you use a computer?" Michelle asked.

"I think so," he answered lightly.

"You're hired. Starting wage—unlimited coffee and the pleasure of my company from time to time," she joked.

"I'll take it."

"Let me grab you a cup and a seat." Michelle made her way to the coffee maker. Well, at least I have minions to manage. More training. She chuckled softly.

———————

Marianne shook her head and laughed when she walked out into the backyard. "What on earth have you two been doing?" she asked Spencer and Cooper.

"Building a moat," Spencer said.

"A moat?"

"Yep!" Cooper pointed to a hole in the dirt next to the barn.

"Why do you need a moat?" she asked.

"It's practice, Mommy," Spencer answered with exasperation.

"Practice?" Marianne questioned.

"Oh my," Pearl's voice came from behind. "What did I tell you two about digging to China?"

Cooper laughed. "No, Grandma—it's a moat!"

Pearl pursed her lips. "Oh..."

"Yep," Cooper said. "Cause it's like the White House where Mommy is gonna be."

"We have to protect Nana," Spencer explained their reasoning.

"The White House isn't a castle," Marianne offered.

"Won't be all that white for long either," Pearl muttered.

Marianne snickered. "Why does Mom need protecting?" she asked Cooper.

Cooper sighed dramatically. "Bad people do bad things to Queens. It's in the stories."

"Mom won't be a queen if she gets elected. She'll be the president."

"Them too," Spencer said.

Pearl narrowed her gaze. *Now, where did this come from?* "What gave you two this idea?" she asked.

Spencer made his way to Pearl and Marianne with Cooper a pace behind. "It was on TV. Bad people do that 'sasnation thing."

Pearl sighed. *What on earth were they watching?*

"Where did you hear that?" Marianne asked.

"It was on TV!" Spencer said.

"Yep. They said that the president got 'sasnated," Cooper said.

Marianne noted the fear in his eyes. She smiled at the pair standing before her. "I think maybe we need to talk," she said.

"It's okay," Spencer said. "We'll build the moat, Mommy."

"And, I know Nana will appreciate that," Marianne told her son. "But, I don't think she wants you to worry about anyone hurting her."

"We can be her knights," Cooper said.

Pearl intervened. "Well then, the first order of business is a bath. Knights are supposed to be in shining armor," she reminded them. "Not muddy jeans."

Cooper and Spencer giggled. Pearl shooed them into the house and turned briefly to Marianne. "They'll be fine," she said.

Marianne sighed. "She's going to flip when she hears this."

"Then let's make sure we make it a funny story," Pearl said.

"Good luck with that," Marianne replied.

"Oh, Spitfire, trust me; I can handle my Candy."

"I've no doubt about that," Marianne chuckled.

"You, however, have charge of the Knights of the Moat upstairs."

"Gee thanks."

"Rank has its privilege," Pearl cracked. She watched as Marianne disappeared into the house. *Oh, boy. I might need to call in reinforcements to spin this one.*

———————

Candace considered the arguments she had been presented. The budget vote was two days away. "Make the concessions," she said.

Dan looked at her with genuine surprise.

"It's reasonable," Candace admitted.

"Candy," Dan cautioned her. "Infrastructure will take a hit."

"We'll make the cut to the infrastructure package that they've requested."

"That's a fifty million dollar cut," her chief of staff reminded her.

"Well, it's better than no budget. Look, we all know that plan was ambitious."

"It was the cornerstone of your campaign."

"One of them, and it's in more danger if we don't make this concession. We've got enough votes to pass this with almost all the additions we've requested. It's a ninety-nine-billion-dollar budget, folks. There are more wins here than there are losses. It's called compromise. No budget is not an option. Make the call." Candace stood up and smiled at her staff. "It's a win," she told them. "Getting a budget passed is no easy task. Don't feel defeated. This is how it's done. You press up to the breaking point, then you bend. It's a solid plan." She turned to Dana. "Coffee in ten?"

Dana nodded. "I'll be there."

"Stop moping," Candace laughed. She began to step through the door and turned back. "You think you've lost the battle. You did. You won the war," she said.

Dan shook his head. "She took that well."

Dana shrugged. "She's right."

"You think she expected this?" he asked. "You're the closest to her."

Dana smiled. "There isn't much that comes at her from left field," she told the group. "At least, not much she isn't prepared to field. Now, if you'll all excuse me I need to find some coffee."

Dana opened the door. She saw Candace grinning at her from a few feet away.

"They're still reeling; I take it?" Candace guessed.

"Not over the budget, over the fact that you expected it."

Candace laughed. "Not much surprises me."

"That's what I told them. So? Coffee?"

"I was thinking more like scotch."

Dana chuckled. "I take it this meeting will be in your office?"

Candace winked.

"Some days, I love this job," Dana said.

Candace laughed. "Me too."

———————

Marianne passed each of the boys a plate.

"Mac 'n cheese!" Spencer pumped his fist in the air.

"Grandma made it special for you two after all your hard work today."

"Can we call Mommy and tell her about the moat?" Cooper asked.

Marianne smiled. "Maybe a little later. Mom is working late tonight, Coop."

"Can we tell Jay Jay?" Spencer asked.

"JD is spending the evening with Aunt Shell," she told her son. "You and Cooper are stuck with me, I'm afraid."

Cooper grinned. He adored his oldest sister. "Can we camp?" he asked her.

Marianne considered the request. "I'll tell you what, we can camp out in the backyard as long as you remember that Maddie has to go to sleep. So, you two can't be loud."

"Okay!" Cooper agreed.

"Spencer?" Marianne looked at her son.

"We'll whisper," he said.

Marianne forced herself not to laugh. *Yeah, right.* She took a few bites from her plate and watched the boys before raising the topic of their project again. "So, tell me about this moat."

Spencer swallowed as quickly as he could. "It keeps bad guys out."

"Yes, I know. Why do you think bad guys will want to get in?"

"Bad guys always wanna get in," Cooper shrugged.

Marianne studied her little brother thoughtfully. "Why do you say that, Coop?"

Cooper shrugged again. "There's always bad guys. They come at night lots of times."

"It's okay, Coop," Spencer said. "Jay Jay will be there. It won't be like your other mommy."

Marianne sucked in a ragged breath. *Oh, Cooper.*

Cooper had adjusted to his new family incredibly well. He loved them all. Marianne knew that. He loved Candace and Jameson most of all. That was as it should be. As the family fell into their new routine, it was sometimes easy to forget that Cooper had been through an enormous amount of upheaval and loss in his short life. The death of his mother might have seemed sudden to a stranger hearing about the situation. For Cooper, it had been a lingering fear. His biological mother had struggled with addiction. Candace had told Marianne that she was positive Cooper had been exposed to frightening situations. It explained his affinity for Aladdin's genie. Genie was funny, magical, kind and could grant wishes; wishes that could keep people safe.

"Well," Marianne began cautiously. "There are people who do bad things in the world," she admitted. The boys looked at her. "But there are a lot more people who do good things."

"Mommy," Spencer addressed her seriously. "Nobody can sasnate Nana."

Marianne felt a stab through her heart. She hadn't given a second of thought to the larger dangers her mother would face as president. The sudden realization took her breath away for a moment. She could vividly recall hearing about President John Merrow's shooting and subsequent death. And, she remembered her mother's voice on the phone when they spoke after the news had broken. The last thing she wanted was to let the boys see her trepidation. She smiled at them as best she could. What would Candace say? She would never promise that nothing could happen to her. She would reassure everyone that she was as safe if not safer than anyone else.

"You know, Nana is an important person."

"Yep," Spencer agreed.

Marianne looked at Cooper. "She's not just our mom. She's someone a lot of people think of like their mom too."

"They do?" Cooper asked.

"They do. They trust her to make things better for them just like we do," Marianne explained.

"Cause she's the gubenor?" Spencer asked.

"That's part of the reason. And, if she becomes the president even more people will look to her—people all over the world."

Cooper looked down at his plate.

"Coop?" Marianne addressed him gently.

"She's our mommy."

"Yes, she is," Marianne agreed. "And, you know that she'll do everything she can to keep us all safe."

Cooper looked up. "What if the bad guys get in?"

Marianne smiled. "There are a lot of people with Mom every day to make sure that no one bad can get close to her," she said. "And, Mom is really good at figuring out what to do," she reminded the boys.

Spencer looked at his mother and then at Cooper. "Jay Jay can make a fort."

Marianne sighed. It seemed none of her reassurances were going to pacify the boys. They remained skeptical. "Where did you hear about assassinations?"

"It was on the TV," Cooper said. "Mommy was with that other president."

Marianne nodded. "You mean President Merrow."

"Yep," Spencer said. "Some guy sasnated him. He had kids too—like Nana."

"Yes, he did." Marianne bit her lip and gathered her thoughts. "He was Mom's friend," she told the boys. They both looked at her. "That's why you saw her on TV with him. They were in the senate together for a while. Do you remember Mom's friend, Jane?" she asked Spencer and Cooper.

"She's funny," Cooper said.

"She is funny," Marianne said. She had always liked Jane Merrow. "She was President Merrow's wife."

"Like Jay Jay and Nana?" Spencer asked.

Marianne nodded.

Cooper looked at her curiously.

"What is it, Cooper?" Marianne asked.

"Is Momma scared?"

Marianne was puzzled for a minute. "Why would your momma be scared?"

"That the bad guys will come."

"I don't think your momma or Mom are scared," she told him.

"But her friend died," Spencer said.

"That's true. Sometimes bad things happen," Marianne admitted.

"Like with Daddy," Spencer said.

"Like with Daddy," she said. "And, like with Cooper's mommy."

"Nana is Coop's mommy," Spencer reminded his mother. Cooper smiled.

"Yes, she is. But Cooper had another mommy first."

"Yeah," Spencer hung his head. "I don't want no one to hurt Nana."

"What do you think Nana would say?" Marianne changed her tactic.

The boys looked at each other.

"She would say that it's okay to be afraid sometimes," Marianne told them. "She'd tell you that you still have to try new things. You can't worry about all the bad stuff," Marianne said. "Worrying about bad things won't stop them from happening."

"But we can still build a moat?" Cooper asked.

Marianne chuckled. *The White House may never be the same again if she wins. Oh hell, maybe I'll help them.* "We'll talk to JD."

Michelle held the door open for the volunteers at her mother's campaign headquarters.

"Any place good to eat around here?" Brad asked.

Michelle smiled. "It's Albany, Brad. You should just ask if there's any place good."

He laughed. "Come on, I don't spend much time in this area."

"Try The Merry Monk down the street," she said.

"Get a little God with my beer?" he joked.

"My mother would say a little prayer and a little wine are good for the soul."

"Care to join me?" he asked.

Michelle looked off in the distance. "I would," she said. "But I have a standing date with my stepmother on Wednesdays."

"Really?" he asked

"I swear. It's painful, but someone has to do it."

He followed Michelle's line of sight to the attractive brunette coming toward them. "That's the governor's wife; right?"

"Yep. My evil stepmother," she laughed.

"Hey, Shell. Ready?" Jameson greeted the pair.

"Only if you're buying," Michelle replied. "JD meet Brad. He's our newest recruit."

Jameson offered her hand. "Thanks for helping out on Candace's campaign."

"Who wouldn't want a beautiful woman in the White House?" he said.

"You'd be surprised," Jameson replied.

"Thanks for your help today," Michelle smiled at Brad.

"Not sure I helped all that much, but you're welcome."

"I hope we'll see you again," Michelle said.

"I have a little time between jobs. I'll stop by sometime tomorrow to see if you need any help."

"Great," Michelle said. "Come on, old lady," she grabbed Jameson's hand.

"Nice meeting you," Jameson said to the man. "Sorry, I need to get this one home before her bedtime."

"Yeah, she's got Bible Study at eleven, and she needs to concentrate," Michelle said.

Brad shrugged, not understanding the inside joke between the two women. "See you tomorrow then," he said his goodbye.

"Bible study? Really, Shell?" Jameson laughed.

"Well, Mom certainly calls God enough after eleven."

"Just rent a billboard," Jameson laughed. "Let's go before I get a ticket for you violating curfew."

———

"Pearl?" Candace looked up from her desk with surprise.

Pearl set down two bags of take-out Chinese food on Candace's desk.

"Uh-oh," Candace said.

Pearl sat down in a large leather chair facing Candace.

"What's going on?" Candace asked suspiciously.

"Haven't seen much of you lately," Pearl said. "Figured you'd take a little time out if I fed your habit."

Candace's eyebrow lifted into her hairline. "The habit that you've been trying to break me of for fifty years? That habit?"

"Gotta know when to give up the ghost, Candy."

"Uh-huh. What's going on?"

Pearl's expression remained passive. "Open that bag and open that bottle I know you have stashed back there and we'll talk."

"Oh no. Please tell me Jameson didn't fall off something again."

Pearl chuckled. "She probably did, but she wouldn't tell me if she did."

Candace opened the bag. "What did you do? Pour my entire stash of cookies into this bag?"

"No, I bribed the lady at the restaurant for a bag full."

"You bribed her?"

"Yeah, I told her you'd probably be needing a chef sometime next year."

Candace laughed. "I see. So, we'll have Chinatown themed State dinners if I get elected?"

Pearl shrugged. "Why not? Everything's made in China anyway."

Candace sat back in her chair. "Okay, out with it."

"Don't you want to eat first?"

"Why? Afraid I'll lose my appetite?"

Pearl shrugged. "The boys decided to build a moat around the barn today."

"Uh-huh."

"You might want to see if they have a mud room if you hope that house stays white when you get there."

Candace sighed. "So, you drove to Albany to bring me Chinese food because the boys got muddy? I'm married to Jameson. Mud is a familiar sight. Now, let's have it."

"It's a practice moat—a not so dry run for the one they intend to build around The White House."

"What?"

"So that no bad guys can get in and assassinate you."

Candace sat dumbfounded.

"Actually, I think the word they used was sasnate."

Candace closed her eyes. "Where in the world…"

"Seems they saw something on television."

"Oh, God."

Pearl gave Candace a minute to process the information. "I let them talk about their plans while they got undressed for their bath. They're quite inventive, those two."

Candace shook her head. "What am I going to do?"

"What do you mean?" Pearl asked.

"Pearl, Cooper and Spencer have both lost a parent. How am I supposed to reassure them?"

"Same way you always do, I'd imagine."

"How's that?"

"Tell them the truth."

"The truth?" Candace rubbed her face. "The truth is there are plenty of people who'd like to hurt me."

"True."

"Big help."

Pearl chuckled. "Candy, we both know that you will be safer as president than you are as governor."

"I'll be better protected."

"What's going on?" Pearl asked. "I knew you'd be upset. There's something you're not telling me."

Candace groaned. "The FBI thinks this serial killer might try to get close—to me."

Pearl's stomach immediately flipped. "What are they doing about it?"

"My security detail has been increased." Candace saw the blood drain from Pearl's face. "Alex doesn't think he'll come after me directly. Maybe someone close to me like a staff member or volunteer."

"But?"

"You've met Alex. She's not one to take any chances."

Pearl nodded.

"I'm not sure what to do about the boys," Candace confessed.

"Marianne was going to talk to them over dinner," Pearl offered.

"Maybe she can put their minds at ease a bit. At least, I feel better about my decision to let Cooper travel with me more. Maybe I should have Spencer join us when he can. It would give Marianne a little break…"

Pearl laughed.

"What?" Candace asked.

"I think that'd be wonderful," Pearl said.

"Then why are you laughing?"

"Because we both know this is as much about you missing those fools as it is making the kids feel better. Got a little more than you bargained for on this one, didn't you?"

"Maybe I did."

"Regretting it?" Pearl asked.

"No."

"And that makes you feel guilty as hell."

"Maybe."

Pearl nodded. "The only thing you've got to be guilty about is how often you feel guilty."

Candace chuckled. "In other words, knock it off."

"Not in other words. Knock it off. Kids are kids."

"Yes, but those boys have both had enough loss in life."

"What's enough? Don't you look at me like that. I see those wheels turning. And, when they had those losses who was it that picked them both up, held them close, made them feel hopeful?"

"Pearl..."

"Oh, no you don't. You. You and Jameson—that's who."

"We've had a lot of help."

"Maybe so. Spencer and Cooper have thrived because they feel loved. That's the only security any of us get in this life, and you know it as well as I do."

"That may be. That doesn't mean some of their anxiety isn't justified."

"No, it doesn't. But look at Spencer. Rick was driving in a car, Candy. That's more likely to happen to you—even as president."

Candace sighed heavily. "I know. They're so young."

"And, they're so lucky. They have more than most people will ever dream of, and I am not talking about the house or the pool, or the trust funds."

Candace shook her head.

"I know you. You take the weight of the world on your shoulders. You always have. You're doing something few people ever will. There are going to be people that want you to doubt yourself. And, some of them are going to come at you through those kids. You know it. That might not be the case this time. It will be the case eventually."

"I know."

"Don't forget who is responsible for that. It isn't you. And, don't forget that those kids, and I don't mean just the little ones, need to see your confidence to feel safe."

Candace smiled. "Thanks."

"You're welcome. Now, why do I think there is more you haven't told me?" Pearl asked.

Candace took a bite out of a chicken wing and mumbled her reply.

Pearl grinned. "You know better than to talk with your mouth full and I don't have anywhere to be, so you can eat that whole carton. I'll wait."

Candace sighed. "There's a lot going on. There's always a lot going on."

"Enlighten me what might be going on now."

"There's a story about to leak about Lawson Klein's overseas interests."

"I will assume these interests don't line up with the nonsense he spews constantly here."

"Not even a little bit," Candace said. "Pearl," Candace stopped and took a breath. "There is some evidence that he's taken money from a group known to traffic young women." Candace watched as disgust played over Pearl's face. "I know. It's horrific."

"Jessica?" Pearl guessed who might have uncovered the link.

Candace nodded. "Not just Jess. There've been allegations for quite a few years now," she explained. "Grant even had a track on some of it. There just wasn't any proof."

"And, now?"

"Now, there are people coming forward with some emails."

"Did Klein know?"

Candace nodded sadly. "It appears so."

"You're hesitant to let it leak because of Laura and Mary," Pearl guessed.

"Partly; I also know how men like Lawson Klein respond when they feel cornered. He's only going to heat up his hateful rhetoric."

"Don't you think it will force Jed Ritchie to part company with him?"

Candace shook her head.

"No? I would think…"

"They're not your typical political breed," Candace said. "They operate outside the scope of the unspoken boundaries we've become accustomed to. That's what worries me."

"Can you stop the story?"

"For a while," Candace said. "I've no intention of stopping it."

"In for a penny, in for a pound?"

"More like I can't play it safe any longer. I don't have the inside track now."

"Grant is leaving FVI, I take it."

Candace nodded.

"Not his choice?"

"Actually, it is his choice." Candace looked at Pearl and sighed. "He wants to help with the campaign."

"And you think that's a bad idea?" Pearl asked.

"Not for the campaign."

"I see."

"Pearl," Candace started and then stopped. She took a deep breath. "He needs time. Everything he has known has been pulled out from underneath him."

"Not everything."

"You mean Jess."

"And you."

"I can't insert myself into that."

"Is that so? From where I sit, you're squarely in the middle of it. Isn't that what your barbecue was all about?"

"He needs time with Jess," Candace replied. "That's not my place."

"Maybe not. But Candy, he looks to you as much as he does to her."

Candace groaned.

"What is it?" Pearl asked. "Are you worried that Jessica wants more from you?"

"No," Candace answered. "I'm not."

"Candy?"

"Pearl... My being in the equation..."

"Candy, you can't protect Grant and you can't feel guilty because he looks to you."

"That's not..."

"That's exactly what this is—guilt. What on earth should you feel guilty for?"

"He's still timid with Jess—afraid somehow he will lose her too, let her down."

Pearl shrugged. "That's their issue to settle."

"One that I'm complicating."

"I see."

"You disagree."

Pear shrugged again. "Jonah has issues with Jonathan."

"Yes?"

"You haven't tried to keep Jameson at a distance from him."

"What does that have to do with Grant?"

Pearl shook her head. Candace had an uncanny ability to understand people in most instances. Pearl had watched Candace navigate many minefields in relationships both professionally and personally. It was interesting to her that when it came to Grant Hill, Candace seemed to have a blind spot. She understood the cause. Pearl knew that Grant was a symptom of a road block Candace was ready to place in her path. Candace was afraid; afraid that wanting to be president was selfish. That only served to conjure more guilt. She needed to get Candace to see it.

"You need to let it go," Pearl said.

"What's that?"

"This idea that it is your fault somehow that Grant felt the need to conceal his relationship with Jessica."

"It is my fault."

"That's a load of malarkey."

"Is it?" Candace challenged Pearl.

"It most certainly is. If Jessica hadn't been with you, she would have been with some other powerful woman and you know it."

"But she was with me."

"And?"

"Pearl, I am the poster child for the right wing's target practice."

"I'd say more like their pin-up girl."

Candace rolled her eyes.

"So, what? Do you honestly think his adoptive parents would have embraced Jessica had she been with someone else?" Pearl said. "He decided to keep it from them. Grant wasn't a little boy when you met him."

"You sound like Jameson."

"She's right."

"He was still young and vulnerable."

"Because aging makes you less vulnerable?" Pearl challenged Candace.

"You know what I mean!" Candace argued.

"I suppose, I do. The point is that he has had years to make a different choice."

"He's been trying to shift things slowly…"

"If you think the only reason Grant Hill stayed at FVI was to martyr himself for your cause, you have a bigger blind spot than I thought."

"What does that mean?"

"It means that he stayed there to play it safe."

"There isn't anything safe about what he has been doing," Candace said flatly.

"But you let him do it."

Candace sighed. "I wish I hadn't."

"Why?"

"Because look where it led!"

"Blinders."

"Excuse me?"

"You—you have blinders on," Pearl said.

"I do not."

"Yes, you do. They're coming after you, Candy—not Grant. He just got caught in the crosshairs."

"That makes me feel better," Candace replied sarcastically.

"I'm not trying to make you feel better."

Candace chuckled.

"I'm telling you to stop blaming yourself for what happens to everyone else. That's what you would tell every one of us. And, stop thinking you know what's best for all of us too."

Candace sighed.

"You can't fix it all. The only thing you can do is what you've always done."

"What's that?"

"Stay true to who you are," Pearl said. "Take off the blinders, Candy. Both where Grant is concerned and where you are."

"Where I am?"

"Right. You want this. You can say that you are hopeful. You can say that you will give it your best. You want this. You want to win."

Candace closed her eyes.

"And, that is why you feel so damn guilty because it's something you want for yourself."

"It's selfish," Candace mumbled.

"The hell it is."

Candace looked up with surprise.

"It's not selfish to want something you deserve."

"I'm not sure I deserve to be president."

"I know," Pearl smiled. "That's partly why you deserve to be there. If you want to do right by all these people, Candy—let them do right by you. It's their turn to stand up and fight for you. Let them. That includes all those kids."

"Pearl…"

"Candace," Pearl began. Candace's eyes immediately began to water. "I'm going to tell you something right now. You listen good. I love my kids. I love your kids. I loved my husband. I loved my daddy and your grandmother. There is not a soul on this earth I could love more than you—not one. I've never sought to explain it. I don't need to."

Candace's tears began to fall.

"You're my daughter in every way that matters. I would walk through the fires of hell for you. I know you better than anyone, except Jameson. And, I'm willing to bet she will tell you the same thing I am telling you now. You came into this world wanting to make it better. That's who you are. You think someone taught you that. You think your granddad inspired it or I did somehow. You're wrong. We nurtured it. That's all we did. We just loved you for who you were and let you be Candy."

"You did a lot more than that."

"No. We guided you just like you guide those fools back home," Pearl winked. Candace chuckled through her tears. "This is your time, Candy. Maybe it feels selfish to want something solely for you. It's never solely for you," she said. "Because you aren't Lawson Klein. You are Candace Reid. Don't you ever forget it."

"It scares me."

"I know. You forget how many people love you."

"No, I don't," Candace said. "That's what makes it so hard."

"Mm. You love hard, Candy. You always have. It's why people stay in your life. You let them fly but you always keep watch in the distance. You don't know how to do anything halfway, least of all love. Let them love you as much. They want to see you fly too."

Candace sniffled back her tears. "I don't know what I'd do without you."

"You'd eat a lot more of that crap in front of you. And, you'd have less money after all the babysitting fees."

Candace laughed. "I love you, Mom."

Pearl allowed a few tears to fall. "I love you too, Candy. Don't forget that."

"I won't."

———

"How was your day at headquarters?" Jameson asked Michelle.

"Pretty uneventful."

"Everything okay?"

"Everything is good."

Jameson sipped her beer without comment.

"Mom checking up on me?" Michelle guessed.

"No," Jameson replied.

"You're checking up on me?"

"Maybe I am."

Michelle smiled. "I'm okay, JD. So is Mel."

"Yeah, I know Mel is okay."

"You do?"

"Yeah. I saw her earlier today when I stopped by the firm to drop off some things." Jameson could tell Michelle was curious. "She was almost bouncing," Jameson chuckled.

"Really?"

Jameson nodded.

"Huh," Michelle muttered.

"Can I ask you something?"

"Like me saying no would stop you."

Jameson shrugged. "Are you nervous?"

"About what? The campaign?"

Jameson shook her head.

"Oh, you mean about getting knocked-up."

"Classy, Shell," Jameson laughed.

Michelle grinned. "No."

Jameson smiled wanly.

"JD?"

"I was just curious."

"What's going on with you?"

"Nothing, why?"

Michelle narrowed her gaze. "Bullshit. What's up?"

"You were a little emotional the other night. I just wondered how you were doing with the decision."

Michelle nodded. "I didn't want Mel to be disappointed. She's always wanted to have a baby."

"And you didn't?"

"I don't know. I never thought about it a lot. I mean, yeah—I've always wanted a family. I guess I never thought about how that would happen." Michelle chuckled. "Now? I'm kind of looking forward to it. I just hope she is too."

"I think you can rest easy there."

Michelle smiled. She watched Jameson as Jameson sipped her beer quietly. "JD? What gives?"

"What do you mean?"

"Why so much baby talk?"

Jameson shrugged.

"Oh shit. Don't tell me you've got the bug?!"

Jameson nearly spit out her beer. "What?"

"You want to have one; don't you?"

"No," Jameson put her beer down and her hands up.

"What gives?"

Jameson sighed.

"JD?"

"I guess, sometimes I just feel like I missed a lot."

"You mean not having a baby?"

Jameson shook her head.

"Oh," Michelle surmised the issue. "You mean never having one with Mom."

Jameson kept her eyes on the bottle in her hand.

"But you do."

Jameson smiled. "It's not about Coop."

"Yeah, I think I get that."

"You do?"

"Yeah. You see all of us having babies. That's a huge part of Mom. It's a huge part that you missed."

Jameson would not meet Michelle's gaze.

Michelle reached over and took Jameson's hand. Not for the first time, she found herself blown away by the reality of how much Jameson loved her mother. "She's lucky," Michelle said.

Jameson looked up.

"I get it," Michelle said. "I really do, JD. For what it's worth, I'll bet she's thought about that plenty too."

"I don't know about that."

"I do. Have you told her?"

Jameson nodded. "That I wished I could have seen you guys grow up sometimes? Yeah."

Michelle shook her head. "No, I mean that you wish you could have done that with her—had that experience with her."

Jameson shrugged.

"Why not?" Michelle asked.

"She'll think that means I want to have one."

"Why don't you? Just curious," Michelle asked.

"Shell, I'm forty. Your mom is likely to become the president, and we have a five-year-old already."

"And?"

"And?" Jameson laughed. "That's not enough for you?"

"It's not about me. It's about you."

"See? The minute I say something everyone thinks I want something else."

Michelle smiled. "Maybe you don't, but that doesn't mean you're not allowed to think about wanting it. Hell, with all these babies how could it not enter your mind?"

"That's the thing, Shell. It never did."

"Until now?"

"No... It isn't that. I'm happy with the way things are. I just..."

"What?"

"I guess I feel a little jealous sometimes."

"I think you should talk to Mom."

"She has enough on her plate without worrying about something she doesn't need to worry about."

"Well, you know Mom. She'll figure it out one way or another. She always does."

"Shell, I don't want to have a baby."

"Yeah, so you said."

"Seriously. You're not getting it. It's not about me wanting to have a baby. It's about missing it with her."

Michelle thought for a moment. She shook her head and sighed. "I do get it, JD."

"You do?"

"Yeah. When Mel and I were first talking about having kids, we… Well, the plan was for her to have them—at least to have the first one." Michelle closed her eyes for a minute. "I started picturing that; you know? I mean, what it would be like to put my hand on her stomach and feel our baby move. Sappy, huh?"

"No."

"I guess that's why I've been sort of emotional. I think I fell in love with that idea."

"I understand," Jameson said. "But you still get to have that with her, and she's on top of the world about it."

Michelle smiled and nodded. "So am I. I guess it took you telling me this to realize what really matters."

Jameson winked. "Your welcome."

"Ha-ha. I still think you should talk to Mom."

Jameson sighed.

"Seriously, JD you might forget sometimes how much Mom loves you too. She wouldn't want you to keep it inside."

"We'll see."

"Well, in the meantime, you can buy me another beer."

Jameson laughed. "Is that so?"

"Yeah, I'm getting my fill while I can."

"On my dime."

"You are the parent."

Jameson laughed. "And you wonder why I wouldn't want any more?"

Michelle grinned.

"Beer it is," Jameson said. She got up from her seat and headed to the bar.

Michelle watched Jameson in the distance. She realized for the first time how much had fallen in Jameson's lap, how much Jameson's world had changed since falling in love with her mother. Michelle hadn't taken much time to think about Jameson's reality. She and Jameson had clicked immediately. They'd been close from the beginning of Jameson's relationship with Candace. Michelle never took much time to think about the age difference that separated Jameson and her mother. They fit. They belonged together. Twenty years was a significant difference. Michelle could imagine that watching Candace's children all begin families, watching Cooper grow—it had to make Jameson wonder about a lot of things. She imagined that her mother thought about the same things, just from a different perspective. *Talk to her, JD. Just talk to her.*

Chapter Nine

Agent Alex Toles closed her eyes and rubbed her temples. She was not looking forward to the conversation she was about to have with the governor of New York, not even a little bit.

"You look like hell," Candace observed as she entered the room.

"Thanks," Alex opened her eyes.

Candace took a seat across from Alex and smiled. "Let's have it."

"I think our guy is close. By that, I mean close to you."

Candace nodded. "You actually think I'm in danger? We haven't had any threats that have been viewed as credible. And, trust me; with Jed Ritchie and Lawson Klein out doing the two-step together about my ineptness, there have been plenty of promises to show me the light."

Alex sighed. "He won't come directly to you," she said. "It's not about you."

"You lost me, Alex."

"The press has been all over my story," Alex said. "My history with Cassidy and with John."

"Yes, I know," Candace said.

"It's not a secret that we've been friends over the years."

Candace began to follow Alex's reasoning. "He's taunting you."

"I think so. Cass is too far out of his reach. He's close to you—in proximity, I mean. Like I told you, I think it might be someone in your orbit; someone that means something to you. You are in the spotlight. He wants that. You're in... Well, you're convenient—no offense."

Candace grinned. "None taken."

"He's here, Candace—in Albany."

"Are you sure?"

Alex nodded. "He's within twenty miles of the airport. It's just a matter of where. We're searching hotels, but so far? Nothing. Which means he's likely renting or purchased something. That could be harder to pin down."

"Do you know who he is?"

"Yes and no." Alex handed Candace a photo of her suspect, Jack Carter.

"John (Jack) Carter? Is this the killer?"

"I'm not sure."

"Explain."

"We have three names to run down."

Candace narrowed her gaze. "You have three potential suspects?"

"No."

"He has three aliases?"

"Maybe," Alex said. She watched as Candace's eyebrow arched in challenge. "He could be working with someone. We're working on some Pennsylvania databases now."

Alex handed Candace another photo. "That's Brad Lawson. This is the most recent photo the DMV had on file."

"You think they are both involved?" Candace tried to understand.

"That's a possibility. I think one person might be giving cover to another. They've been friends since their teens. Listen," Alex said. "He doesn't have to go after you to get the notoriety you bring. Like I said before, it could be anyone close to you, even someone working on your campaign, a member of your staff."

"We don't have the resources to watch everyone who might be considered close to me. I asked Shell to stick close to campaign headquarters and keep her eyes open. Although, I'll be honest, Alex your news is making me rethink that decision. I'll pass this along to the paid staff. But you need to know; we already have a tribe of people coming and going. That's the nature of a campaign. It's the nature of an open society."

"I know. I want to put some eyes closer," Alex said.

"Someone to pose as campaign staff?"

Alex nodded. "It can't be me or Claire."

"No, I wouldn't imagine so. FBI agents?"

"Yes. I have two agents that will be there in the morning. It's important that no one knows who they are, not even Shell."

Candace considered Alex's direction for a moment. Michelle was running her campaign office. Michelle was her daughter. That put her in the crosshairs, and that was not something Candace felt comfortable with. "No."

"Candace, if she knows she might inadvertently give someone away. Shell is great. She's not trained for this."

"No," Candace repeated. "If what you suspect is true, Shell is the person in the most danger."

"You have to trust my judgment," Alex argued. "I'm trying to protect anyone who might end up in his line of sight."

Candace nodded. "No," she repeated. "If you want to place agents in that campaign office then we tell Shell—either that or I pull her out of there. She needs to know who she can go to. I'm not going to hand her this picture and let her think she's by herself in there."

Alex understood her friend's concerns. Michelle needed someone to go to should she see or suspect anything was amiss. "I figured you'd say that."

"Let me guess; you have a solution."

"We have a powerful mutual friend who knows what to look for, and who we both trust. Someone who has a direct line to me, and someone Shell will trust."

Candace immediately understood. Alex wanted to bring former First Lady Jane Merrow into the equation. "Alex, I don't think Jane wants to spend time in Albany. It's Albany, for heaven's sake."

Alex chuckled. "She wants you to win this election. That means you need to stay safe first and foremost. She'll do it if I ask her. I need you to give me the green light to do that. I'm not a politician, Candace. I do know that sometimes a high-profile figure can hinder a campaign more than help it too early in the game. I don't want to hurt your campaign. Jane," Alex hesitated. "She's familiar with both our worlds."

"I'm aware that Jane is more than the picture painted for the people, Alex."

Alex smiled. Candace Reid had been around politics her entire life. She'd also served on the Senate Intelligence Committee for years. That committee had held inquiries into President John Merrow's assassination and into the possible obstruction of justice by his successor Lawrence Strickland, who had left office disgraced by innuendo and ineffectiveness. Jane Merrow shared the same intelligence training and background as her former husband, President John Merrow had. Jane's connections ran deep in both the political and the intelligence worlds. Alex doubted that Candace knew the full scope of who Jane Merrow was or that something called The Collaborative worked under cover of the CIA. It was clear that Candace Reid had surmised there was more to Jane Merrow than a former Hollywood actress who became a fairytale First Lady.

"But?" Alex asked.

"There's no but. You're right. She could be an asset to both of us right now. I'm guessing that you ran this idea by Cassidy?"

"She knows the drill," Alex said. Alex's wife, Cassidy had been married to a congressman for years—a congressman who had once been thought to be headed for the top. Cassidy knew the ins and outs of campaign life and the political arena. She also was a close friend of Candace's. "She lived it for years."

"Yes, she did. So, what was her thought on this idea of yours?"

"She thinks that with the media feeding on Ritchie's drama, having Jane take up a presence might help you with the press."

Candace smiled. "I agree. The former First Lady would be an asset."

"But?"

"I should make that request of her, not you."

"No," Alex disagreed. "Candace, she needs to know all the reasons she's there."

"I think we both know she's ahead of the curve," Candace grinned. "You can fill her in on all the details after I speak with her."

"Candace..."

"Alex, this isn't up for debate. I've heard your case, and I agree with your assessment. Nonetheless, you need to understand that I put myself in a vulnerable position when I decided to run for the White House. I can't appear vulnerable. Do you understand? This kind of thing goes with the territory."

"What kind of thing? A serial killer wanting to exploit you?"

"Anyone wanting to exploit me," Candace said. "The reason isn't important. I entered this race on a promise to see it through to the end. I knew the risks. We both know that the road to hell is paved with good intentions and the road to the White House is the road to hell."

"You sound like John."

"President Merrow wasn't just our friend, Alex. He was the leader of the free world. That's not something you seek unless you are prepared to sacrifice yourself when the time comes—whether that's your reputation or your person."

Alex shook her head. *If only that were true.* John Merrow and Candace Reid were cut from the same cloth. They both believed in serving something greater than themselves.

She also knew that many people who sought higher office only sought to serve their private interest. In Alex's view, that put people like Candace at greater risk. She cared. Like it or not, that made Candace more vulnerable.

"All right," Alex reluctantly agreed. "But, you have Jane call me after you speak to her."

"You have my word. Alex?"

"Yes?"

"You find this son of a bitch and put him where he belongs," Candace said.

"You have my word, Governor."

———— ◆ ————

Candace hung up the phone with Jameson and sighed. Amid the chaos of the campaign as it heated up, the last thing Candace had needed or expected was a psychotic killer closing in on anyone close to her. The story was featured on the news nightly. When— the media kept asking—would the FBI and state police capture this killer? Lawson Klein and Jed Ritchie continued to fan the flames every chance they got. What was Governor Reid doing about it? The newest line claimed that Candace was unwilling to dedicate state resources to the case, fearing it would jeopardize her ability to pass the state budget. Despite Alex's press conferences emphatically making the point that the governor's office had offered every possible resource, the narrative continued. Right now, Klein and Ritchie's assertions were the furthest thing from Candace's mind. The slightest possibility that a killer might target someone close to her made Candace sick to her stomach. Her motherly instinct told her to pull Michelle out of the campaign office immediately. Jameson had reminded

Candace that Michelle would never forgive her if she did that. Candace groaned. "Damnit."

"Hey," Dana popped her head into Candace's office.

"Is Shell here yet?" Candace asked.

"Not that I've seen. Candy, what's going on? Why was Alex here this morning? Did they find someone?"

"They have some solid leads."

"Why do I think Jane Merrow's call was not just about your campaign?"

"It wasn't," Candace said. She sat back in her chair and rubbed her eyes. "She might be the one bright spot in this mess."

"No doubt having her spend a couple of days will shift the narrative."

Candace nodded.

"That's not what you were referring to; is it?"

"Cooper and Spencer saw something on the television about John's assassination."

"Oh boy."

"Yeah—oh, boy. They've decided they need to build a moat around The White House if I get elected to protect me."

Dana chuckled. "I'm sorry. I know it's not funny but those two really are something."

Candace smiled. "Yes, they are."

"You think maybe Jane can make them feel a little better?"

"I do," Candace said. "Actually, I was thinking when this is over I might invite Alex and Cassidy up for a weekend."

"There's more to this. I know it."

Candace shrugged. "Dana, there aren't many people outside of my family and you that I trust completely right now."

"I know."

"I trust Cassidy."

"I know that too. You want to bring her into the campaign, don't you?"

"Yes. But I know that she'll balk at that request."

"You think Jane can help with that too."

Candace smiled.

"Smart."

"I need people I can trust right now," Candace said. "Things are about to get messier."

"Why do I think we are not talking about the FBI's case?"

"The New York Times is working a piece on Klein's affiliation with Petru Rusnac."

Dana let out a long breath. "I haven't heard that name since you left the senate."

"Mm. I know. If it weren't for this debacle now, I'd consider asking Alex for some help."

"Are you going to tell Jane?"

"About the story or about Rusnac? As far as Rusnac goes, I'm confident that she's aware of his dealings."

Dana flopped into a chair. Petru Rusnac was a Moldovan oligarch. He was one of a few principal players thought to have begun to turn the tide in the small country away from western democratic governing and toward a more sympathetic alignment with Russia. One of the worst allegations against the man was his investment in the trafficking of young Eastern-European women throughout the world.

"Are you telling me that Lawson Klein is involved with Petru Rusnac?"

"I am."

"How closely?" Dana asked.

"Closely. He's taken substantial money from Rusnac's businesses. And, wait for it—he's sold property to Rusnac here in the states."

"You're sure?"

Candace nodded.

"How long have you known?"

"I've known there were potential ties to Moldova and Serbia for years. About his friendship with the Moldovan oligarchy? About eight years now."

"What changed now?"

"I knew about his potential ties—his unsavory friendships. Dana," Candace started and then stopped herself.

"What?"

"That property he sold Petru?"

"Yeah?"

Candace shook her head.

"Oh, my God. You think they brought women in that way?"

Candace nodded.

"Jesus. Is that the story they are going to run?"

Candace nodded.

"Holy shit."

"I know," Candace said. "They'll wait to run it until they have a few more sources. I can't hold it up forever."

"You know he is going to fire back with everything he has."

"That's why I need people I can trust close. He's thrown the kitchen sink already. I'm betting the whole house is on its way."

"What can I do?" Dana asked.

"What you do every day."

"What's that?"

"Have my back."

"Always."

———

Jameson walked back into the kitchen and headed straight for the coffee maker. It was only eleven in the morning and she was feeling uncharacteristically exhausted.

"Momma?"

Jameson turned to the sound of Cooper's voice. "Hey, buddy."

"Are we going to Mommy now?"

Jameson chuckled. "Are you tired of me, Coop?" she joked.

Cooper looked at her sadly and shook his head.

Jameson mentally berated herself. She had been joking. Cooper was incredibly sensitive and still had his worries that he would somehow upset one of his parents. She set down her cup and crouched down. "Come here, Coop."

Cooper walked slowly to Jameson.

Jameson smiled at her son and pulled him into her arms. "I was kidding, sweetie," she assured him. "I know you want to see Mommy. We're going to leave in about an hour; okay?"

Cooper nodded.

"Cooper," Jameson addressed him again. "I'm not upset. It's okay that you miss Mommy. I miss her too."

"You do?"

"All the time," Jameson said. "Just like I miss you when I have to go somewhere."

Cooper smiled and hugged Jameson tightly.

Jameson closed her eyes and reveled in his affection. *Think before you open your mouth, JD*. "Why don't you go and play in your room for a little while?" she suggested. "I'll come up when it's time to go."

"Okay," he agreed happily before scampering off.

Jameson stood to her full height and shook her head. "Way to go JD," she admonished herself.

Marianne walked into the kitchen and narrowed her gaze. "Was that Jessica's car I saw pull out of the driveway a few minutes ago?"

Jameson nodded.

"JD? Are you okay?"

"Yeah, I'm fine."

Marianne was skeptical but let her suspicions lie. "Was Jessica here for Mom?"

"No. Actually, she was here to talk to me."

Marianne's brow shot up.

Jameson chuckled. "That's surprising?"

"A little."

"She wanted to talk about Cooper."

"Cooper? Is there an issue with his grandmother again or…"

"No, nothing like that." Jameson noted Marianne's unspoken question. "She's just trying to find her way with Grant. I think she just wanted to talk to someone who had adopted a child. She's carrying a lot of guilt."

"For putting him up for adoption?"

"I'm sure that's on her mind but she's feeling conflicted."

"About him being in her life?"

"Not the way you are thinking. It's more like she feels responsible for coming between Grant and his parents."

Marianne nodded. "That's not her fault from what I understand."

"No, it isn't."

"What do you think about it? I mean, Mom mentioned that he wants to go work on her campaign."

"Does that bother you?" Jameson wondered.

"Doesn't it bother you?" Marianne returned. "It's kind of like the past smacking you in the face."

Jameson grabbed her cup of coffee and took a sip. "Your mom loves Grant."

"Yeah, so she's said. I know Mom. But, JD this is a little weird, don't you think? I mean all of a sudden…"

"Most things in life feel like they happen suddenly," Jameson interjected. "You know your mom. She's got a big heart. Jessica was a big part of her life. I think that she took the lead with him in some ways because Jessica was so afraid she'd do something wrong."

"Did Mom tell you that?"

"No, Jessica did."

"Huh."

Jameson decided to change the subject. She had no issue with Candace's relationship with Grant Hill or with Jessica Stearns. Candace was not someone to completely cut ties with someone because a romantic relationship ended. Jameson felt no insecurity in her marriage. She was cautious where Grant was concerned only because she didn't know him well. She did trust Candace.

"So? You are headed to Scott's for the weekend, huh?"

Marianne nodded. She smiled, but Jameson detected that something was bothering her step-daughter.

"Is everything okay with you two?" Jameson asked.

"Everything is more than okay," Marianne said.

Jameson smiled. Marianne was in love. It was written in her eyes. Jameson suspected that Marianne was also terrified. "And, that is a bad thing?" Jameson asked.

"It's not that," Marianne said.

"Listen, I know it's probably weird talking to me about this. He is my cousin."

Marianne laughed. "Actually, JD I think you're about the only person I would talk to about this."

"Coffee?" Jameson asked.

"Don't you need to leave for Albany?"

"I'm not leaving for a while," Jameson said. She grabbed Marianne a cup of coffee and directed her to have a seat at the table.

"I'm not sure what my problem is," Marianne confessed. Jameson listened. "It's—God, JD—I love him; I really do."

"You don't say?"

"It's crazy. It's just that when I start thinking about where it all might be heading, I start to feel... I don't know; conflicted?"

Jameson nodded. "You mean guilty."

Marianne sighed. She hadn't expected to fall in love again after her husband's death. She'd assumed that if she ever decided to marry again, it would be with someone who served as a companion. In some ways that seemed acceptable. Loving someone else sometimes felt like a betrayal of Rick. She struggled with her desire for a future with Scott and the future she had planned with Rick.

"I guess, I do," Marianne admitted. "It isn't just that. I do feel that sometimes. I admit it. I never expected it—loving someone again."

"Well, I think I can understand that. But Rick would have been happy that you found someone that loves you and that you love too. And, I have to tell you I think he would have been glad it was Scott. It's like Coop having three moms. It's even like Jessica and Grant. You don't have to stop loving Rick because you love Scott."

"I know." Marianne sighed. "JD... There's also the reality of what Scott wants."

"Which is you."

"Yes, but one day I think he would like to have a child of his own."

"And you don't want that?"

Marianne sighed again. "It's not that. It's just—how do I explain this? I know he loves Spencer and Maddie but they aren't his kids. You know?"

"Is that what he said?"

"No, of course not. It's just that when we've talked about the kids, he's mentioned how much he would like one."

"With you."

Marianne nodded.

"And you think somehow that means he doesn't think of Spence and Maddie as his?"

"I... That's not what I mean. I just..."

Jameson smiled. "He couldn't love those kids more if they were his," she said.

"But having Spencer and Maddie isn't enough."

"I don't think that's it."

Marianne looked at Jameson hopefully.

"He loves you, Marianne. It's not easy, acting as someone's parent when you aren't—when they have another parent that they love. It's kind of like walking a tightrope."

"Speaking from experience?" Marianne asked lightly.

Jameson took a deep breath. Family was the center of her thoughts lately—Candace's kids and Cooper most of all. "Yes."

"JD?"

Jameson smiled. "I understand where he's coming from," Jameson said. "He probably wishes sometimes that Spencer and Maddie were his. And, if I had to guess that makes him feel like shit."

"Why?"

"Because Rick is their father. And he doesn't want to diminish that or to overstep his boundaries. That's not easy when you love someone."

"Rick isn't here," Marianne pointed out. "I mean, Maddie won't even remember her father. Scott is the only father she knows."

Jameson smiled. She wondered if Marianne had realized what she had just said. "Maybe so, but you have to think about how Scott sees that. He doesn't want to do anything that might push you away or the kids one day."

"Okay. I think I understand what you are saying. What does that have to do with wanting more children?"

Jameson shrugged. "He loves you. Why did you want to have kids with Rick?"

"We both always wanted a family."

"And?"

"And we loved each other."

"Exactly. Marianne, Scott is surrounded right now by people starting and growing families. Maddie and JJ, Laura is expecting again, Shell and Mel are starting to try to have a family—It makes a person think."

Marianne tipped her head curiously. *It makes a person think?* "JD, are you thinking about having a baby?"

Jameson laughed. "No," she said.

Marianne raised her brow.

"Stop," Jameson laughed harder. "God, what is it with you and Shell? No, I don't want to have a baby."

"If you say so."

Jameson groaned. "Maybe Scott does, and I don't blame him. I get it. You think it's about having one of his own. It's not. It's about being a part of that with you all the way through."

"What does that mean?"

"It means that he has all the gaps he can't fill. He's watching Jonah and Laura right now and wondering what it was like for you."

"He could just ask."

Jameson shook her head. "He could. That won't allow him to feel that. You've been with Spencer and Maddie since the moment they were conceived. You felt the ups and downs, the excitement and anticipation with Rick. Scott loves you, Marianne. And, yeah, he loves the kids. I'm sure he wonders what it would be like for you to come home and tell him that you're pregnant. It's about wanting to share everything with you, not about wanting his own."

Marianne took a deep breath and let it go slowly. She looked at Jameson and saw something she'd never taken the time to see before. Jameson didn't want a baby. Jameson was wondering what she had missed with Candace. In her own way, Jameson was mourning that. Marianne hadn't stopped to think how Jameson must feel at times. She hadn't had the chance to be with any of Candace's children or even Cooper from the beginning. One thing that Marianne did know, Jameson loved all of them as if they were hers.

"Did you ever tell Mom?" Marianne asked.

"Tell her what?"

"That you wish you could have done that with her?"

"She knows."

Marianne nodded. She suspected that her mother had an inkling. She also guessed that Jameson had never shared with her mother how deeply her feelings ran. Jameson's explanation opened Marianne's eyes to things she hadn't considered about family.

"I'll bet she thinks about it too," Marianne told Jameson.

Jameson smiled. *Maybe.*

Candace watched the news and shook her head. *Great.* She looked up when Dana walked into the room.

"You saw it?" Dana guessed.

Candace nodded. Her primary rival for the Democratic nomination, George Keyes had just finished a round of interviews expressing his concern that Candace's lengthy political career put her in jeopardy in a general election. He'd also adopted the argument that Candace was beholden to the establishment that had deliberately positioned her for a run for the White House. She would inevitably be forced to do their bidding.

"I can't believe this is his argument," Dana said.

Candace shrugged. "It's politics, Dana. He wants to win."

"You're not pissed?"

"I'm disappointed," Candace said. "I'd hoped that we

would debate policy and not politics."

"He's pissed because he knows you have President Wallace in your corner."

"The president will be in the corner of whoever is nominated."

"Candy, they want you to…"

"It's part of the game, Dana."

"How do you want me to respond?"

"Use the facts."

"Not very glamorous."

"Well, that's the contrast. Stick to the narrative," Candace instructed. "For now."

Dana shook her head. "You're the boss."

Candace smiled. "Yes, I am."

Chapter Ten

Michelle walked into Candace's office nervously. It was unusual for Candace to request Michelle meet her at the office in the evening unless something unexpected had occurred. Those unexpected things seldom fell in the happy times category of life.

"Mom? What's going on?"

Candace smiled. "Relax, Shell. Just sit down."

"Oh, this can't be good. I saw Keyes on TV. Please tell me you're not quitting the campaign."

"Hardly."

"Then why are you telling me to sit down? Oh, God! You and Jameson decided to have another kid!"

"You have a vivid imagination, Shell."

"Well, what? Someone's sick?"

"Shell!" Candace sniggered. "Take a breath."

"Sorry, too much coffee."

Candace nodded. "Jane's flying in tomorrow."

"Jane Merrow?"

"Yes."

"Are you planning to campaign together?"

"Eventually," Candace said. "She's going to spend a few days at headquarters taking the lead with the press."

"Why? Did I do something that…"

"No," Candace held up her hand. "Hopefully, it's only for a few days. Jed Ritchie is out making the rounds on the morning shows. Frankly, Senator Keyes new tactic isn't helpful. Having a serial killer on the loose is not helping bolster confidence in me either."

"Yeah, well they're all full of shit, Mom. And, you're not the FBI," Michelle pointed out.

"Facts are sometimes less important than optics, Shell. You know that better than most."

"I hate those assholes."

Candace laughed.

"What else?" Michelle wanted to know.

Candace sobered. "Remember when I told you to keep your eye out for anyone that seemed to be lurking?"

"Yeah?"

"No concerns?"

"No lurkers," Michelle replied. "Some new volunteers. No one that has made me suspect anything."

Candace nodded. She made her way over to her desk and retrieved the pictures that Alex had given her earlier that day. "I need you to let me know immediately if you see either of these men."

Michelle looked at the picture of Brad Lawson first. "Nope." She put it behind the second photo and froze.

"Shell?"

"This is Brad."

"What?" Candace asked.

"This—this picture is of our new volunteer, Brad Lawson."

Candace looked over Michelle's shoulder. "Shell? That's a picture Alex gave me of some man named Jack Carter."

Michelle shook her head. "No, that is Brad Lawson."

Candace grabbed her cell phone.

"Mom? What are you doing?"

Candace ignored Michelle. She held her breath waiting for an answer. "Alex?"

Alex Toles looked at her partner and shook her head with frustration. Another body. She suspected it was that of Brad Lawson. She looked down at the corpse and pinched the bridge of her nose. She was tired of working on this killer's ticking clock. She wanted him to work on hers. "Something doesn't fit," she said. She groaned when her cell phone rang. "Candace?"

"Alex…"

"What's wrong?" Alex asked.

"Shell recognized the photo of Jack Carter as someone who started volunteering a couple of days ago."

Alex held her breath.

"But, she knows him by the other man's name—Brad Lawson. What's going on?"

Shit. "I'm not totally sure. Is Shell with you?"

"Yes."

"Keep her there."

"What?"

"Candace, if he knows Shell, he might know where she lives. She's secure with you. No one's coming after any of you there."

Candace sighed. "I can't keep her in the dark."

Alex groaned. "I know. I can't get there right now. I'm in the middle of something."

"Alex..."

"Listen, I am going to send someone to you. Don't let Shell or Jameson leave alone."

"Jameson isn't here. She dropped Cooper off and went to do some work."

Alex groaned. "At her office?"

"Yes. Do you think Jameson is in danger?"

Alex took a deep breath. "Jameson can handle herself," she said. "Just call her and tell her to stay put until someone gets there."

"Someone? Alex..."

"Candace, please—trust me on this one."

"What do you want me to tell Shell?"

"Tell her I will fill her in when I get there."

"You're coming here?" Candace asked.

"As soon as I can. I need to deal with some things where I am first."

"All right. I don't know why, but I feel like I need to tell you to be careful."

"I always am," Alex said. "Shit."

"What's up in Governor land?" Claire Brackett asked.

"He's been to Candace's campaign office. Shell recognized him. We need to look through that house again."

"What do you hope to find?"

"Some idea of where he might be. What he might be driving. I don't like the idea of using anyone as bait."

Claire nodded. "What are we waiting for? Nothing we can do to help him," she gestured to the body.

Alex grimaced. *No, nothing at all.*

———————

Jameson sat on the edge of Cooper's bed letting her hands comb through his curls. Candace stepped into the doorway.

"You all right?" Candace asked.

Jameson sighed.

"Jameson?"

"I was just thinking about everything he's been through. I can't imagine losing him."

Candace moved beside Jameson. "Worried about Shell?"

Jameson nodded. "I'm worried about everybody," she said. She looked up at Candace. "I saw Keyes on the morning shows."

"It's just politics, honey."

"It's bullshit. I thought he was your friend."

"He is. He's also my rival right now."

"I wish I could say that I understand. Would you do that? Accuse him of being less than honest?"

"No—not unless he was."

Jameson shook her head.

"Come on," Candace coaxed Jameson.

Jameson made her way to her feet with a sigh. "How can you take this all in stride?"

"I'm not," Candace replied. "Not really. What can I do? I have to see it through—all of it."

"I know. I just wish I could help more. Jesus, I upset Coop this morning."

"Upset him how?"

"He was excited to come see you. I asked him if he was tired of me."

197

Candace smiled. "He loves you. He doesn't want to hurt your feelings."

"I was joking."

"Yes, I know. He didn't seem any worse for the wear when you dropped him off. So, whatever you did to reassure him it worked."

"I hope so."

"What were you doing at the firm?" Candace asked.

"Jonah asked me to look at some plans."

"Difficult client?" Candace asked.

"Not really. To tell you the truth, I'm not sure why he thought I could help."

"Did you? Help?"

"I made some suggestions. They didn't need them."

"Mmm."

"What?" Jameson asked.

"I think maybe Jonah is missing you at the office."

"What?"

Candace shrugged and led Jameson out of Cooper's bedroom. "He's used to having the time with you."

Jameson considered Candace's observation. "Maybe we should plan a camping trip. Invite Scott. Might be good for both of them."

Might be good for you. Candace smiled. "I think that's a great idea."

"So, when do you think Alex will get here?" Jameson asked.

"Not sure. She was tied up with something. Whatever it was, it wasn't something she could walk away from."

Jameson groaned. "I can't believe I was talking to that guy."

Candace shuddered slightly. "He didn't send off any warning bells?" she asked.

"Not a one."

"Well, we'll see what Alex has to say."

"Candace, if he comes back..."

Candace sucked in a deep breath. "I don't know whether to hope he does or he doesn't. I just know we need to get him off the street before he hurts anyone else."

Jameson made no reply. *How do these things always end up in her lap?*

"Absolutely not!" Candace raised her voice.

"Candace, just listen," Alex implored the governor.

"Mom," Michelle pleaded for her mother's attention.

"You want to use Shell to lure this sadistic son of a bitch? You've lost your mind."

Alex shook her head. "We have a window."

"You know what he looks like. Arrest him!"

"We have a warrant out. We've notified law enforcement that he might be driving a Crow Electrical van and issued their plate numbers. Nothing. There's been nothing, Candace."

"You said he's close to the airport," Candace said.

"I did—within twenty miles. There's no record of Brad Lawson or John Carter owning or renting property here. We tried pinging the phone number his wife gave us. He's not using the numbers that either Jack Carter's wife or Brad Lawson's receptionist gave us—nothing, Candace. He's a serial killer. Serial killers are sadistic. They're not stupid."

"I don't need a lesson," Candace bit. "I'm well-aware of

the intellect he likely possesses. That in no way engenders confidence in this idea you have."

"Let me do it," Jameson chimed. All eyes turned to her.

"What?" Candace asked her wife. "Let you do what?" she asked sharply.

"Shell said she told this guy I might have some work for him. Let me offer him something."

"Are you insane?" Candace shot.

Jameson shook her head. "It would get him away, Candace. Marianne is leaving for Scott's tomorrow morning. I can come up with some project to do at the house."

Candace stared at her wife in disbelief. "I'm not risking you either."

Jameson nodded. "Can we have a moment please?" she asked the group.

"That means get out now," Shell said. "Coffee?" she asked Alex. Alex nodded.

Jameson waited for the door to close.

"No," Candace said. "It's too risky."

"Alex is not going to let anything happen to me. Besides, I can take care of myself."

"Jameson…"

"Candace, you know that I'm right. You heard Alex. There are at least thirty victims if she's right. If I can help; I have to."

Candace sucked in a shaky breath.

"I know that house like I know you," Jameson said. "I've been in every nook and cranny. Alex will be able to put people close without him knowing. It's their best chance to end this without anyone else getting hurt."

"What about you?"

"I need to do this," Jameson said. "I have to."

Candace closed her eyes. "I don't have to like it."

Jameson moved to her wife and pulled Candace close. "I'll be fine. Just think how much it'll piss off Klein. Keyes will have a hard time saying you toe the line," she teased.

Candace chuckled nervously. "Promise me that you will do whatever Alex says."

"I promise."

"I mean it, Jameson."

"I promise. Now, let's go talk to Alex. And, Candace?"

"What?"

"This is not her fault. Don't put this on her. Alex is just..."

"I know."

"Overnight, Connecticut State Police made a grisly dis-covery—not far from where the bodies of seven women were found buried just over a week ago. Sources say the remains of an unidentified male was found in the barn of a vacant prop-erty nearby. Investigators are working to piece together the puzzle of how the man ended up there," a reporter said.

The morning news anchor threw him a question. "Is this related to the other victims?" she said

"Difficult to say. We have seen an FBI presence here, but that doesn't necessarily mean they suspect the two are re-lated. My sources say that until they determine the identity and cause of death; it's unclear if this individual met with foul play at all."

"So, it could be an accident?" the anchor inquired.

"At this point, they are not ruling any possibilities out."

Candace looked at Dana. "I hope that works."

Dana nodded. "It's the truth," she said. "All I did was make certain it filtered down a certain way."

Candace shook her head. There was no doubt that the person Alex had found the previous day had met with foul play. Alex had filled her in on her theory that Jack Carter had killed Brad Lawson. Alex hoped that the story might entice Jack Carter to make a move. "I wish to God it was the truth."

Dana regarded her boss thoughtfully for a moment. Candace prided herself on honesty, even when it was uncomfortable. There were times when politics required artful spin. Reality existed in perception. It was Dana's job to shift perception in Candace's favor. "Candy, you heard Alex. She suspects it's this Brad Lawson person. They don't know anything yet. It was the truth."

"Truth is a funny thing sometimes, Dana. They say it sets you free. Sometimes, it just bites you on the ass. Let's hope we don't have to deal with the latter on this one."

———————

"Are you sure that you're ready for this?" Alex asked Michelle.

"I think so."

"All you have to do when he shows up is smile and tell him that Jameson is looking for some last-minute help. Jane will be here in less than an hour. She'll give you cover if you need it; okay?"

"What if he doesn't show up?" Michelle asked.

Alex forced herself to smile. "Then we go to plan B."

"Is there a Plan B?"

"There's always a Plan B. Listen, Shell... Agent Robbins and Agent Johnson are here. They know how to blend in, just like Jane knows how to work this."

"What about you and JD?" Michelle asked. "If he goes to the house..."

"I can take care of myself," Alex assured her. "Jameson can handle this. Claire will be close to her the whole time without him knowing. There'll be a small invisible army ready to take him down. Trust me; I have no intention of pissing off your mom."

Michelle chuckled nervously. "Did you try the address he listed?"

"It doesn't exist," Alex said. "Sorry, Shell. That would've been the easy way."

"And, Plan B?"

"Not for you to worry about," Alex said. "I'll see you later." Alex made her way to Agent Robbins. "Agent Brackett vouched for you," she said.

"But you have your doubts."

"This isn't a chance for you to make a name for yourself," Alex said. "It's your responsibility to give me ears, and to keep Michelle steady if needed. That's it."

"I got it."

"Make sure you do, Robbins. You and Johnson aren't the only eyes I have in this office," she warned him. With a deep breath, Alex turned and walked out the door. *Please let this work.*

Alex stepped aside. She wanted to call her partner and check on how things were progressing at the farm house.

She'd spent over an hour with Candace and Jameson the previous evening filling them in on the details of the serial killer case. Candace had already been apprised of the killer's penchant for nursery rhymes and strangulation. Alex had worked nearly a dozen serial killer cases in her career. This one stood as the most unsettling, convoluted, and sadistic she'd encountered. She'd been impressed with Jameson's questions—to the point she'd found herself musing that Jameson would have made an excellent investigator.

"Checking up on me?" Claire Brackett joked when her phone rang.

Alex and Claire had a long, interesting, if not always happy history. Alex did trust Claire. That didn't stop Alex from worrying about the situation that she was sending Jameson into.

"How's Jameson holding up?" Alex asked.

"Seems okay to me."

Claire's response didn't surprise Alex. Jameson Reid grew up in a law enforcement family. She had two brothers, which meant she could hold her own physically, and Alex had learned from their visits that Jameson possessed a quiet confidence. Using a civilian as bait was never an option that Alex cared for. This civilian was a friend. That made the stakes infinitely higher for Alex Toles.

"I take it he hasn't shown yet?" Claire guessed. She heard Alex sigh. "He will."

"Unless he got spooked."

"Nah. He's probably playing Patty Cake in his basement by himself," Claire replied. "Give him time. He'll show."

"I hope so."

"Hey," Claire softened her tone. "He'll show. You said

it yourself; he can't resist. Besides, did you see that piece on the news this morning? I'll bet he did. He's coming, Alex."

"Just stick close to Jameson."

"I think I might worry about him more than JD."

"JD?" Alex asked.

"That's her name; right?"

"You like her," Alex surmised. Claire did not click with people easily. It didn't surprise her that Claire felt comfortable with Jameson Reid. Jameson was what Alex liked to call a 'no bullshit' person. She was a straight-shooter, thoughtful and in command of herself.

"She's real," Claire said honestly. "And, she's no pushover, Alex. Pretty sure she could do what we do if she wanted."

"Probably so," Alex agreed.

"Even without us, he'd be getting more than he bargained for with her."

Alex snickered. *Probably so.*

"You just make sure you don't tip his ass off following him here," Claire joked.

"You want first crack, huh?"

"You have no idea," Claire said.

"I'll let you know," Alex promised.

"I'll be waiting for your call," Claire replied sweetly.

"Fuck you, Brackett."

"So much fucking with you, Toles. No wonder Cass is pregnant every time I see you."

Alex laughed. "Goodbye, Claire."

Claire placed her phone in her pocket and laughed. "She is so easy."

"Nothing yet?" Jameson asked.

"Nope. He'll show."

Jameson nodded.

"You know, your wife is going to kick your ass when she finds out how close you're letting him get," Claire said.

"No, she won't. Well, maybe a little," Jameson laughed.

"You seem calm. It's not every day you let a serial killer into your home."

"I guess not," Jameson replied. "I heard what Alex said. If he makes a move toward me, if he starts to chatter it gives you even more to nail his ass to the wall. That's if I don't pull out my nail gun and beat you to it."

Claire grinned. "You're not as mild-mannered as people think; are you?"

Jameson shrugged. "I am as long as you don't hurt someone I love."

Claire nodded. She looked around the kitchen. "Big kitchen."

"Big family," Jameson replied.

"How come you offered?" Claire asked curiously. "To do this; I mean?"

"Shell is Candace's daughter," Jameson replied. "That makes her my daughter—as strange as that might seem to some people."

"Nah, I've seen strange," Claire said. "That ain't it."

"I can only imagine. You? Why do you do this?" Jameson asked.

"Don't know if I can answer that. It's just kind of the thing I always seemed destined to do."

"Catch criminals?"

Claire laughed. "More like find a way to cause trouble without going to jail."

"Married?" Jameson asked.

"Me? No."

"Really?"

"Do I seem like the marrying kind?" Claire asked.

"Is there a kind?"

"If there is, it isn't me."

Jameson nodded and turned to start a pot of coffee.

"Oh, no. Alex does that all the time," Claire said.

"Alex does what?"

"Nods her head and goes to do something else when she thinks I'm nuts."

"Does that happen often?" Jameson asked.

"Pretty much."

"I don't think you're crazy," Jameson said.

"You don't?" Claire asked.

"No. I swore I'd never get married."

"What changed?"

"Candace."

Claire chuckled. "Just like that?"

"I don't know," Jameson said. "Coffee? I'd prefer a beer, but something tells me that's frowned upon."

"Got any?" Claire asked.

"Beer?"

"Yeah."

"In the fridge."

Claire made her way to the refrigerator and pulled out two bottles. "Pour that shit out," she gestured to the coffee cup in Jameson's hand. "Tell me you can hold one?"

"I think I mastered that in the ninth grade."

"Good." Claire popped off the caps with a key and handed Jameson a beer. "Now, if we both survive this nightmare nursery rhyme, I'll buy you a shot to celebrate."

"And, if we don't?"

Claire held up her beer and clicked it against Jameson's. "We will."

"You sound sure."

"Hell, serial killers are nothing compared to marriage."

Jameson lifted her beer. She loved being married to Candace. Managing a family, particularly one the size of the Fletcher-Reid clan presented constant challenges. "Here's to survival mode."

"Is that what you call it?"

"What?" Jameson asked.

"Marriage," Claire said.

Jameson laughed. "Something tells me we'll need more than this for that conversation."

Claire shrugged and took a pull from her beer. *Definitely*.

───────

Candace smiled at Jane Merrow as she approached.

"Governor Reid," Jane greeted her friend. She pulled Candace into a hug.

"I'm glad you're here."

"I wish it were under different circumstances."

"Me too," Candace admitted.

"How are you doing?" Jane asked as Candace ushered her through the door.

"Terrified."

Jane put her arm around Candace. "Alex and Claire are the best at what they do. I'm not just saying that. They wouldn't do this if they weren't confident in the outcome."

"I know," Candace sighed. "This is so close to home."

"I understand."

Candace led Jane into a small sitting room.

"There's more, isn't there?" Jane guessed. "Another reason you asked me to come."

Candace nodded. "More than one."

"When this is over, you and I will discuss it all over a bottle—or two of wine," Jane promised.

"Mommy!"

Candace chuckled when Cooper ran into the room. His face was covered in maple syrup. It was exactly the distraction she needed. "What have you been doing?" she asked him.

"Me and Mel had waffles," he said as he collapsed into Candace.

Candace raised her brow. "Is that so?"

"Yep. Hi," he waved to Jane.

"Hello, Cooper."

"Cooper, do you remember my friend Jane?"

Cooper nodded.

"It's good to see you again, Cooper. Last time I saw you, you taught me all about dinosaurs," Jane reminded him.

Cooper grinned from ear to ear. "Momma likes dinosaurs. Mommy likes trains better."

Jane looked at Candace and smiled. She wished that she had a camera. Candace had the same look in her eyes as Cooper—pure happiness. She looked back at Cooper. "Well, before I leave again you will have to show me your trains."

"Okay!" he said.

Melanie appeared in the doorway. "Sorry," she apologized to Candace. "He was determined to come find you, I guess."

"That's okay, Mel," Candace said.

"You remember Jane?"

"Of course. Hello, Mrs. Merrow," Melanie extended her hand.

"Just Jane," Jane replied.

Melanie smiled as best she could.

Both Jane and Candace felt tension emanating from Melanie. Candace looked at Cooper. "Cooper, why don't you run and wash your hands and face? As soon as I'm done with Jane I'll come up and we'll spend a little time together."

Cooper grinned from ear to ear. He nodded and took off in a sprint. Melanie called after him. "Do you need me to help?"

"By myself, Mel!" he called back.

Candace sniggered. "He's determined."

"He's happy to be home with you," Melanie said.

Candace nodded. "I needed him close today."

"Yeah, I get that," Melanie replied.

Jane looked back and forth between the two women. She smiled. "I know you're both worried."

"Is it that obvious?" Melanie asked.

"I know you might not believe this, but Alex and Claire have handled more dangerous situations."

"More dangerous than a serial killer?" Melanie asked.

Jane sighed lightly. Alex and Claire had both spent years working as agents within the intelligence complex. They dealt with serial killers constantly. The difference was in that life serial killers were called assassins. "I told you it would be hard to believe. Trust me; it's true. I've known Alex since she was in her twenties. There is no way she would take a chance with Michelle or Jameson's life—neither would Claire."

"What if he doesn't take the bait?" Melanie asked.

"He will," Jane said. "They probably know him as well as he knows himself by now—at least, they know what he will do."

Melanie nodded. "No offense, I will feel a whole lot better when Shell and JD are home."

"None taken."

"I'm going to go keep Coop company until you're done," Melanie said.

Candace offered her a smile. "He's been drawing a plan for a new train track to show Jameson. Maybe you could help him with it," Candace suggested.

"Sure. I hope he isn't as picky as she is," Melanie said as she took her leave.

Candace chuckled.

"Jameson will be okay," Jane said. "They both will be."

"I know. Mel is right, though. I won't be able to relax until they're home."

Jane nodded. "I should make my way down to your campaign office. But I get the feeling that there is more than today's plan or this campaign that's troubling you."

"The boys—Cooper and Spencer—they've been devising a plan to keep anyone from assassinating me."

Jane sighed heavily.

"I'm not sure how to reassure them," Candace confessed. "They saw something on TV with John and I in it."

Jane shook her head. It had been ten years since her husband's assassination. Sometimes, it felt like yesterday. "I'd be happy to talk to them," she said.

Candace noted the sadness in Jane's eyes. "I miss the son of a bitch," Candace said.

Jane laughed. "He would enjoy watching you now," she

said. "He never wanted to be there," she said. "He let other people's aspirations dictate his life."

"I know."

"You've put a lot of the pieces together," Jane guessed. "About his death, I mean."

"I don't know about that. I wasn't born yesterday. Presidents don't tend to get shot by strangers."

Jane nodded. "No, they don't."

"I don't want to pretend there aren't risks. I don't want any of the kids worrying all the time about my safety."

"They will anyway," Jane said. "But I understand what you mean. I'm not sure how much I can help. I do have a few ideas."

"I knew you would."

Jane took a deep breath and stood. "As for the campaign," she began. A sly grin crept onto her face. "I will enjoy helping you eviscerate Bradley Wolfe and his capricious cronies."

"They do seem to change tactic on a whim."

"Easy to do when the only thing you value is power."

Candace couldn't argue with Jane's assessment. She walked Jane to the back door. "I know you must have a million things on your plate."

"Me?" Jane waved off the idea. "My girls are married and playing mom. As much as I love doing all those things retired grandmothers do, I could use a little adult diversion."

Candace raised an eyebrow. She was sure that Jane still had both her ear and her hand pressed to many things that effected the "adult world."

"What's that look for?" Jane asked.

"Somehow, I don't see you sitting in a rocking chair knitting booties."

Jane laughed. "That would be a sight."

"Thanks," Candace said.

"You don't need to thank me. I'm always happy to help knock an arrogant psychopath off his self-appointed throne."

"Are we talking about this serial killer?"

Jane smiled.

Candace chuckled.

"I'll see you."

"Jane?"

"Yes?"

"It means a lot to me."

Jane nodded. Candace was a great deal like her husband had been. She loved people but she only let a few people outside of her family close. That was one of the pitfalls of high-level politics. Trust was a precious commodity. The higher a person climbed, the more treasured trustworthy, loyal friends became. Candace had been a staunch supporter and an honest friend to President John Merrow, and not only on the campaign trail. She'd been a lifeline for Jane more than once after his death. Candace didn't expect anything from Jane. She appreciated Jane's friendship just as she had John Merrow's. There was little the former First Lady would not do for Candace Reid.

"I know," Jane replied. "That's why I'm here."

———

Alex sat in the back office at Candace's Campaign Headquarters nervously drumming her fingers on the desk.

"Should I know that tune?" Jane Merrow asked when she

walked in.

"You're here."

"In the flesh," Jane replied.

"Thanks."

Jane nodded. "Always happy to help."

"Does that mean me or Candace?"

"Both," Jane said. "I am curious, Alex; why not just arrest him here?"

Alex groaned. "There's more than one reason," Alex said.

"Enlighten me."

"You have to promise not to tell Candace."

"Let me guess; the powers above don't want a take-down of a serial killer in Candace's campaign office." Politics permeated everything.

"Something like that."

"I figured as much. What else?"

"The best evidence we have against this guy is what we found in that house yesterday. If that body is Brad Lawson—between that and the trophy case we found in the basement it gives us a pile of circumstantial evidence."

"And, that's the problem, I gather."

Jameson shrugged. "You know the drill, Jane. This isn't the CIA. The FBI still operates in the courts and the court of public opinion. It falls prey to just as much political influence as intelligence. The difference is the outcomes end in a court of law. Juries like forensic evidence. I've got nothing in that department but hope."

"Explain."

Alex sighed. "Well, Claire and I collected a few things in that house we think are likely to have the killer's DNA on them. The best possibility was a Coke can in the basement. Just so happens we have a few soda cans from a place we think he frequented—a place where he could visit his burial plots undetected. It's a long shot. If there is DNA from the can in that house that matches even one of those cans we found in the woods…"

"And, if that matches this person you expect will show up here, you'll have some compelling evidence."

Alex nodded.

"And?" Jane asked.

"Well, if we get him on tape making a play toward Jameson or even some type of backhanded confession…"

"Oh, Alex."

"I know. I hate this. This office has people coming and going all day. It's a risk to pursue him here. This plan is the best chance to get him without having anyone else compromised."

"Including Candace."

"Yeah," Alex admitted.

"What about Jameson?" Jane asked.

"Claire's with her."

"Whose decision was that?" Jane inquired.

"Mine."

"Is that so?"

Alex groaned. "She won't let Jameson get hurt, Jane. And, she won't let this asshole slip past us either."

"You don't need to convince me," Jane said. "I've been at this a long time, Alex. I've seen this from both sides of the street—if you know what I mean."

"I do. So, why the questions?"

Jane smiled. "Based on that drumming and the expression on your face when I walked in here, you needed to hear yourself say that. It's not me, Alex—it's not Candace or Jameson, or Claire or any one of the agents out in that office behind us that need to trust you—it's you."

Alex sighed and began to massage her temples. "There are risks. We both know it."

"There are always risks. You know that better than anyone."

"Thanks. That makes me feel so much better," Alex rolled her eyes.

"You're welcome."

"Remind me not to call you when I need a confidence boost."

Jane laughed. "If you didn't think this was the right course, we wouldn't be standing here. Stop second-guessing yourself. Doing that will only increase the risk to everyone."

Jane was on point. Alex was about to continue the conversation when the door opened.

"He's in the parking lot," Agent Robbins said.

Alex nodded. Alex looked at Jane. "Showtime," she said.

Chapter Eleven

Michelle attempted to ready herself to greet the man she knew as Brad Lawson. *Keep cool, Shell. Act normal. It's all good.*

Agent Robbins whispered in her ear. "Relax," he tried to calm her. "If he senses you are nervous, play it off as Jane Merrow being here today."

Michelle looked at the agent beside her and smiled. "Thanks."

Robbins nodded and stepped away, heading back to where a coffee maker was kept. It would give him a line of sight to the suspect and Michelle.

Michelle moved to a large bulletin board and began pinning volunteer names to it.

"Hi," a voice called to her.

Michelle turned and met the gaze of the man she knew as Brad Lawson. "Hey. I'm glad you're here."

"Really?" he asked.

Michelle smiled and finished pinning a cut-out to the board. *You can do this, Shell. Just like it was yesterday.* She stepped up to him. "I was hoping you'd show. I looked to find your number, but we don't seem to have one here for you."

"Yeah, I sort of dropped my cell phone a few days back. I need to replace it."

Michelle nodded.

"You were going to call me? Need somebody to change a lightbulb again or clean a chimney?" he asked.

"Close," Michelle said. She reached into her pocket. "I mentioned to my stepmother that you were between jobs. She called this morning to say she was in the middle of a project and could use an extra hand."

"What kind of project?"

"Who knows?" Michelle said. "It's JD. She might be building Noah's Ark for all I know."

Alex watched and listened carefully to the conversation taking place in the other room. She smiled. "She's good," Alex said.

Jane stood over her shoulder watching the scene unfold. "She has a future."

"In the FBI?" Alex asked without diverting her eyes from the screen in front of her.

"No."

"Always recruiting," Alex commented. "Bring it home, Shell. Bring it home."

"Your stepmother wants to build an ark?" Brad asked.

"Could be. I think she's bored. She called me early this morning—wondered if you had any carpentry skills."

"I can handle a saw."

Michelle forced herself not to shiver. "I don't have any idea what she's up to. My sister and her kids took off for the weekend. I guess that gave JD the bright idea to bite off more than she can chew," she laughed.

He tipped his head.

"Her number is on that card," Michelle explained. "If you're interested. I hate to lose you, but she pays better," Michelle joked.

———

Alex chuckled. "She pays better? Nice, Shell."

"What do you think?" Jane asked.

"If he doesn't take the bait, we take him. I'm not risking losing him again."

Jane nodded.

"Did you get that Robbins?" Alex asked.

Agent Robbins picked up the phone on the table in front of him and answered Alex. "Understood."

———

"Lots of people here today," Brad commented to Michelle.

"Oh, yeah," Michelle glanced around the office.

"Sudden surge?" he asked.

"No, just sort of happens when someone is occupying the back office," she gestured with a nod.

He brightened. "Your mother?"

"No," Michelle shook her head. "Safe to say she's tied up at the Capitol."

He grinned. *Tied up?*

Michelle noticed the feral look in his eyes. Fearing her stomach might revolt, she recalled Agent Robbins' advice.

"Jane Merrow is fielding some press calls and meetings to-day."

"You're kidding?"

"Nope. She's good friends with my mom."

"Huh."

"Like I said," Michelle continued. "I'd love you to stay and help me manage all the excitement, but JD pays better. In other words, she pays money, not just bad coffee."

He smiled. "She doesn't have a crew?"

"JD?" Michelle laughed. "JD likes to do everything her-self. She should build herself a doghouse for the trouble it gets her in."

He chuckled. *Oh, I'm sure we can arrange that.* "I'll give her a call."

———————————

"Bingo," Alex commented. "Robbins, I'm on my way. Johnson, you have the make on his car?"

"Yep, he arrived in a 2012 Toyota Camry—black. Li-cense plate, 203 XDG Connecticut. It's registered to a Jennifer Benjamin."

"Son of a bitch!" Alex replied. "Smart bastard. It's regis-tered under his wife's maiden name." She picked up her jacket and headed for the back door.

"Be careful, Alex," Jane said.

"Keep an eye out in case he circles back," Alex said. "Robbins will be here. Johnson and I will tail him to Scho-harie."

"Just be careful," Jane repeated.

"I promise."

Jameson picked up the phone. "Hello?"

"Um, hi. Shell gave me your number. We met briefly the other night..."

"Oh yeah, Brad; right?"

"Yeah. She mentioned you might need some help with something."

"I could. I seem to have taken on a little more than I bargained for."

"What kind of project?"

"Well, it's supposed to be a surprise. Our grandson and our son have taken to building forts all over the house," Jameson explained. "And moats, it seems. I started the framework—a castle of sorts, but I think I might have been too ambitious for a weekend project. Candace's daughter will be back Sunday, and if I leave a mess, I'll probably be forced to live in the little shack I've yet to finish."

Brad chuckled. "What kind of help do you need?"

"I have a lot of wood out in the old barn. Someone to help me carry it out here. I've done most of the cutting. It's the piecing together that seems to be tripping me up. Two hands and two feet aren't fast enough. If you're interested, Shell can give you the address. It's about a forty-five-minute ride from there; well, unless you drive like Shell. Then it's half an hour."

"You need help today?" he asked.

"I needed help yesterday if you ask my wife," Jameson said. "The sooner, the better. I'm happy to kick a couple of hundred bucks your way if you have the time."

Brad smiled. "Sure, I have plenty of time."

"Great. Shell will give you directions," Jameson said. "I'd better get back to it."

"Sure. I'll head your way shortly."

"Sounds good," Jameson said. She hung up the call and looked at Claire Brackett.

Claire smiled. "Shit, you almost made me believe you were building a fort."

Jameson moved to the back door and opened it. She pointed a short distance away.

"Holy shit," Claire said.

"I figured it'd be better to have something when he arrived."

"When the hell did you do that?" Claire wondered.

"I got here at about six this morning and started."

"By yourself?"

Jameson chuckled. "You might have given me an excuse to start something I've been meaning to."

Claire shook her head. Jameson had framed out what looked to be a play castle not far from the back of the house. "You did that in less than six hours?"

"Been doing it a long time."

"We need to meet with the team and position them."

Jameson nodded. "Like I said, I know every nook and cranny of this property."

"Good," Claire said. "I looked at your drawing. I've got some ideas. You're the expert. We've got less than an hour and fifteen people to position. Let's take the tour."

———

Alex pulled her car over and let the Toyota Camry make its final turn out of her sight,

She pulled out her phone. "He's coming to you now," she said.

"Understood," Claire replied. "We're ready," she promised.

"As we planned?" Alex asked.

"Better," Claire replied. "Jameson really does know every inch of this place. I've got surveillance set upstairs in her son's room," she told Alex. "Corrigan is up there. You should have eyes and ears the whole time."

"Is Jameson wearing a wire?"

"Yeah. Not easy to place in that tank top," Claire chuckled.

Alex rolled her eyes. "You're both taken."

"Yeah, doesn't mean I didn't enjoy it."

Alex chuckled. There was no denying that Jameson was an attractive woman. The playful statement was an appreciated moment of levity.

"Be careful," Alex said.

"Worried about me?" Claire asked lightly.

"If Candace hears you talking like that about her wife, we might not need to worry about Carter," she said. Alex sobered. "Besides, I'd like to keep my partner around."

Claire closed her eyes for a second. *Me too.* "Ditto," she said. "See you in a few."

"You will."

———

Jameson wiped some sweat from her brow and started to make her way toward the car pulling up the driveway.

Claire watched from the position she had taken in the top of the barn. The plan was for Jameson to lead him there. Claire wanted to be as close as possible when that happened. *Just be cool, JD.*

"Hey," Jameson waved. Brad stepped out of the car. "Thanks for making the drive."

"Thanks for the chance to make a few bucks."

"Believe me; it's well-worth the investment."

"Hot out today, huh?" he commented. His eyes raked over Jameson's body appreciatively.

Jameson smiled despite feeling her stomach roil. *Gross.* "It is."

"So, you want to show me what you've got?" he asked.

Claire rolled her eyes as Jameson's conversation unfolded in her ear. "And, people call me obvious?"

"You are," Alex's voice came over the com. "You're also crude."

"Nice of you to join us, Agent Toles," Claire said.

"Thanks for the invitation. How's your view?" Alex asked.

"From up here, I can see everything out there."

"Good. What's Jameson's plan?" Alex asked. She watched the computer screen in front of her as Jameson led their suspect to the backyard.

"She'll get him working a bit. Hot day—cold beer."

"She's going to bring him in the kitchen?" Alex asked.

"Nope. Too confined. She'll bring him to me."

Alex sighed. *The barn—good plan, Claire.* "Good plan, Brackett."

"I know."

Alex snickered. "Going silent until he moves."

"Understood. Buy you one of Jameson's beers later," Claire said.

Alex smiled. "You're on."

———

224

"Any news?" Candace asked.

"He's at the house," Jane told her over the line. "That's all I know."

Candace sighed.

"They'll be okay, Candace."

"I believe you. For some reason, I still feel sick."

Jane understood that emotion. She'd felt it more than once as a military wife, a First Lady, and as a CIA operative. She did believe that today's outcome would find everyone they cared about returning home safely. She also knew that didn't mean they would return unscathed.

"Hang in there, Governor. This will pale by comparison one day."

"Not a ringing endorsement for the job I'm applying for," Candace quipped.

Jane laughed. "You're the fool who put in the application."

"Thanks."

"Anytime, Madame President."

Candace snickered. "From your lips to the Republicans ears."

"One can hope. Try and relax. I'll bet the next call you get is from Jameson."

"I hope so."

———

"How old are these kids of yours?"

Jameson laughed. "Four and five; why?"

"Big playhouse."

"They won't stay four and five," she pointed out.

He heaved a long 2x4 onto a pile and wiped the sweat from his face with the back of his hand. "Right, but don't you think they'll outgrow it?"

Jameson finished nailing two boards together and leaned against the structure. "Maybe. I don't know. I thought I'd out-grown castles and nursery rhymes."

Alex sat up. "Holy shit! She's baiting him."

He cocked his head slightly. "You thought you outgrew them?"

"Yeah," Jameson said. "Until I started reading them to the kids. I don't know; it brought back lots of memories, I guess." She looked at the frame of her creation. "Sometimes, I would finish reading to one of the kids or I'd hear Candace reading to them and I'd find myself remembering my mother doing the same thing with me. Funny."

"What's that?" he asked.

"I thought I'd forgotten all the words and stories; you know?" Jameson said. "Spencer, our grandson—he loves Old King Cole." She laughed. "Maybe that's why I wanted to build this. He's four. He and my son are always making up some story about a castle. I think he wants to be Old King Cole," she explained. "Now that Candace is running this campaign, I think they've decided The White House is a castle. They were out here building a moat the other day."

Claire grinned. Jameson had told her the same story while Claire got her set up with a microphone. Claire had sug-gested looking for the opening to tell Brad or Jack or whoever the hell this guy really was the tale. *Perfect, JD—perfect.*

He shrugged.

"What? Not a fan of Old King Cole?" Jameson asked. She directed him to help her hold another board in place while she fastened it.

"A merry old soul?" he laughed.

"That's what they say," Jameson said as she hammered a nail in.

"And his fiddlers three," he said. "Not every nursery rhyme is a fairy tale," he told her.

"Don't like fairy tales either?" she asked.

"I love fairy tales. They seldom have the ending you see in a movie."

"Oh, I don't know," Jameson replied. "Mine has had a pretty happy ending." She moved to fasten the other end of the board. "To tell you the truth, I feel a bit like Old King Cole a lot of the time, emphasis on the old—and the merry," she said. She finished her task and looked at him. "Thanks. It is hot. I think I could use something cold. You? I have some beer in the barn if you're interested."

"Did King Cole drink on the job?" he asked.

"If I am him—yes," Jameson replied.

He nodded.

Jameson removed her tool belt and directed him to follow her. She had made it her mission to focus on the project at hand. For Jameson, that was building the playhouse. It allowed her to fall into a groove with the man beside her. Now, as they approached their appointed destination, Jameson began to feel the gravity of the situation pressing in. This man wasn't an extra hand or a comrade. He was a killer; a killer who was likely setting her in his crosshairs as they walked.

Claire watched as Jameson's gait slowed slightly. "You've got this, JD. Keep going. Just get him in the barn."

Alex listened as Claire mused aloud. It was evident that Claire and Jameson had spent time talking. Alex had noticed Jameson's pace slow as well on the screen. She could only see Jameson's back now, at least, until Jameson entered the barn. She suspected Claire could see Jameson's expression as well. There would have been no safe way to give Jameson ears. They could hear and see her every move; Jameson was deaf and blind. She had to trust that Alex and Claire were prepared. "I wish she could hear us."

Claire sighed. "She knows we're here. Time for you to move closer, Toles."

"I won't have eyes," Alex said.

"I'll be your eyes," Claire promised.

Alex looked at Jill Corrigan. She nodded. "Go," she told Alex.

"It's Claire's call," Alex said. She could almost hear the gasp of surprise of everyone listening. "She says when to move and where. Not before her direction."

Corrigan nodded. "That's you, Agent Brackett."

Claire took a deep breath. Alex's words meant one thing—she trusted Claire. "Understood," Claire said. "On my call."

Jameson opened the cooler that she had placed in the barn and handed her helper a beer.

"Thanks," he said.

Jameson took a seat on a pile of wood. "You think my King Cole story is silly."

He took a long pull from the beer in his hand and looked at the bottle. "No," he said. "I'm a bit more like Simple Simon."

Claire moved carefully toward the ladder she had pulled up to the upper level of the barn. She sprawled out flat, looking through a crack between boards at the figures below. "Stay steady, JD. He's following those breadcrumbs we talked about."

"Simple Simon the pie man?" Jameson chuckled before taking a sip from her beer.

He grinned. "Simple Simon wasn't the pie man," he told her. "He met the pie man going to the fair."

Jameson nodded. "And, that's you?"

"No. Later Simple Simon goes fishing," he said.

"Yeah? I don't remember this one? Does he catch anything?"

He smiled. "No. He wants to catch the whale. But, all the water he had got was in his mother's pail."

Jameson tried to understand his pun. "Doesn't he prick his finger or something?"

"He does. You see, Simple Simon is innocent. He's a curious boy."

"So, you were curious as a kid?"

He lifted the beer bottle in his hand to his lips again and swallowed greedily. He wiped his mouth with the back of his hand and offered Jameson a sickening smile. "Curiosity is a funny thing," he said. "Simon wants to try everything, but at every turn, someone like Old King Cole stops him."

"This is it," Claire said. "Be ready." *He's telling you, JD. He's telling you.*

"Claire," Alex's voice called cautiously. "He's cracking."

"Trust me," Claire said.

Alex took a deep breath. *I do. It's him I don't trust.*

"How did I end up in your story?" Jameson asked. *Claire, I hope you are there.*

He inched closer to her. "How do we all end up in each other's stories?" He looked her in the eye. "Take Little Tommy Tucker who sings for his supper," he said. "Or, what about Little Miss Muffet? They all have something in common. Someone takes something from all of them," he said. "They think they are safe. They're curious, hopeful, minding their own business until something stops them in their tracks. Tommy Tucker has no knife. He has no wife," he explains. "Miss Muffet? A spider takes over her tuffet. There are no happy endings," he said. "We're all living in The House That Jack Built."

"Go!" Claire said.

He reached behind him and picked up a hammer from the ground. "You're just the latest resident," he whispered to Jameson.

Jameson's stomach flipped over violently. She anticipated his move and lifted her hand to grab his. Their motion sent them both falling backward, leaving him hovering above her.

"Fuck the ladder," Claire said. She jumped through the small opening in the floor. She landed with a small thud on what she imagined was a rolled-up tent. "On the right, Toles. On the right! They're on the ground!"

Alex drew her gun and started into the barn. A small army of agents followed on her heels. "Where!" she asked.

"Behind the woodpile."

Jameson struggled to match the strength of the man above her. She caught a glimpse of Claire behind him. *Thank God.*

In less than a second, Claire had grabbed the hand holding the hammer. She whisked the man off Jameson and threw him to the ground. "Son of a bitch." He got up before Claire could draw her weapon and cocked his arm to swing the hammer at her. She ducked.

Alex ran up behind the man as cries of "FBI!" rang out behind her. Her focus remained squarely on the man. For a split second, she considered firing her weapon. Her foot seemed a better option. She landed a kick squarely in the middle of his back. He tipped and Claire's fist sent him backward onto the ground with a thud.

Alex held her gun on him. She shook her head. "FBI," she said. "John Carter, you are under arrest for the murder of Kaylee Peters…"

Claire heard Alex reading the suspect his rights. She moved a few short paces to where Jameson was finding her feet. "You okay?"

Jameson nodded.

"You did good," Claire said. Jameson stared at the scene

unfolding a few feet away. Claire took hold of her arm. "JD," she said. "You did good. Go call your wife."

Claire's words finally pulled Jameson's focus away from the organized chaos in the barn. She nodded. Claire watched her walk away and sighed. An approaching voice caught her attention.

"The legend," he said when Alex spun him around, his hands cuffed behind his back. Alex stared at him passively. He laughed. "What's the matter, Agent Toles? Ding Dong Bell," he said. "How'd you like the well, pussycat?"

Alex's expression remained unchanged. "Your rhymes are over, Carter. We know everything."

He laughed again. "You haven't begun."

———

"Candace?"

"Jameson? Are you all right?" Candace could feel the trembling in her hand as she held the phone.

"Other than really sweaty, I'm fine."

"Alex?"

"They got him."

"Jameson?"

Jameson closed her eyes. "I don't want to talk about it—not right now."

"I'm coming home."

"Candace..."

"Don't bother," Candace said. "I'll see you in as soon as I can get Cooper ready."

Jameson set her phone on the table and sighed.

"Hey," Claire poked her head in the kitchen.

"Hey."

Claire stepped in. "Afraid I'll have to take a raincheck on that shot," she said. Jameson smiled weakly.

Claire took a deep breath. It wasn't in her nature to reassure people. She had seen the hint of ghosts in Jameson's eyes. And, Claire Brackett knew a thing or two about ghosts. While Claire was sure that the conversation in the barn had unsettled Jameson, she suspected the experience had conjured old demons and fears.

"I told you; you did good," Claire said.

"Glad it worked."

"Listen, JD, shit like this? Dealing with people like that asshole in the barn? It messes with you. He's not just sick," Claire said. "He's an asshole without a conscience. I get it. You were out there working with him for two hours—talking. You know why you're there, but he makes you forget for a minute. You think maybe, just for a second he's not the guy you know he is. Then, just when you think he's someone else, he shows you his true colors. I've lived it," Claire said.

Jameson sighed. "How could I be so comfortable with him?"

"How do you think he managed to lure all those women?"

"Hey," Alex peeked inside. "Sorry. We gotta' roll," she said to Claire.

"I'll be right there," Claire replied.

Alex nodded and offered Jameson an understanding smile. "We'll talk soon," she promised.

Claire waited until Alex had shut the door to continue her thought. "Killers are people, JD. The worst of them are the most charming. It's what makes them sinister. You held your own. You looked him in the eye. That takes more than guts. It takes resolve. Don't second guess anything you said or did."

Jameson nodded. "I don't know how people end up like that."

"People will say they're sick. Maybe. Maybe someone fucked with their life at some point. That's not what makes them kill for pleasure."

"Then what does?"

Claire shrugged. "I don't know," she admitted. "You have a soul, so you think everyone else does. Maybe sometimes that piece is just missing." She reached out and put a hand on Jameson's shoulder. "Raincheck on shots and marriage?"

Jameson smiled. "I look forward to it."

"Me too."

———————————————

Candace walked through the door in search of Jameson. The eerie quiet in the house unsettled her. It had taken her longer to leave Albany than she had hoped. Jonah offered to take Cooper for the night. Cooper was delighted and Candace was grateful. She knew that Jameson was physically safe. Jameson's voice had sounded hollow to her over the phone. That concerned her. A faint banging met her ears when she reached the kitchen and she followed the sound to the back door. Candace looked outside and sighed. It appeared that Jameson was putting the finishing touches on a play scape for Cooper. She took a deep breath. The last thing Jameson needed was to see how rattled Candace felt. Candace opened the screen door and took a step onto the back porch.

"Been busy, I see."

Jameson looked up from her task. "How long have you been there?"

"Only a minute," Candace replied. "Quite the project."

Jameson looked at her creation and shrugged. "I hope they enjoy it."

Candace stepped off the porch and made her way to Jameson. She shook her head affectionately. Jameson was a mess. She was covered in several layers of dirt, sweat, and wood stain. She reached out for Jameson.

"I'm filthy," Jameson protested.

Candace ignored Jameson and stepped directly into her arms. "You're safe."

Jameson closed her eyes when Candace's head fell against her. In less than a second, she heard soft cries escape Candace.

"I'm okay," Jameson promised.

Candace pulled back. "You are a horrible liar."

Jameson smiled. "I'm okay."

Candace cupped Jameson's cheek in her palm. "Don't lie to me, honey—or for me. I have eyes."

"It was a long day," Jameson confessed.

"You kept at it."

"I needed to stay busy."

Candace could tell that Jameson was not quite ready to talk about the events that had unfolded earlier. "Are you finished yet?" she gestured to the structure Jameson was in the process of staining.

"About twenty more minutes," Jameson said.

"Have you eaten?"

Jameson shook her head.

Candace sighed. She desperately wanted to keep Jameson close. She sensed that was not what Jameson needed at the moment. "How about I work on that? When you're done, you go shower and I'll have dinner waiting."

"Where's Coop?"

"He's spending the night with his big brother."

Jameson nodded.

"Jameson, if you want Cooper to come home just say so. Jonah will bring him here."

"No. I'm sure he was excited."

"He was, but when he sees what you've been working on, I think he will forget all about his plans."

Jameson shook her head. "It needs to dry," she said absently.

"Jameson..."

Jameson leaned in and kissed Candace's lips gently. "Let me finish so I can get washed up."

Candace nodded. She kissed Jameson one more time and made her way back into the house. She was relieved to see Jameson was all right. She wasn't sure how to reach her wife. *I wish she would talk to me.*

"What's all this?" Jameson asked when she reached the living room.

"All this?"

"You cooked."

"I do have that ability," Candace quipped.

"I know," Jameson said. "I thought maybe we would have take-out."

"I thought I might be able to entice you to eat with something you enjoy."

Jameson smiled. The coffee table was set for dinner with a bottle of wine placed in the corner. Candace had made pasta with shrimp and scallops. Jameson had never pinned down exactly what Candace used to season the dish other than garlic. It was her favorite thing on earth to eat. Candace hadn't made it in longer than Jameson could remember, mainly because Cooper didn't care for shellfish and neither did Marianne.

Jameson took a seat on the sofa. "Thanks."

"It's just pasta."

"No, it isn't."

Candace looked at Jameson with concern.

"I'm okay," Jameson said again. "I really am. I just—I realized how close he came…"

"To hurting you?" Candace asked.

"No," Jameson said. "I wasn't worried about my safety."

Candace listened with interest.

"I knew he would make an advance," she said. "I knew that Claire and Alex would be there."

"But?"

Jameson sucked in a deep breath. "For a few minutes, I forgot all about why we were there. We were working on the play scape and I just—Candace—it'd be so easy for someone not knowing who he was to be caught off guard by him." Jameson closed her eyes and rubbed them. "If he'd gotten to Shell before…"

Candace moved to Jameson's side and rubbed her back. "He didn't."

"I know. He could have. I can't imagine what those girls..."

"Jameson," Candace called soothingly. "He can't hurt anyone anymore. You made sure of that."

"You talked to Alex, didn't you?"

"She called, yes."

"Did he confess?"

"I don't know," Candace said. "I would imagine they are still grilling him."

Jameson looked at the bowl in front of her. Her stomach revolted.

"You don't have to eat," Candace said.

"You went to the trouble..."

"Taking care of you is no trouble," Candace said. "If you can't eat—don't."

Jameson looked at Candace apologetically.

"What can I do?" Candace asked.

"Nothing. I'm so tired."

"Let me wrap this up, and we'll go lie down."

"You need to eat," Jameson replied.

"I need to be with you. Go upstairs. I'll be there in a few minutes."

"Candace, I..."

"Don't make me give you a time-out."

Jameson snickered. She was exhausted mentally, physically and emotionally. Candace could always cajole her out of a funk. Having Candace close had already begun to lighten her spirits. "If time-out involves our bed and using you as a pillow, I will be happy to be punished."

"Well then, time-out it is."

Jameson leaned in and pecked Candace on the cheek. "I don't think I can talk tonight," she said. "I just need to…"

Candace smiled. There were times in life when a person needed the simple solace of an embrace. Words had their place and their time. Now, was not that time for Jameson. Candace was less concerned about hearing a play by play of the day's events as she was making certain Jameson was all right. She could get the details other ways if she desired. "Your human pillow will join you shortly."

Jameson nodded and started for the stairs. "Candace?"

Candace looked up.

"I love you," Jameson said.

"I love you too."

Candace rolled over when she heard her phone. Jameson grumbled. "Go back to sleep," Candace told her. She pulled herself from the bed and made her way out of the room to take the call.

"Alex?"

"Hey, did I wake you?"

"No," Candace answered honestly.

"How's JD?"

"Truthfully?"

"Yeah."

"I don't know, Alex—quiet. She's quiet. She was so exhausted she couldn't eat." Candace heard Alex sigh. "What is it? What's wrong?"

"Nothing," Alex replied. "He confessed."

Candace let out a relieved breath.

"I'm not sure we would have gotten his confession without JD."

"Alex, what aren't you telling me about today?"

"Nothing pertinent if that's what you are thinking. Listen, it's normal—JD being quiet. It's normal."

"Alex, she built an entire playground out in our yard."

"She finished it?"

"Yes."

Alex chuckled.

"Is that amusing?" Candace asked.

"No, it's not that. I just understand. Sometimes after a day like today, I just need to run. Exhausted or not, I just need to clear my head. I'm sure building is the same outlet for JD. She'll be okay. She just needs to process it."

"I hope so."

"Trust me on this one. She could easily have been in law enforcement."

"She grew up around it."

"I know," Alex said. "She's smart. And, I have to tell you she can hold her own physically."

"Well, she was the only girl in a brood of boys."

"I wanted you to know that he is going away forever. I wanted JD to know that too."

"Thank you."

"It gives a person a new perspective," Alex offered. "Being that close to evil."

"Evil?"

"I know you don't see it that way."

"I wouldn't say that," Candace disagreed.

"I would. I know you. You and Cass are a lot alike. You see the deed as evil, not the person."

Candace took a deep breath. Lately, she had been finding it increasingly difficult to find the best in some people. "You might be surprised."

Alex sighed. She was aware of the nastiness being flung at Candace and her family in the public sphere. She had lived through that with her wife. Cassidy had seldom wavered in her ability to see the good in people. People could hurl wild accusations and spread vicious rumors about Cassidy Toles—Cassidy would take a deep breath and shrug it off. Attacking or hurting someone Cassidy loved crossed the line. Alex had come to know Candace well. Jameson had been affected by this case. Candace's daughter had been touched by it. At the same time, Candace was enduring an onslaught of hurtful rhetoric hurled towards her children.

"I get it," Alex said. "I do."

"I know you do," Candace said. "It's not just today— not for Jameson or me."

"Yeah, I kind of figured. Anything I can do?"

Candace smiled as she listened to Alex. She valued her friendship with the FBI agent and her wife. "Actually, there might be," she said.

"Whatever it is, just let me know. I owe you both."

"No, you don't. If anything, it's the other way around."

"Nah. Don't worry too much about JD, Candace. She'll feel better after a good night's sleep and a little time with you."

"It that your expert opinion?"

"Well, it's the remedy that works for me—so, yeah. A little distraction sometimes helps too. That shouldn't be an issue for you two."

"Why is that?"

"Well, you have as many kids as we do and we don't have grandkids yet. I'd wager something will happen to take her mind off things in less than twenty-four hours."

"Probably so."

"Tell her that Claire is eager to finish their conversation." Alex laughed. "And, I have no idea what that means so don't even ask."

Candace laughed. "I will. I'll be in touch. You keep me apprised—of what is happening with Mr. Carter."

"Never a question, Governor."

Candace made her way back into the bedroom and slid into the bed beside Jameson.

"Everything okay?" Jameson asked.

"Everything is fine. Go back to sleep."

Jameson turned and strained to make out Candace's expression in the faint light. "Who was on the phone?"

Candace sighed. "Alex."

"What happened?"

"Jameson, why don't we talk about this in the morning?"

"Just tell me."

"He confessed."

Jameson closed her eyes and let out a long sigh of relief. "Thank you."

"For what?"

"Telling me. I think I'll sleep better now."

"I'm sorry about today," Candace said.

Jameson's eyes flew open. "Why? I'm not."

"You're not?"

"No. Hell, I'm glad I could help even a little."

"From what Alex said you helped a lot more than a little."

"I don't know about that. It felt good." Jameson chuckled at the evident surprise in Candace's eyes. "Probably didn't seem that way when you got home, huh?"

"Not really, no."

"I can't explain it—how it felt knowing what he had done—sitting there drinking a beer with him."

"I can't even imagine."

"The thing is, it felt good to be able to help."

Candace sighed inwardly. "You're always helping everyone."

"Maybe. It doesn't feel that way, though. Watching the things you deal with—Candace, sometimes I want to beat the shit out of people."

Candace grinned. "You don't say?"

"You know what I mean."

"Yes, I do."

"I was so mad when he lunged toward me." Jameson heard Candace faintly gasp. "He didn't hurt me. Claire was on him in less than a second. And, anyway, I think he was surprised at the grip I had on his hand." She chuckled.

Candace's heart skipped several beats. She had known that John Carter had gotten close. She hadn't realized how close.

"I'm fine," Jameson assured her wife. She kissed Candace's lips gently. "When everybody finally left? I mean, everybody?"

"Yes?"

"That's when I got pissed. I had to keep working. He was so close to Shell. If I had the chance again, I think I would have gotten the better of him before he had a chance to know what was coming."

"I'm glad you didn't."

Jameson closed her eyes.

"What is it?" Candace asked. "There's something else; I can feel it."

Jameson took a deep breath for courage.

"Jameson, you can tell me anything."

"I know." Jameson smiled. "All of it—everything— this guy coming so close, the situation with Grant, Laura being pregnant, Shell looking to start a family—hell, Marianne was talking to me about her future with Scott—even Cooper, it just makes me think sometimes."

Candace could guess what was on Jameson's mind. "About?"

"What it would have been like if they were all ours."

Candace smiled. "I know. I think about that too sometimes."

"You do?"

"Of course, I do. I wouldn't change anything because that would change everything," Candace said. "That doesn't mean I don't wonder what it would have been like to walk that road with you." Candace was surprised to see tears brimming in Jameson's eyes. "Does that surprise you?"

"No, not really. Shell seems to think I should have a baby."

Candace chuckled. "She would."

"It's not that."

"I know."

"I would have, you know?"

"That would have been a neat trick," Candace said. "Having a baby with me when you were six."

Jameson laughed. "I never think about it like that."

Candace stopped her teasing. "If things were different, Jameson; if I were twenty years younger, this conversation would be completely different."

"Really?"

"Really. I love Cooper more than anything."

"Me too."

"I would love to have been making the plans Shell and Melanie are making with you."

Jameson smiled. "Thanks."

"For telling you the truth? Did you really think otherwise?"

"No," Jameson said. "But hearing you say it means more than I think you know."

Candace leaned in and captured Jameson's lips with a tender kiss. She'd never told Jameson about her private musings, about the fact that when Shell announced she and Melanie were going to try and conceive that she felt a momentary surge of jealousy. Candace shared more with Jameson than she ever had anyone in her life. She shared every part of herself. There was one thing she would never be able to share. It wasn't a void, but it was a silent longing that she was certain would always make itself known from time to time. Knowing that Jameson felt it too gave her solace.

"There isn't anything I wouldn't share with you," Candace said. "Or anything I wouldn't give you if you asked."

"I know." Jameson placed her head on Candace's breast and closed her eyes.

Candace kissed Jameson's head. She could feel the tension leaving Jameson's body as Jameson succumbed to her exhaustion. *You really are a lunatic if you didn't know that.* "I love you." *More than you know.*

Chapter Twelve

Two Months Later

"What are you doing?" Jameson asked Candace.

Candace looked up from her computer. "Hey."

"Hey? You never came to bed last night."

Candace removed her glasses and sighed. "I'm sorry."

"What's going on?"

"The Times is finally getting ready to run a story on Klein's dealings in Moldova."

"And, that's a problem for you?"

"It will be."

"How?"

Candace sighed heavily.

"Candace?"

Candace massaged her brow.

"Candace?" Jameson repeated.

"Someone has made the claim that the reason John Merrow was killed can be traced to his Russian connections."

"And?"

"And," Candace took a deep breath. "They are claiming that I was one of the people on the Intelligence Committee that paved the way for him to lift sanctions through back channels."

"Excuse me? It's not true."

Candace looked up at Jameson and shook her head.

"Candace, is it true?"

"No," Candace said. "It's far more complicated than this suggests."

"But?"

"Jameson, everyone on that committee was aware that John's defense team was pushing contracts through to Russian contractors."

"Why?"

"That's... It's classified."

"Jesus, Candace. Everyone knew?"

Candace nodded.

"And no one did anything?"

Candace was growing frustrated. She was tired, and she had no desire to defend herself to anyone. International relations were never handled the way the public believed. An intricate web of diplomatic, defense, business, and intelligence entities existed. Everything was connected, and everyone was connected—far more than the American people would ever realize. Presidents and politicians took calculated risks. Sometimes, alliances with demons were necessary if one hoped to keep the devil from doing his bidding. She looked back at Jameson. "A lot of people work to keep this country safe, Jameson. That sometimes requires dealing with people you and I might consider less than desirable."

"How bad is this?"

"It depends on the line my former colleagues choose to deliver."

"What do you mean?"

"Well, Senator Keyes is gaining some ground in the polls."

"It's only August," Jameson pointed out.

"Almost September," Candace reminded Jameson.

"I don't understand. Primaries don't even begin until February."

"That gives Keyes four months to court the establishment."

Jameson sighed. "What are you going to do?"

"Make sure the *establishment* remembers it is likely implicated in this."

"Candace, is any of this…"

"It's policy, Jameson. It's not legislation; it's policy. There's a lot that goes on out of public view."

"I know that," Jameson snapped.

"I didn't mean," Candace sighed. "I didn't mean that you have no idea," she said. "There are things that none of us can share when we come home. That has nothing to do with a lack of trust."

"I'm sorry. I know that too."

"Don't be sorry. Nothing that was done was illegal or in my opinion unethical. It was all weighed carefully. The decisions we made were bi-partisan. But…"

"But?"

"Not everyone agreed with the decisions, Jameson."

Candace took a deep breath. Seven years earlier, the American embassy in Moscow had been attacked leaving twenty-two people dead including Ambassador Russ Matthews. She expected that those seeking to derail her would attempt to connect the dots somehow to the committee and ultimately to her. It was a complete farce. That didn't change the fact that a simple accusation could cause her campaign massive damage. Candace was now preparing for the inevitable political and media war she saw on the horizon. She looked at Jameson. "We have a complicated history with Russia."

"So, your committee was divided?"

"Not divided. There are always corners that have a different idea and an entirely different agenda. Sometimes what they say in front of a camera is at odds with what they do behind closed doors."

"You mean like Klein?"

"Lawson Klein is like a pesky mosquito," Candace said. "He leaves a mark every now and again hoping to spread the plague."

Jameson understood Candace's meaning. There were forces larger and more powerful than the likes of Lawson Klein. Klein pedaled their agenda and any innuendo that might further that agenda. He was a minion, not the master. "So, what now?"

"Well, at least they are coming at me this time," Candace said.

"Can I do anything?"

"Put on some coffee."

"You need to get some rest."

"Well, what I need and what I will get are not always the same thing. Dana will be here in an hour."

"Coffee it is."

"Jameson?"

"Yeah?"

"I will make this up to you and Cooper."

Jameson smiled. She and Candace had planned to take Cooper to the train museum that afternoon. She'd learned to roll with changes in Candace's schedule. "There's nothing to make up. I'll get some coffee going."

Candace watched Jameson leave her office. She let her face fall into her hands. *Is this even worth it?*

———

Pearl turned to the sound of footsteps. "Well, look what the cat dragged in."

"Very funny," Jameson said. "Where is Jinx anyway?"

"He's upstairs with Spencer, I think. That cat doesn't leave his side unless Candy is here."

Jameson sighed.

"Oh boy, what happened?" Pearl asked.

"Nothing out of the ordinary if the ordinary is your wife running to be president."

"That good, huh?"

Jameson shrugged.

"Don't worry too much," Pearl said. "It always seems worse than it turns out to be."

"I wish I had your confidence."

"What will be will be."

"You're not worried?"

"What is it that you are worried about?" Pearl inquired.

"I hate watching her have to pivot constantly."

Pearl grinned.

"What?"

"Seems to me you've done your share of pivoting as you call it the last year."

"What are you talking about?" Jameson asked.

"Let's see; you signed over your business to Jonah and Mel. You adopted a little boy. You've been traveling with Candy whenever you can. You helped catch that depraved lunatic. Should I go on?"

"It's not the same. That's just going with the flow."

"Right."

"Oh, just say what you want to say," Jameson rolled her eyes.

"Okay, I will. You're right. Candy has to change on a dime. She has to adjust to whatever gets thrown in her path. I don't see how you think that's any different from what you do."

"I don't have the same pressure."

"Is that so?"

"Pearl, Candace has the weight of an entire state and millions of people's hopes on her. That doesn't even begin to cover the demands the kids put on her."

"And what about you?"

"Me? I try not to put any demands on her."

"You don't say."

"Pearl..."

"Maybe you should."

"Should what?"

"Not demands. Maybe you need to pivot to your needs a little more instead of always putting hers first."

"What is that supposed to mean?"

"It means that you get to have a life too, and not always on Candy's time."

"I don't think I..."

"No, you don't think that you are sacrificing yourself. You are."

"She needs me to..."

"She needs you to be Jameson."

"I..."

"I know you," Pearl said. "You are worse than her. You put everyone else before you. What about that idea you had?"

"What idea?"

"That you were going to help build houses for people? Help in some places that need someone with your experience?"

"I would love to."

"So? What are you waiting for? Someone to pick you up and drop you off?"

Jameson chuckled. Pearl was nothing if not candid. "I want to help her."

Pearl let out a heavy sigh. "Then be yourself, Jameson. Go do something for you."

"Pearl, it isn't that simple. There's Cooper and..."

"And an army to help with all of it. I'll bet your mother would love to spend a weekend with Cooper."

Jameson sighed.

"And, that's good for him. It's good for you too."

Jameson scratched her brow. "I don't want her to have to handle..."

"Horse shit."

Jameson's head snapped to attention.

"It is. It's horse shit. You're afraid that you are going to let Candy or Cooper down somehow. Has she?"

"Has she what?"

"Let you down?"

"Candace? Never."

Pearl grinned.

"Oh, no... It's not the same, and you know it."

"Seems the same to me. She didn't fall in love with you because you followed her around like a puppy dog. She's got plenty of people willing to do that."

"Is that what you think I'm doing?"

"I think that you love Candy. I think that you love your family, and I think that you have some hair-brained notion that you need to be available for every one of them 24/7. That's what I think."

Jameson took a seat at the kitchen table. Pearl's words stung with the truth.

"Jameson." Pearl pulled out a chair and sat across from Jameson at the table. "I remember this cocky, witty, beautiful young woman sitting here at this table giving Candy hell."

Jameson smiled. "I still give her hell."

"I'm sure she'd agree. Things this last year have turned your world upside down more than you expected," Pearl said. "It happens. You can't lose yourself in loving them."

"So, what do I do?"

"I can't answer that. You need to do something solely for you. Candy can say that she didn't want to run this campaign; she did. She wants it, and she wants it as much for herself as she does any cause she cares about."

"I know."

"Then you should realize that you're also allowed to have something meaningful in your life outside of this family."

"I..."

"You know, Jameson tending a family isn't just about being physically available. It's about being able to be present even when you can't be right with them."

"That doesn't make sense."

"No? Sure it does. What do you do when Jonah calls or Marianne for that matter?"

"I don't see what that..."

"What about when Candy was in Washington most of the week? Do you think she'd say you weren't there for her? Did you think she wasn't holding up her part of your relationship?"

"Of course not."

Pearl smiled.

"Okay, I understand what you are saying. Pearl, there is Cooper to think about now, and the family has changed since Candace and I met. It's..."

"It's bigger," Pearl said. "Closer and probably a whole lot more complicated." She laughed. "And, I hate to tell you, but it's not going to get any easier as you go."

"Speaking from experience?"

"I am. I'll tell you a secret."

Jameson was genuinely curious.

"It's not easy for me to give you all your space. Surprised to hear that?" she asked. "It isn't. I don't enjoy watching people lash out at Candy or any of those kids. I worry about her. I worry about you."

"We worry about you too, you know?"

"Well, I should hope so!"

Jameson laughed.

Pearl held up a finger. "I have something for you," she said.

Jameson watched as Pearl got up from her place at the table and walk out of the room. She chuckled. Pearl was in many ways the thread that held the family together. Pearl was Candace's rock. She was the person everyone could count on for a healthy dose of the truth—straight, honest, but always with love. "What is she up to?" Jameson mused.

"You know; I ask myself that same question about you almost daily," Pearl replied as she walked back into the room. She handed Jameson a piece of folded paper.

"What's this?"

Pearl shrugged. "Something I thought you might be interested in."

Jameson opened the paper and read the notes written on it. She looked up at Pearl.

"Well?" Pearl said. "Seems there are some people besides Candy and this crazy crew that could use your help."

Jameson looked back at the paper. She'd seen a story in the paper about a house that had been devastated by fire in nearby Berne. It was a short piece. She sighed as she read the note Pearl had written. "Do you know these people?" Jameson asked.

"No. I know Reverend Howe," Pearl replied. "His name is there at the bottom. He's been raising some money to help the family."

"Where are they staying?"

"With family, although not all together. The father is with the oldest son in Maryland. The mother is staying with her sister in Cobleskill. She has the younger two with her."

"I'm not sure what I can do to help."

"Well, maybe you should talk that over with Reverend Howe."

Jameson looked up at Pearl.

"He told me they have to tear the whole thing down," she explained.

"Insurance?"

Pearl shook her head.

Jameson sighed.

"The Greers don't have much money, Jameson. Reverend Howe told me Chris Greer was laid off from his construction job two years ago. Not a lot of building happening in this area. You know that."

Jameson shook her head. She did know. Development or lack thereof was a constant sore spot with Candace. There were parts of New York State that were falling into disrepair. The once thriving agricultural communities had been hit hard by industry and conglomerates. Albany had not been spared either. While parts of New York were thriving, there were pockets where whole communities struggled to get by. That reality drove Candace's initiatives as governor. It was a reality that was mirrored across the country, and Jameson knew that was one of the reasons Candace had felt compelled to seek the presidency.

"Do you know..."

"What I know about the Greers and their situation is on that paper," Pearl said.

Jameson nodded.

"What I suspect is that you might be able to help the good reverend piece together a solution."

"Pearl, I can design a house—no question. With some help, I can even build it, but I have no idea what they are looking for or what resources they have."

"You can do a lot more than design a house and build it."

"I don't think…"

"Jameson, you are one of the most gifted people I know when it comes to solving problems. It's one of the reasons Candy loves you. She respects you. You know how to take the pieces of what looks too broken to fix and make it into something even better. Not many people can do that. And, I'm not just talking about that damn leaky roof in the barn."

Jameson smiled. "I think you give me too much credit."

"The hell I do," Pearl put the thought to rest. "Most of this family thinks Candy is the glue that holds it together."

Jameson chuckled. "You're the glue," she said. "You hold Candace together."

"Mmm. Sometimes I still do," Pearl admitted. "But I have taken a back seat to this snarky architect who wandered into my kitchen about five years ago."

Jameson shook her head. "You don't take a backseat to anyone."

"Yes— I do, and that's how it should be. It's not the easiest role to play," Pearl admitted. "You need to step away from it occasionally—get your mind into something else. Besides, if you don't do something soon, I'm apt to find the yard's been turned into a replica of London or something."

Jameson laughed. The day Pearl had seen the castle Jameson built she had rolled her eyes and asked Jameson whatever happened to letting kids play with boxes and blankets. "It's not that big."

Pearl's brow shot up. "It's big enough. It's up to you," Pearl said. "I will tell you this; if Candy gets elected your life is going to be less your own than ever before. It won't last forever, but you will need to find something to preserve your sanity—start now." She offered Jameson a wink. "Now, I have to pick up Marianne and the kids from the pediatrician and take her to get her car."

"What's wrong with her car?"

Pearl shrugged. "Mice."

"Mice?"

"Or squirrels. Can't really say. Chewed through some wires. Had to have it towed this morning."

"Why didn't she call?"

Pearl laughed. "She did. She just didn't call you. I'm down the street; remember?"

Jameson sighed.

Pearl shook her head. "Call Reverend Howe. That's probably the closest I'll ever get you to church. I'm not getting any younger," she said. "I need to score some points."

Jameson laughed. She looked back at the paper. *Call the reverend, huh? Maybe I will.*

"Slow down, Coop!"

Cooper ran through the Executive Mansion in search of Candace. "Mommy!"

Candace came around the corner from the kitchen and laughed. "My goodness, what have you been up to?"

"Momma and me went to the Rebrend's house. He's got a huuuge tire swing!"

Candace looked over at Jameson curiously. "No trains?" she asked.

"Long story," Jameson said.

"Did you eat dinner yet?" Candace wondered. Jameson shook her head.

"I had cookies," Cooper said excitedly.

"I can't believe it," Candace teased him. "Does that mean that you don't have any room for my lasagna?"

Cooper's smile widened further.

Candace grinned. "Well, why don't you go wash up. Dinner will be ready in about half an hour."

"'Kay!" Cooper barreled up the stairs.

Candace chuckled.

"You made lasagna?" Jameson asked. "I thought we'd find you tucked away in the office—well, that or asleep."

Candace sighed. "I closed the office door a little after noon."

"Everything okay?"

"The things that matter are."

Jameson nodded. "The campaign matters, Candace."

"Not more than you and Cooper, it doesn't."

"It matters to me and Cooper too."

"I know."

"You must be exhausted," Jameson observed.

"I told you; I closed the door on work hours ago. What I didn't tell you is that I took a nap."

Jameson smiled. "What prompted that?"

"I can't control what anyone is going to do."

"No, but you can plan for it."

"Can I? Really?" Candace sighed. "I've been spinning, spinning in so many directions. I don't know why. It's not like me."

"I know why."

"You do?"

Jameson nodded. "You want this."

Candace groaned.

"Don't apologize for that. You want to win this election." Jameson looked up at the ceiling. "I want you to win this election."

"Do you?"

"Yes."

"This is still only the beginning. I keep telling everyone to prepare for the long haul. I need to take my own advice."

"Just your own?"

Candace laughed. "Okay, so maybe Pearl called."

Jameson leaned in and kissed Candace.

"What was that for?"

"Seems Pearl set us both straight today."

"Do tell."

"Do you remember that story a couple of weeks ago about the family in Berne whose house nearly burned to the ground?"

Candace nodded. "Of course, I spoke to Mayor Laughlin that week. Awful. I know the community was trying to raise money to help them."

"They are."

Candace narrowed her gaze.

"Insurance lapse," Jameson explained.

Candace's eyes closed in defeat. "Shit."

"Yeah. The house is a total loss, Candace."

Candace opened her eyes and looked at Jameson.

"I told you; it's a long story. Probably an after-dinner story to explain it all. The short of it is that Pearl is friends with the pastor at the Congregational church there."

"Ah, that explains rebrend," Candace mimicked Cooper's pronunciation. "You went to see Gabe Howe."

Jameson nodded. "Yeah, and I think we might need a tire swing after that visit."

Candace rolled her eyes. *Just what we need another way to support the emergency room.*

"Anyway, he filled me in on most of the details, took me out to the property." Jameson shook her head. "It's a mess."

"Why do I think you have an idea how to clean it up?"

"I have a few."

Candace smiled. *Of course, you do.* "And?"

"They need to raise a lot more money," Jameson admitted.

"How much more?" Candace asked.

"A lot."

"A number might be helpful, Jameson."

Jameson sighed. "They've raised a little over twenty-thousand."

"And?"

"Even if I can get contractors to donate their time, and materials donated—Candace, to rebuild that house the way it was would cost at least fifty-thousand."

"And?"

"And, I can't build it the way it was. It wasn't safe. They're lucky they all got out."

"Jameson," Candace began cautiously. "What are you telling me?"

"I want to help them out."

"By helping rebuild this house or by funding the project?"

Jameson sighed.

"Honey, you can't fund every person who faces tragedy."

"I know."

Candace sighed knowingly. She wished that she could finance the recovery of every lost soul or struggling family. That would never be possible. "How much do you need to get it started?"

"Candace, I'm not asking you..."

"How much?"

"Probably another fifty-thousand."

"Have they applied for any programs?" Candace asked.

"A few. You know how long that takes."

Candace did know how slowly the wheels of assistance turned. They turned like the wheels of justice, in a painfully slow rotation. "What do you want to do?"

"I want to make an anonymous donation—not from you. I don't want this to..."

"Jameson, you've been extremely successful financially. You don't need my permission."

"I would never make this kind of decision without you; elections or not."

"I know. Neither would I. Listen, there might be another option."

"I'm all ears."

"Do you remember Len Stacey?"

"Senator Stacey?" Jameson asked.

"Right."

"Lost me."

"When he retired, he set up a non-profit that helps families like the Greers."

"Yeah, but Senator Stacey is from New Hampshire."

"I know they have worked with families in Connecticut and in Maryland. Let me make a call."

"You'd do that?"

"Jameson, I wish I could make those calls for every family. I can't."

"Candace, I…"

"Let me call Len. This has obviously struck a chord with you."

"It has."

"I can see that."

"I wish I could do more. Reverend Howe said the lowest estimate they got was three-hundred-thousand. That's worse than highway robbery, Candace."

Candace grinned. *Ever the protector.* "Sometimes, it's not your wallet that makes the greatest impact."

"No, but you still need money to get things done."

"And, knowing what you can work with and where to find that money is the biggest battle. It's just like politics."

Jameson laughed.

"So, why don't you figure out what you can work with, and I will work on what you need to finish."

"You have enough on your plate without…"

Candace pressed two fingers to Jameson's lips. "This is a partnership, Jameson. Maybe we both lost sight of that for a minute. It's give and take and give some more. Lately, you've been doing most of the giving."

"Candace, you give to everyone until you…"

"Until I'm so dry that I'm not giving enough to the one person I love the most," Candace said. "I'm sorry."

"Sorry? You don't have anything to be sorry for."

"But I do. Loving you is my anchor. Maybe you don't realize that. I do need you by my side, but no more than you need me at yours. I told you when we set off on this road not to forget that you are the most important part of my life. You are."

"I know. You're the most important person in mine."

Candace smiled. "So, maybe it's time we took the time to remember that. I want you to be happy, Jameson. I don't just mean with us or with this family. I want you to do the things that make me crazy."

"Oh, you mean like the climbing ladders and the…"

Candace silenced Jameson with a kiss. "Let's not get into the details."

Jameson sniggered.

"I can't promise I will always be able to step away like I did today."

"I know."

"But I promise that when I can, I will make a point to. You can't wait around for those breaks in my schedule, honey. You need to do the things you love and trust that I will be waiting right here, just like I trust you to be there when I need you."

"I promise."

"Good. Now, what do you say to a glass of wine be-fore Cooper comes back looking for dinner?"

"I'd love to as long as mine can be beer."

"Negotiating already?" Candace teased.

"No, I'll save the negotiations for later."

Candace grinned. "I look forward to that presenta-tion."

So, do I.

Chapter Thirteen

December

"This is bullshit." Jonah shook his head at the television.

"Jonah," Laura called for his attention.

"They're trying to call Mom a traitor."

"Jonah."

"What? Did you hear that?"

"Yes, I heard it."

"How can you be so calm?"

Laura took hold of Jonah's hand. "Your mom will handle it."

"It's bullshit. I'm tired of those assholes."

Laura's eyes closed.

"Shit," Jonah groaned. Laura's father was still leading the charge against Candace, at least, he was on the television screen. The latest was to demand an investigation into her knowledge of the embassy bombing in Russia after John Merrow's assassination. "I know that this isn't easy for you."

"It's not that," Laura said. "Your mom knows what she's doing."

"Maybe she does. She looked so tired last time I saw her."

"She is tired," Laura said. "She's juggling an important job, a campaign and a family."

"I don't know why she does it."

"Why don't you ask her?"

"Ask mom why she does it?"

"Yeah."

"She'll play it down."

Laura grinned. "I'm not so sure. Why don't you give her a call? See if she has some time this week."

"I don't want to stress her out."

Laura shrugged. "I think you underestimate her."

Jonah was about to answer when his phone rang. "Hey, Shell."

"What are you two doing?" Michelle asked her brother.

"Not watching the news," Jonah grumbled and shut off the television.

"Probably a good idea. Stay away from that shit. It'll rot your brain."

"Why are you in such a good mood?"

"Me?" Michelle feigned innocence.

"Yeah, you."

"I'm not in a good mood."

Jonah laughed. "Okay. Why are you in a bad mood?"

"I'm not in a bad mood either. I am in a pizza mood. Thought you guys might want to join."

"Uh-huh."

"What's going on?" Laura whispered.

"Shell wants to have pizza."

"With us?" Laura asked. He nodded and Laura grabbed the phone. "When are we having this pizza?" she asked Michelle

"I thought around two," Michelle answered.

"You want to meet somewhere?"

"Actually, yes," Michelle said. "I'll send you the address."

"What?" Laura asked.

"Just be there," Michelle said.

"Oooo-kay."

"What did she say?" Jonah asked.

"She's up to something."

"I knew she was in a good mood. Holy shit! Do you think she's pregnant?"

Laura shrugged.

"You don't think so?"

"Since when does pizza herald pregnancy?"

Jonah smirked.

"What?" Laura asked.

"You've eaten your share this time."

Laura rolled her eyes. "I'm going to go give JJ a bath."

"She's pregnant. I'm telling you."

"Anything is possible." Laura laughed. *At least, he has something else to obsess over for a few hours.*

———————

"What do you think this is about?" Jameson asked Candace.

Candace shrugged. "I've no idea."

"Seriously?"

"When it comes to Shell I learned long ago to expect the unexpected."

"Pizza? Shell never asks us to meet for pizza."

"That's because Shell usually comes here looking to be fed," Candace replied.

Jameson laughed. "True. You're not worried?"

"No."

"Curious?"

Candace chuckled. "You're almost as bad as Cooper."

"What are you talking about?"

"Cooper has been snooping for Christmas presents."

Jameson bit her bottom lip gently.

Candace offered her a knowing smirk. "You wouldn't have any idea where he got the idea to do that?"

"Me? No. I'll bet Spence taught him."

"Mm. And, where do you suppose Spencer learned his detective tactics?"

Jameson shrugged. "Hey, he's spent years mastering new places to hide. Maybe he just wants to be on the other end for a change."

Candace burst out laughing. "That must be it."

"Makes sense to me."

"I'm sure it does, honey." Candace let out an exasperated breath when her cell phone rang. *What now?* "Dana?"

Jameson gauged the shift in Candace's mood as Candace listened to Dana on the phone. *Oh, no.*

"No, no," Candace said. "They certainly can call me to testify. No, I know. Well, they're opening up a can of worms as bait. They might want to careful. Exactly. They might end up catching a fish they hadn't expected. I'm not sure. What does Glenn think?" Candace listened attentively to Dana. "I agree. We should get out in front of it. She would be, but she's due in a couple of weeks. Somehow, I don't see her traveling. You did? What did she say?"

Jameson tried to busy herself, but she was keen to discern what Candace's conversation pertained to.

"Why am I not surprised?" Candace chuckled. "Is that right? Oh, I'm sure Jameson will be up for that."

Jameson's interest piqued.

Candace laughed. "There is a bright side to everything. Thanks for the heads up. I'll talk to Jameson and then give her a call. You too."

Jameson waited for Candace to address her.

Candace smiled.

"Well?" Jameson asked.

"It seems Congressman Drury and a handful of others are making a plan to call me to testify in front of the House Intelligence Committee."

"Why are you smiling then? And, what is it I will be up for?"

"Dana and Glenn think it might be a good idea to give a speech on foreign policy."

"Uh-huh."

"Dana called Cassidy to see if she would be willing to work with me on it."

"Uh-huh."

Candace chuckled. "Since Cassidy isn't traveling these days, she suggested perhaps a speech at Yale might be a good idea. Jane's youngest teaches there."

"And?"

"And, Cassidy suggested to Dana that perhaps you and I could drive down and spend a couple of days there. She was going to give Jane a call."

Jameson nodded.

"I thought that would be something you'd enjoy?" Candace looked at Jameson quizzically.

"Seeing Alex and Cassidy? Yes. The fact that this jerk Drury is making waves? No."

"It's part of the game."

"Cheating?"

"I'm not sure I would..."

"I would call lying to gain ground cheating," Jameson said.

"I don't have anything to hide."

"Exactly my point."

Candace sat down on the end of the bed, took a deep breath and looked at Jameson. "Most people will not regard foreign policy as my strong suit," she said.

"So, I've heard you say."

"They won't. Despite serving on the Intelligence Committee as the ranking minority member, the public sees me largely as a social issues candidate."

"And?"

"This plan the hard right has could easily backfire on them."

"You think this is a good thing?"

Candace shrugged. "Cassidy is probably the best speech writer I've ever had. She understands my voice. She also knows this issue like the back of her hand—so does Jane."

"There is a lot you haven't told me," Jameson surmised.

"I've told you..."

"No, I understand the whole classified thing. Most of it, I don't need or want to know. When it might hurt you, then I..."

"It might," Candace conceded. "It's my job to turn adverse situations into opportunities."

"When do we leave?"

Candace smiled gratefully. "I have to call Cassidy."

"Are you sure you want us to go with you?"

"Positive; unless you don't want to."

Jameson smiled. "Just let me know how much I need to pack."

———

Jameson looked at Candace when the car rolled to a stop in front of a large white house.

"Don't ask me," Candace said. "I told you; I've no idea what she's up to."

Jameson opened her door and stepped out. Officer Evans opened Candace's. Cooper slid out after Candace and caught sight of Michelle walking onto the porch.

"Shell!" He took off in a sprint for his sister.

"What is going on?" Candace muttered.

"Only one way to find out." Jameson took hold of Candace's hand just as Jonah and Laura pulled in the driveway.

"I wish Pearl could've been here," Jameson whispered.

Candace laughed. "Why? Think we need protection?"

"Never know."

Michelle stood on the front porch smiling. "I guess you're the only one who's excited about pizza," she said to Cooper.

Cooper laughed.

"Why don't you go inside and find Mel?"

"I don't know where to go," he reminded her.

"You'll find her. She's with Marianne and Spencer in the kitchen. Go on."

Cooper looked at Michelle again for reassurance.

Michelle smiled and opened the front door again. "Mel! Incoming!"

Cooper giggled and stepped inside. He looked at his feet.

"You can leave on your shoes, Coop. Go find Mel and Marianne."

Jonah sidled up to Jameson. "Do you know what this is about?"

Jameson shrugged.

"I'll bet she's pregnant."

Jameson smiled. "Guess we'll see."

Candace scooped a wobbling JJ from his feet and carried him toward the house. "How are you feeling?" she asked Laura.

"Good. A little tired, but good."

"Only a couple more weeks," Candace said.

Laura looked down at her belly. "For me."

"Ah, you think Shell has some news," Candace surmised.

"News—yes. What it is, I wouldn't begin to guess. Whose house is this anyway?" she asked.

Michelle heard Laura's question. "This would be Mel's and my house as of about 10 a.m. yesterday. So, you'll have to forgive the lack of formal seating."

Candace lifted her brow. Michelle and Melanie had bought a small house a little over a year earlier. She was genuinely surprised that the couple would want to upgrade so soon.

Michelle grinned at her mother. "Well," she said as she looked at the rest of the family. "I may not have much besides lawn chairs and paper plates; I do have heat. And, I know the curiosity is killing you. Either that or you all really love pizza." Michelle chuckled. "Come in."

"Nana!" Spencer ran straight for Candace when she walked through the door.

"Mommy! Momma! Shell's got a new house!" Cooper exclaimed.

"We heard," Jameson chimed.

"It's big," Spencer observed.

Melanie laughed as she entered the room. "It's not that big. It's just bigger than the one we sold."

"You sold your house?" Jonah asked. "How did you sell your house and none of us knew you were even trying to sell it?"

"That was a mouthful," Michelle laughed. "Why don't you take off your coat and we'll explain."

"Seriously," Jonah said. "I don't get it. How did..."

Marianne and Scott stepped into the room.

"I bought it," Scott said.

"What?" Jonah asked.

"I bought Shell's house," he said.

Jonah looked at Candace and Jameson dumbstruck.

Michelle and Marianne both burst out laughing.

"Good God," Michelle said. "Pull up a camp chair and we'll explain."

"Is there wine?" Candace asked.

Michelle's eyes sparkled. "For you—yes."

"Oh, my God!" Jonah's eyes flew open. "Scott bought the house… Marianne are you pregnant?"

Marianne rolled her eyes. "Uh—no."

"Huh," Jonah muttered.

"Why are you so determined to get one of your sisters pregnant?" Laura asked.

Jameson coughed.

"That's not what I meant!" Laura said. "Jonah is convinced someone is pregnant, someone besides me."

Michelle looked at Candace and smiled. Candace immediately anticipated the coming news.

"Well, Jonah is on the right track—for once," Michelle said.

Jonah gloated.

"We didn't want to say anything at all until we were sure," Michelle said.

Melanie took Michelle's hand. "We're expecting."

Michelle held up her hand before anyone could speak. "Before you say anything. You should know it looks like we'll have our hands full."

Candace smirked. "Twins?" she guessed.

Michelle shrugged.

"I thought you weren't trying until this month?" Laura was confused.

"Call it a woman's prerogative," Michelle quipped.

"Congratulations," Jameson said.

"Thanks," Michelle replied.

Candace moved to embrace Michelle. "I'm so happy for you both."

"Me too," Shell said.

"When can we expect the new additions?" Candace asked.

Melanie answered. "June."

Candace's surprise was evident. Michelle shrugged. "We took an easier road," she said. "No one was more surprised than us that it happened so quickly."

"Why the bigger house?" Jonah wondered.

"There's an in-law apartment in the back. Mel's grandmother is going to move in there. She can't be totally independent. At least, neither of us feel comfortable with that. She's not ready for a nursing home. So…"

"And you?" Jonah looked at Scott. "Are you two…"

Scott chuckled nervously. "We don't have any announcements." He looked directly at Jameson. "I'd like to be closer to Marianne and the kids. It made sense."

"What about the clinic?" Jonah asked.

Candace noted Jameson's smile. *You knew all about this.*

"Well, we have the funding for a new clinic. Seemed like Albany was the ideal place. So…"

"That's great," Laura interjected.

"If everyone has had enough news, there's pizza in the kitchen—and wine—for those of us allowed to drink it," Michelle offered.

Candace waited for the room to clear. She pulled Jameson back and whispered in her ear. "You knew."

Jameson smiled. "Yeah."

"You didn't tell me?"

Jameson shrugged. "Mel sort of let it slip when she brought me out to look at the house. She felt horrible about it, but I think she needed to talk. I promised I would let Shell tell you herself. For the record, I didn't know they were going to do this today."

Candace leaned in and kissed Jameson' lips.

"What was that for? Not that I'm complaining."

"I think you know."

"Are you two coming or what?" Shell poked her head into the living room.

Jameson caught the expression in Michelle's eyes. "I'll make sure they save you a piece," she told Candace.

"Make sure they save me some wine," Candace quipped. She turned and looked at a sheepish Michelle.

"Are you mad?" Michelle asked.

"Mad?"

"You figured out JD knew."

Candace nodded. "I'm not mad. I'm thrilled for you."

"I wanted to tell everyone together. Just… Mel was nervous, I think—when JD came out here. We didn't know yet about it being twins. We just knew the test was…"

"Shell," Candace giggled. "It's okay. I'll confess, I am surprised. June?"

Michelle sighed. "We decided to go the simplest route—for now, anyway. If we decide to have more kids maybe we will try something else. It's the right time for us. And, we were lucky."

Candace smiled.

"I know that Mel told JD. No one else knows. Mel's brother offered to be our donor when he visited in September," she explained. "When he did, it just seemed to all fit. We decided waiting was pointless."

"That's wonderful, sweetie."

"You're really not mad? I mean, you're not mad at JD; right? Mel made her promise not to…"

Candace pulled Michelle into a hug. "I love you, Shell."

Michelle sniffled. "I love you too. Tell you a secret?"

Candace pulled back and smiled.

"I'm scared shitless," Michelle said flatly.

"About having twins or about raising them?"

"Both. And, I have to do the first without wine."

Candace laughed. She put her arm around Michelle's shoulders and began to lead her toward the sound of voices. "Trust me, sweetheart; you will have years to make up for that lost time—trust me."

Jameson walked into the bedroom and hovered in the doorway. Candace was lying in bed reading. Her glasses were perched on the end of her nose as she studied the paper in her hand. Jameson let out a soft sigh. Candace looked peaceful—happy. Jameson wondered when the last time she'd seen that expression on her wife's face had been. Michelle's news had lightened Candace's spirits. And, Jameson was sure that the plans Candace had made for them to visit Cassidy and Alex had given the governor something to look forward to.

"See something interesting?" Candace flirted without looking at her wife.

Jameson made her way to the bed. She straddled Candace's waist, removed Candace's glasses and placed them on the bedside table.

"What are you up to?" Candace's eyes twinkled.

Jameson took the paper that Candace held in her hand and put it on the table with her glasses. She tucked a strand of hair behind Candace's ear, leaned in and kissed Candace soundly. "Any more questions?" she asked.

Candace moaned in contentment. "No."

"Good."

Jameson lowered her lips to Candace's again tentatively. Hearing the sigh that escaped the back of Candace's throat, Jameson deepened their connection. She felt Candace's hands reach around her back; Candace's fingertips pressing into her flesh and pulling her closer.

Jameson pulled back slightly to look at Candace.

"What is it?" Candace asked. She stroked Jameson's cheek.

Jameson's reply came in the form of a passionate kiss. She held herself above Candace, delighting in the way Candace's fingers moved up her shirt. Her lips strayed to Candace's neck, seductively nipping and tasting the softness she found there. She let her lips hover next to Candace's ear and whispered. "I don't want you to think about anything," Jameson said. "I don't want you to feel anything but me touching you."

Candace's heart raced like that of a teenager. Jameson's ability to send her soaring had never dwindled. The warmth of Jameson's breath on her neck sent a hot rush of excitement through every nerve of her body and settled in her core. Jameson's touch was tender and communicative. Candace was confident she could never tire of the woman above her. "Jameson," she sighed.

Jameson had become lost to the sensations that making love to Candace produced within her. She loved everything about Candace—the softness of her skin, the faint hint of her perfume that lingered between her breasts and behind her ear, her soft sighs gradually becoming more desperate, the look of fiery passion mingling with intense emotion that lit Candace's irises when she looked at Jameson. When Jameson took the time to think about it, Candace had commanded her attention and her love from the moment they had met. Jameson had never considered herself a hopeless romantic. Although, Candace often accused her of that affliction. No, it wasn't about romanticism; what existed between them was not a sentiment realized. The connection Jameson shared with Candace went far deeper than thought or sentiment. It defied reason. It just was. It always had been, and Jameson felt sure nothing in the world could ever change the love they shared.

Candace sensed an emotional tide brewing in Jameson. She reached out and caressed Jameson's cheek. "Jameson, look at me."

Jameson opened her eyes. Tears welled in them. She sucked in a ragged breath and closed them again.

Candace smiled, taking a moment to trace the outline of Jameson's face with a fingertip. *So, sensitive.* "Jameson," Candace called lovingly.

Jameson took a deep breath and opened her eyes again.

Candace looked at Jameson adoringly. "Tell me."

"I don't know how."

"Then show me."

Jameson's heart thundered so wildly at Candace's direction that Candace could feel it.

"Jameson," Candace whispered. "It's just me."

Jameson had found herself needing to be close to Candace all afternoon. She wasn't sure what was driving her need. Sometimes watching Candace do the simplest things overwhelmed Jameson's senses. She'd spent the day admiring her wife in the distance. Jameson loved to watch Candace with her children. She loved the way Candace's hand would lovingly play with Cooper's curls when he fell asleep in her lap. She marveled at the way Marianne, Shell, and Jonah could transform into small children in their mother's presence. During the afternoon, Jameson had looked over to find the day's excitement challenging Shell's ability to stay awake. Shell's head had fallen on her mother's shoulder in contentment. Candace had captured Jameson's gaze from across the room. Jameson marveled at the way her heart ached from a simple exchanged glance. Simple things— those things might have seemed trivial to many people; for Jameson those moments meant everything.

Jameson often spoke the words, "I love you." Tonight, she thought the emotion behind them might choke her with its potency. She looked in Candace's eyes. "I love you so much it hurts," she confessed.

Oh, Jameson if you only knew how much I understand. Candace smiled and gently reversed their positions. Jameson's intention to seduce Candace had shifted without warning, and Candace instinctively understood what was called for. She removed Jameson's T-shirt and tossed it aside, then removed hers. Jameson reached for her and Candace pressed her back on the bed with gentle force.

"I wanted to make love to you," Jameson feebly protested.

"I want to make love *with* you," Candace replied.

Jameson watched in rapt fascination as Candace continued to undress them both, pausing every so often to kiss Jameson's flesh tenderly, never lingering long enough to solicit more than a slight shiver from Jameson's body. Jameson's eyes were riveted to Candace's every move.

Candace threw the last bit of Jameson's clothing on the floor. She looked down at Jameson's flushed skin and felt a rush of excitement travel through her body. There was nothing Candace enjoyed more than making love with Jameson—nothing. That reality unsettled her at times. She'd always enjoyed sex. She'd realized the first time she and Jameson made love that making love dramatically differed from sex. Making love was infinitely more rewarding. In this place, everything disappeared except the two of them. The demands of careers, the needs of children, the opinions of strangers evaporated in this place. She tenderly brought her lips to Jameson's. The kiss started slowly, an achingly powerful search for connection and acceptance. Candace pulled back slightly and sighed. *How is it possible to love you more?*

Jameson's hands traveled up Candace's stomach to her breasts. She let her palms gently graze over Candace's nipples, enjoying the way they responded to her touch. Candace's eyelids fluttered for a brief second. Jameson bit her bottom lip as the blue of Candace's irises deepened with de-sire.

Candace's hands reached out and explored Jameson's breasts, playfully tugging at Jameson's nipples until Jameson's eyes closed in submission. She smiled. "Jameson," she called to her wife. Jameson forced her eyes open. "Stay with me."

Jameson loved it when Candace made love to her this way. It was erotic. Her hands took hold of Candace's as Candace began to move against her sensually. The sight was mesmerizing. As entrancing as it was to watch Candace, Jameson had to fight to keep her eyes open. Candace commanded all her senses, all her emotions—desire squelched reason, love drowned reality. Jameson's head spun pleasantly. She could feel heat building between them as Candace's hips continued their slow dance against her.

Candace was enraptured by the sight of Jameson beneath her. Jameson's body lifted, pleading for release, but her eyes told a different story. Jameson's eyes implored Candace to lift her higher, to hold her steady until she had no choice but to allow her body to freefall into blissful surrender. Candace felt Jameson's hands hold onto hers more tightly. She lowered her lips to Jameson's with a tender kiss.

Jameson's eyes finally closed. She could taste the sweetness of white wine that lingered on Candace's lips. Her lips parted and invited Candace in to explore. Jameson sighed into the kiss. She loved kissing Candace. Often, Jameson mused that if she could spend the rest of her life simply kissing Candace, she would. Her tongue snaked out to taste Candace's top lip. She felt the first quivers begin to travel through her core at the sound of Candace's appreciative moan.

Candace sensed that Jameson was about to spiral out of control. She whispered in Jameson's ear. "Let go, Jameson."

Jameson's hands gripped Candace's back, holding her as a tether to the earthly plain. "Candace!"

Candace slowed her movements gradually. Her body tingled pleasantly everywhere. She brushed the sweaty bangs from Jameson's eyes and smiled. "I love you."

Jameson released a long, contented breath. She shifted their positions to lie beside Candace.

"What is it?" Candace asked.

"I wanted to love you."

"Did I miss something?"

Jameson shook her head. "I wanted to make love to you."

"Jameson." Candace kissed Jameson on the forehead. "You just did."

"No, I mean…"

"I know what you mean," Candace replied.

"I need to."

Candace smiled with understanding. *Oh, Jameson.*

Jameson's lips traveled methodically from Candace's lips to her shoulder, back across to her throat and slowly down until Jameson's mouth claimed Candace's nipple. She playfully tasted and tugged until Candace's hips rose. Jameson followed the silent requests Candace's body conveyed. She placed a delicate trail of kisses down Candace's body until she reached Candace's center. Jameson stole a glance at Candace before continuing. Candace's eyes had closed, and her lips had parted in anticipation. Slow and soft—that is how Jameson intended to make love to Candace. She closed her eyes and let her lips fall onto Candace's center.

Candace's entire body was immediately lit on fire. The warmth of Jameson's tongue as it bathed her in a series of tender caresses made her body hum with pleasure. She prayed that Jameson would prolong the torture. And, it was torture—the kind of torture that intense pleasure delivers. It was almost painful. Bliss was a strange thing. Candace could feel Jameson coursing through her veins. "So, perfect," she murmured.

Jameson moaned, enjoying the way Candace's body moved in time with hers. Her hands gripped Candace's hips and pulled her closer. She was quickly losing her resolve to make love to Candace slowly.

"Jameson," Candace barely managed to speak the name. "Please," she begged.

Candace's plea was Jameson's undoing. She pulled Candace even closer and sucked softly, tasting and teasing until she heard Candace begin to repeat her name over and over.

Candace forced her eyes open. She looked down at Jameson making love to her and instantly felt her body submit to Jameson's will. "Oh, God! Jameson!"

Jameson held Candace steady, guiding her through a violent crash of ecstasy and into a series of gentle waves that caressed them both. She felt Candace reach for her and moved to look in Candace's eyes. Jameson kissed Candace sweetly. "Beautiful," she said.

"You are," Candace agreed.

Jameson chuckled. "Take the compliment," she told Candace.

"Thank you."

Jameson collapsed beside Candace and pulled Candace into her arms.

"Not that I am complaining—at all, but what brought that on?" Candace wondered.

"It's been a while since I've felt you so relaxed," Jameson admitted.

Candace sighed regretfully.

"No, no," Jameson kissed Candace's temple. "I'm just glad that you seemed to be able to let go a little today."

"It was a good day."

"Why do I think your mood is about more than Shell's news?" Jameson inquired. One thing Jameson did know, Candace was dealing with a host of stressful situations both as governor and with her campaign. There was no doubt that Michelle's news would have brightened Candace's spirits. Despite the fact Candace and Michelle could go head to head at work, Jameson was aware that the two adored each other. And, no matter how much Candace might desire to win this election and regardless of how much she enjoyed the challenge of her job, nothing mattered more to Candace than playing the role of mom and nana. Still, Jameson had sensed a shift in Candace's mood ever since she had spoken with Cassidy.

"I guess, I'm looking forward to getting away for a few days."

"To see Cassidy?"

Candace nodded against Jameson. "I think there's something she wants to talk to me about."

"Other than the speech, you mean?" Jameson asked.

"I think so."

"You don't think anything is wrong..."

Candace chuckled. "If you mean with Cassidy and Alex—no. Whatever it is, it's political in nature."

"You're not worried?"

"No. Not really."

"Candace?"

"Yeah?"

"Why do I think I am in the dark?"

Candace turned in Jameson's embrace. "What do you mean?"

"Just a few things Claire said," Jameson said.

Candace considered her reply. Jameson had kept in touch with Claire Brackett after the serial killer case had closed. Candace knew that. She had no idea what Claire Brackett might have said to Jameson. She did know that both Alex and Claire had worked in the intelligence community for years. Candace knew enough to have inklings about what Alex and Claire might have been involved with. She also understood that there were secrets that even the president was unlikely to discover. She sighed. "I don't know as much as you might think I do."

Jameson pulled Candace a little closer. "They've both seen things," she said.

"Yes, they have." Candace heard Jameson sigh. "Jameson?"

"I just want you to be safe."

Candace turned to Jameson and smiled. "Safety is an illusion. We both know that. I have people in my corner that

I trust, Jameson—not just our family. If I didn't, I would never have taken this on."

"That's why you're looking forward to seeing Cassidy."

"I've known Cassidy and Jane longer than I've known you. Few people have been through what they have in the public arena."

"You mean Chris's death and the assassination."

Candace was referring to those events. She was also referring to much more. Cassidy's ex-husband had been disgraced publicly before being killed in a car crash, at least, according to the public narrative. That hadn't been long after President John Merrow's assassination. John Merrow had been a close friend of Alex's. It had been a difficult time in both Cassidy and Jane's lives. Grieving in public was no easy feat, and compassion in the press often ran short.

"Yes, but also all the fallout from those events." Cassidy had been married to Christopher O'Brien for years. Most of the mainstream press fell in love with her early on.

"But?"

"We all have our detractors, honey."

Jameson closed her eyes. Candace shared a camaraderie with Cassidy Toles and Jane Merrow. In some ways, Jameson envied that. She always endeavored to support Candace, but Jameson would be the first to admit she preferred to stay out of the know when it came to politics. She chuckled.

"What's funny?"

"Just thinking it will be nice to play some billiards." Alex Toles was no fan of politics either. Jameson knew that.

Candace shook her head. "Better get your rest then. Last time we stayed there a night, I didn't see you until breakfast."

"I couldn't let her win!"

Candace laughed. "Of course not." *Lunatics.*

Chapter Fourteen

"How did Mom seem before they left?" Michelle asked Marianne.

"Actually, she seemed to be in a great mood."

"She likes giving speeches."

Marianne laughed. "I think it has more to do with getting away and seeing Cassidy and Jane."

"Yeah."

"Shell? You okay?"

"Huh? Yeah. I just haven't talked to her much since Sunday."

"Shell?"

Michelle smiled. "Were you ever nervous?"

"What do you mean?" Marianne asked. She sighed when Michelle's meaning struck her. "About being pregnant?"

"No."

"Lost me, Shell."

"That you'd disappoint Mom. Why? Should I be nervous about being pregnant?"

Marianne laughed. "No."

"Oh."

"I mean, no you shouldn't be nervous about being pregnant."

Michelle nodded.

"Shell, why are you worried about disappointing Mom?"

"I don't know. The doctor just warned me that I might have to pull back on travel when things get closer."

"And, you think that will disappoint Mom?"

"I'm due at the end of June."

"And?"

"And? And the convention is in July. Do you know how much will be on her plate in June?"

Marianne smiled at her younger sister genuinely.

"What?" Shell asked a bit defensively.

"Shell, Mom was thrilled to hear your news."

"Do you think so?"

Marianne's initial inclination was to set Michelle straight bluntly. She took a deep breath. Michelle was clearly worried. "Why would you doubt that?"

"I don't. It's just... Well, when Mel and I started talking we'd thought we would start trying this month. We figured it'd take time; you know?"

"Mom cares more about you than any campaign."

"Yeah, but I committed to helping her."

"And, you are planning on quitting now?"

"What? No! Of course, not!"

Marianne grinned. "You don't have to be joined to her hip to help her."

"I just don't want her to think that it doesn't matter to me."

"She doesn't think that. No one thinks that." Marianne laughed. "We all care, but, Shell, I seriously don't think anyone is more passionate about Mom's campaign than you are. She knows that." Marianne studied her sister closely. "Want to tell me what this is really about?"

"What if I suck?"

"Come again?"

"At this."

"This?"

"This! You know, *this*!" Michelle looked at her stomach. "Being someone's mom!"

"You'll be a terrific mom."

"I don't even know how to be pregnant correctly."

Marianne struggled not to break out in laughter. "What are you talking about?"

"I threw up for three hours last night! This morning I'm fine. Does that make sense? Isn't it called morning sickness?"

Ah, and so it comes together. "It doesn't always work the way it sounds."

"Huh?"

"The morning part," Marianne explained.

"Oh." Michelle groaned. "I thought my head was going to come off. That ever happen to you?"

"Only with Spencer. Which I hope means I won't have to deal with that ever again."

Michelle's ears perked. "Marianne?"

"Hum?"

"Do you want more kids?"

"Not right now."

"But do you?"

Marianne nodded. "One."

Michelle smiled. "What's going on with you and Scott?"

Marianne held up her hand. "Don't go printing any extra birth announcements; you have double duty as it is."

"Ha-ha. Come on, what's going on?"

"Don't get all excited. I just sort of think we are heading in that direction."

"Seriously?"

Marianne nodded. "I'm still not ready."

"I know. Would you be mad if I told you that I think it's awesome, though? That you found Scott, I mean."

"Me too."

"You really love him."

Marianne's eyes grew misty. "I do. I still miss Rick."

"Me too."

"It's totally different. But yes, I love him. And, to be honest, it scares the hell out of me."

"I'll bet. JD's gonna freak," Michelle chuckled.

Marianne shook her head. "Nah. She already expects it, I think."

Michelle tipped her head thoughtfully. "You talked to her."

"Yeah, I did. Weird, huh? I seem to talk to her a lot now."

"A little, but I get it. JD's easy to talk to."

"She is," Marianne agreed.

"Do you think they ever would?"

"Huh?"

"Mom and JD," Michelle said.

"Do I think they would what?"

"Have a baby."

Marianne smiled. "I don't think so."

"Why not? Because JD is in her forties now? Lots of women have babies in their forties."

"I don't think that's the issue."

"Really? JD just seems—I don't know, like it's bothering her."

"I don't think what's bothering her is wanting to have a baby."

"I don't get it."

Marianne smiled at her younger sister. "I thought the same thing until I talked to her about Scott wanting children."

"And?"

"She understood it in a way that I couldn't."

"What do you mean? I thought you wanted to have that with Scott?"

"Someday," Marianne replied. "I was wondering if it wasn't enough for him; Spencer and Maddie."

"Scott loves Spencer and Maddie."

"I know he does. He mentioned he'd like to have a baby."

"And that made you think he didn't love Spencer and Maddie?"

"No," Marianne replied. "I just felt—I don't know, a little nervous about it. JD put it in perspective."

"Really?"

Marianne laughed. "JD might be goofy at times, Shell, she's not shallow."

"I don't think she's shallow. I'm just curious what she said."

"Imagine you were her. She walked into a family and became an instant parent and grandparent. None of us are hers, but we are."

"Uh-huh. Cooper is hers."

"Yes, but even with Cooper, she didn't get to be there from the beginning. She sees you and Mel now, she watched Rick and I have Maddie, Jonah and Laura—I think it makes her wonder what that would have been like to have that with Mom."

Michelle nodded. "Do you think that's why she's doing all this volunteer work all of a sudden? To fill up that void?"

"No, I don't. I think she knew she needed to vacate her business for Mom right now. You know that JD's firm holds government contracts. There's enough that could be thrown at Mom with Mel and Jonah running the firm. Imagine if it were JD?"

"And?"

"And, JD doesn't love politics like you do, Shell. She loves Mom. She needs something too."

"I guess I never really thought about that. Mel mentioned that she and Jonah were tabling any government jobs."

"Probably wise."

Michelle groaned.

"What is it?" Marianne asked.

"These new accusations about Mom..."

"They're not true."

"No, but they could do serious damage if she gets called to testify."

Marianne shrugged.

"That doesn't worry you?" Michelle asked.

"Mom can handle it."

Michelle sighed.

"Shell, don't worry so much."

"I can't help it. I've seen her behind the scenes, Marianne. It takes its toll sometimes."

"I'm sure it does. What would you have her do; quit?" Marianne was surprised to see Michelle shrug. "She never quits."

"I don't understand why people hate her."

"They don't hate her."

"Have you read some of the articles?" Michelle challenged her sister.

"I don't waste my time. I know what they say."

"How can you say people don't hate her?"

"Because they don't," Marianne said. "They hate a fictional character that they've created."

"You mean they hate Governor Reid."

"No. I mean they hate someone completely different. They don't *know* Mom. They don't know her as a governor or a person. She's an image, Shell."

Michelle sighed. "She's a person."

Marianne smiled. "Yes. It's easier to make someone into a thing. It's easier to love a thing or hate a thing. People are more complicated."

"You sound just like her," Michelle observed.

"I told you; I've learned to listen to her."

Michelle sighed again. "She doesn't deserve it."

"No, but she expects it."

"That doesn't make it okay, Marianne."

"I have to admit; I'm surprised to hear you talking like this."

"I want her to win," Michelle said assuredly. "She would be a fantastic president. I've seen her at work. I hate seeing the toll it takes," she admitted.

"Mm."

"What?"

"You're feeling protective."

"I guess maybe I am. Sometimes, Marianne, I want to come out swinging."

"I hear you."

"You too?"

"She is my mother. Imagine how JD feels."

"No thanks. No wonder she wants to be out pounding on things."

Marianne laughed. "I'm sure JD appreciates the outlet. I'm sure Mom does too."

"I wish I could help more."

"I think you sell yourself short," Marianne said.

"Thanks for that."

"Don't thank me. You've done a lot to help Mom's career. You just have to remember sometimes that she is Mom."

"And Nana."

"Good Lord," Marianne said. "Pretty soon we're going to need name tags for family gatherings."

Michelle laughed. "Distinct possibility."

"Are you making the trip for her speech?"

Michelle nodded. "Yeah, it's Friday. I leave on Thursday night."

"Staying with the Toles?"

"Yeah, I think Mom wants Cassidy to train me on twins."

Marianne laughed. "Let me know how that goes."

"Why? Think I need lessons?"

"No, but I can guarantee dealing with twins will be more challenging than dealing with the campaign."

"No way."

Marianne laughed. *Oh, I am going to enjoy this.*

Cassidy Toles closed the door to the office Alex and she shared and flopped onto the couch.

"Tired?" Candace asked.

Cassidy grinned. "Surprisingly, no."

"You make sure to tell me," Candace said.

Cassidy winked at her friend. She was at the end of her fourth and what would be her final pregnancy. "I promise, but I wouldn't worry. Oddly, I seem to have more energy than usual lately."

"I give you credit. Four kids are enough to make anyone need a nap."

"You should know."

Candace smiled. "Yes, I should," she agreed.

"You must be excited about Shell's news."

"I am. I can't wait to see her face when she spends a night here with Connor and Abby." Candace laughed. "Maybe you could loan them to her and Mel for babysitting duty."

Cassidy laughed. She and Alex had five-year-old twins. She'd be the first to admit they could give the most energetic adult a run for his or her money. "I'd be happy to."

"So? Why do I think there is more to this visit than helping me with this speech?" Candace asked.

Cassidy took a deep breath. "Because there is."

"More than helping me devise ways to torture Shell too, I am guessing."

"I do want to help you with the speech."

"I know."

"I also think you should know a few things before we continue," Cassidy said.

Candace nodded. She heard Cassidy sigh. "Cassidy, if you…"

Cassidy held up her hand. "No. Alex and I discussed this at length. We discussed it with Jane."

"And, you get the privilege to break it all to me."

Cassidy laughed. "It's not all dire," she promised. "Do you remember telling me that Cooper and Spencer were trying to redesign the White House to protect you?"

"I do. Even after an hour with Jane, they still have their plans."

"I think maybe Cooper should spend a little time with Dylan tomorrow."

"Dylan?"

Cassidy nodded. Dylan was her eldest. He was seventeen.

"I'm sure Dylan has things he'd rather be doing than entertaining a five-year-old."

"I think Dylan would love to spend a little one on one time with Cooper."

"I'm missing something," Candace said.

Cassidy took another deep breath. She rubbed her belly and raised an eyebrow. She decided to just lay the truth on the line. "Chris wasn't Dylan's biological father."

Candace was stunned. She'd met Cassidy while campaigning for Cassidy's ex-husband Congressman Christopher O'Brien nearly nineteen years ago. "Cassidy?"

Cassidy shrugged. "That's not all," she said.

"I'm listening."

"John was his father."

"John?"

"Merrow."

Candace picked up her glass of wine and took a sip. She was surprised, although less so than she imagined most people would've been. It was no secret to her that President John Merrow had his share of affairs, and she had always known that Cassidy was unhappy with Christopher O'Brien who had been a well-known philanderer.

"I know," Cassidy said. "Crazy."

"Not really."

"It wasn't an affair," Cassidy set out to explain.

"Cassidy, you don't owe me an explanation."

"I do," Cassidy disagreed. "I agreed to work on your campaign. My past and my life can now be used for or against you," she said. "We both know how it works."

"Who knows?" Candace inquired.

"The family, Jane and the girls. We've never made it public."

Candace thought for a minute. "If working for me is too great of a risk…"

"Not for me," Cassidy said. "Not for our family. Alex and I spoke with Dylan. He's comfortable with the truth and his family. Jane and the girls have always accepted him. He expects that one day the truth will come out. I'm more concerned about how it might impact you right now."

"Do you have some reason to think someone knows?"

"No," Cassidy replied. "But with people digging into the embassy bombing in Moscow, it concerns me more."

"Because of John's ties to Russ Matthews?"

Cassidy nodded. "Partly."

Russ Matthews had been a longtime friend of John Merrow's and had served as Ambassador to Russia. He had been the highest-ranking official killed in the bombing.

"You think that inquiries into my dealings on the committee might lead to Dylan's parentage?"

"Maybe. Like I said, that concerns me less than other things."

"I'm listening."

"Candace, you know that Alex worked in Intelligence."

"I do."

Cassidy sighed. "She can give you more details, and she will."

"About?"

"About what she was doing. About who Christopher really was. About why that embassy was attacked."

Candace scratched her brow. "Cassidy, I don't want to compromise Alex or your family."

"I know that. Look," Cassidy took a deep breath. "I can tell you this much; you need to win this election. Bradley Wolfe cannot sit in the Oval Office."

Candace nodded. She knew that Bradley Wolfe was a threat to many things. "I haven't even secured the nomination, Cassidy."

"You will. That's part of the reason Jane is coming tomorrow. This speech is important. We all know that. Jane knows far more about the details of what these congressmen are trying to dig into. She knows what they will look to exploit to create scenarios they think might serve them."

"And?"

"And, she knows how to shut them down."

Candace considered Cassidy's words. "I mean what I am saying. I love having you on my team. I don't want you to feel obligated to stay."

"I don't. Look, I've seen enough, learned enough over the years to understand more than I ever wanted to about how politics work, what role they play in a much larger world."

Candace nodded.

"When John was killed," Cassidy paused to gather herself.

"Cassidy, you don't have to…"

"Yes, I do. It was a one-night stand, Candace. We were at a fundraiser for Chris's campaign. Chris was making time with one of his aides. It was so blatant. I had a few too many. John was in the senate. We just… It sounds crazy. It just happened."

Candace smiled. "Sometimes, it does."

"I never regretted it in the sense that it gave me Dylan. I've always regretted the lie."

"Did John know?"

Cassidy nodded. "It was an impossible situation. At least, it seemed that way. When he died? Candace, it rocked me to my core. Alex was devastated. He was her best friend."

"I know."

"Everything changed that day—all our lives. She needed to know why. I needed to know too. Jane needed answers."

"And, those answers landed in Russia," Candace guessed.

"Many of them. The truth is, Candace I don't know if what Alex knows will help you at all. I don't know if it will make you safer. I'm confident there is no one other than Alex and Jane who will tell you the entire truth. And, you need to know it if you want to win this election and be successful as president."

Candace smiled. "Not what I expected this visit."

"I'm sorry."

"Don't be," Candace dismissed the thought. "I was just thinking how smart I was to ask for your help."

Candace chuckled at the curious look Cassidy gave her. Alliances and acquaintances were common place in Candace's world; just as common as adversaries were. Friendship was a rare commodity. Friendship required trust. The office Candace was currently seeking required a level of confidence in advisers and staff like none other. Cassidy's honesty and her candor did not surprise Candace. It solidified her affection for the woman sitting across from her. It engendered a sense of trust that Candace placed in few people.

"Friends are hard to come by in this life, Cassidy."

"Yes, I know."

"You have no idea what your trust means to me," Candace said honestly. "And, no idea how grateful I am that you still want to be on this team."

"Adversity is a great teacher," Cassidy said. "Loss is part of that adversity. What you're seeking to do is something few people can," she told Candace. "Most people will never understand how much it does matter. They've never been close enough."

Candace nodded. "I meant what I said. If being involved with this campaign or God willing, my administration is too risky or too stressful…"

"You'll be the first to know."

Candace took a sip from her glass of wine. "Okay, that's enough dark and dreary. Let's talk about how to torture my daughter with your twins."

Cassidy laughed. "You do have a dark side."

Candace winked. "You trust me with your secrets; I'll trust you with mine."

Jameson sipped her beer and watched Alex line up a shot on the pool table. "Think they're talking about us?" she joked.

Alex laughed. "I'm sure they'll get around to that eventually." She took her shot, effectively ending their current game.

"Damn," Jameson shook her head.

"Hey, I have a place to practice daily and a kid who won't leave me alone about it."

"Thanks for the reassurance that I don't suck."

"I never said that," Alex poked. Jameson chuckled. "How've you been, JD?"

"You mean after having a serial killer try to hammer me?"

Alex shrugged. She gestured to the couch for Jameson to have a seat. "I kind of think that might be less stressful than campaigning."

"You might be right." Jameson regarded Alex for a moment, sensing something was on her mind. "Why do I think this visit is about more than some speech Candace is making?"

Alex laughed. Jameson was no pushover. "It's an important speech," Alex observed. "Most people have no idea how small the world really is."

"Probably true."

"It is true," Alex said. She took a sip from her beer bottle and sighed. "Cass loves working for Candace."

Jameson smiled. "Can I tell you something?"

"Sure."

"I think Cassidy has been a lifeline for Candace these past few months."

"They have a lot in common," Alex said. "I could say the same thing about Cass. It's good for her. I know she loves being a mom, but I also know she needs something for herself."

Jameson chuckled. *Where've I heard that before?*

"I get the feeling you've heard that before."

"Yeah, well… You know, what Candace is doing now is more than a full-time job. It isn't always easy to balance things."

"Yeah, I get it." Alex sighed. "I've never cared too much about politics. To be honest, politics tend to piss me off."

"I get it."

"I figured. Funny thing, I've always thought Cass would've made a great senator or something like that."

"I could see that."

"I think she likes being able to be a part of it without having to be the face of it, though. She'd never admit it, but she enjoyed a lot of the things traveling in those circles brought into her life," Alex said.

"It has its ups and downs," Jameson said. "The hardest part for Candace is how her choices affect all of us."

Alex nodded. She believed that. In fact, Cassidy had made mention of that several times. She took a deep breath. "JD," she began.

"Yeah?"

"Cass wanted you to come down for a few reasons."

Jameson listened curiously.

"I'm sure she's told Candace by now."

"She's not quitting..."

"No," Alex dismissed the thought. "I think it's safe to say that she's committed to helping Candace get elected."

"I'd understand, so would Candace. I mean, you're going to have your plate full in a couple of weeks."

Alex shrugged. That was the truth. "True. We're lucky to have a lot of support. I don't think a baby is going to change Cass's feelings about working for Candace."

"But?"

Alex sighed again. "She mentioned that Cooper was nervous about assassinations."

"He and Spencer saw something on the TV a few months back."

"Yeah, that happens sometimes," Alex commented. "We went through that with Dylan when O'Brien was splashed all over the news. No matter how much we tried to shield him—Well, he either caught a glimpse of the TV or he heard things at school."

"Couldn't have been easy."

"No, it wasn't. He was only seven. It was hard for all of us. Sometimes, I am amazed how well-adjusted he is," Alex admitted. "He's had more than his share of upheaval and loss."

Jameson nodded. Dylan had only been seven when his father died.

Alex continued. "JD, there's something that Cass and I thought Candace should know. Actually, there's more than one thing."

"What?"

"Christopher O'Brien was a son of a bitch," Alex said flatly.

"So, I've heard."

"Yeah, so the world heard," Alex replied. "The truth is it was much worse than anyone in the public knows. He was not who people thought he was—not in any capacity."

Jameson was curious.

"I won't go into all the details. Let's just say his agenda was not to serve The United States."

"I kind of gathered that."

"Yeah, well, he didn't actually serve anyone but himself most of the time. His allegiance was to another government."

"Are you saying he was a spy?"

Alex shrugged. Spy was a stupid word in her opinion. "He was working for another government. Well, at least, he was supposed to be. I'm not sure at all what he was hoping to do. He was a shitty husband, an absentee father, and a crooked politician who took orders from the Kremlin."

Jameson's choked on the sip of beer she'd just taken.

"That's pretty much how I feel about it all too," Alex said.

"Holy shit. You're not kidding."

"Nope. That's part of the reason Cass wanted Candace and Jane here this week. All this digging into the embassy bombing—she wanted Candace to have all the information possible."

"Do people know?"

"Some people know. I can't say who knows. That's the thing about working in the intelligence sector. There's a lot of competing agendas. Some of it overlaps politics—more than you might imagine."

Jameson sighed nervously.

"I'm not telling you this to worry you. Candace wasn't born yesterday, JD. She's probably one of the smartest politicians I've ever met. She might not know the details, but she knows the drill. The details will help her down the line. Most people won't give her them straight. Jane and Cassidy will."

"Cassidy knows?"

Alex nodded. "I probably should have kept more from her. That's just never the way it's been. There are lots of little things I would never tell her. She doesn't need to know everything I have seen. She knows enough. I wouldn't have made it without her to confide in. That's how it was for John with Jane. Everyone in this life needs someone they can tell everything to that has no stake in it other than loving them."

Jameson rubbed her face. She'd known that Candace pursuing the presidency came with both overwhelming responsibility and considerable risk. Alex's revelations brought that home in an unsettling way.

Alex smiled at her friend. "She'll be okay, JD. If that's what you're worried about."

"I am worried. You say that. Look at what happened to President Merrow."

Alex nodded. John Merrow had been her commanding officer in Iraq and later her closest friend. His death had devastated her. "John was in a different position than Candace."

"What do you mean?"

"I mean that he wasn't just a politician."

"You're talking about his military service."

Alex nodded. "He worked for the CIA, JD."

Jameson was stunned.

"I told you; worlds overlap."

"Jesus."

Alex couldn't help but chuckle. It sounded absurd, like a spy novel. Alex had come to accept that truth was stranger than fiction. "Crazy, huh?"

"A little."

"That's not the only thing people don't know about John."

"I'm not sure I want to know," Jameson said.

"He was Dylan's biological father."

Jameson's jaw dropped.

"That was my reaction when Cass told me," Alex chuckled.

"Holy shit."

"I might have said that too." Alex winked at JD. "It's a lot to take in."

"Alex, why are you telling me this?"

"If you mean about O'Brien and John's background, because Candace will only tell you parts of it. Not because she doesn't want to tell you, because she won't want you to worry about her. It'll eat away at her. Me telling you takes that pressure off. You can handle it. I saw the way you worked Carter over without him knowing. If I didn't think you could handle the truth, we wouldn't be having this conversation."

Jameson nodded.

"And, as far as Dylan; Cass felt Candace needed to know that. No one knows but the family—all our family."

"You mean Jane?"

Alex nodded. "And her girls. That doesn't mean no one will ever figure it out."

"Hey, listen, if that's too risky for Dylan, Candace will understand. She..."

"We both know that. Dylan is all right. I think, if I'm honest, it might be a relief for us all if it did get out there. Right now, might not be the best time for that where Candace is concerned—not with Cass and Jane so close to the campaign."

"Probably not," Jameson conceded. "She won't want Cassidy to quit, though."

Alex smiled. "Yeah, I figured as much. Look, I told you; I hate politics. Unfortunately, my wife has a taste for it," she laughed. "She still thinks someone like Candace can make a real difference."

"You don't?"

Alex sighed. "I do. At least, I think Candace will try."

Jameson smiled. "She will."

"John tried too," Alex said. "He was caught between worlds. Candace isn't."

"But?"

Alex groaned. "There are people who will be less likely to give her all the information she needs," Alex said. "Not just to win this campaign."

"I think I understand."

"I figured you'd catch on quickly."

"Alex, can I ask you something?"

"Shoot."

"No bullshit, do you think Candace is in danger?"

"Not physically."

Jameson sighed.

"They won't want to martyr her, not ever," Alex said. "And, believe me, JD crazy strangers don't kill presidents or presidential candidates."

"There's a but coming."

"They also don't want her in that office."

"Because she's..."

"Because she will make her own decisions," Alex said.

"You think they'd rather that Keyes be the nominee?"

"No. Jane and Cass have a better pulse on that stuff. But, no; I don't. They want Wolfe in the White House."

"Who does?"

"The people with the power," Alex said. "They'd love to send Candace packing. They don't want a politician. The last thing they want is to negotiate. They want a flunky; someone they can control."

Jameson shook her head. "I wish I knew how to help her."

Alex smiled. "The one thing I do know, JD is that the best way you can help her is by giving her someone to let it all out with. That's why I'm telling you. She needs you to be that person. She'll want to protect you from the truth. I've just given it to you; enough that she won't need to think about whether she should."

"Do you think she can win this?" Jameson asked.

"She has to."

Chapter Fifteen

"Nervous about the speech?" Jameson asked.

Candace smiled. "No."

"You were locked away with Cassidy and Jane all night."

"We had a lot to talk about."

Jameson nodded.

"I already know that Alex filled you in."

"Are you mad?"

Candace sighed. "I was at first."

"Why?"

"Jameson, I don't want to burden you."

"I don't see it that way."

"I know you don't."

"I worry about you," Jameson conceded.

"I'm okay."

"I want you to be able to tell me anything that you need to," Jameson said.

"So, do I."

"Really?"

"Yes." Candace chuckled. "Cassidy made me realize how important that was."

"Do you think they will call you to testify before congress?"

"Before the Intelligence Committee, yes."

Jameson sighed.

"It's all right," Candace said. "I have what I need."

"What's that?"

"Knowledge."

Jameson nodded. "Knowledge is power; is that it? Can't it also be a liability?"

Candace closed the distance between them and kissed Jameson. "I suppose, it can," she admitted. "But only if you don't know how to employ that knowledge and who to trust with it."

"I'm glad you have Cassidy and Jane in your corner."

"Me too. I'm glad that I have you."

"You do."

Candace placed a gentle kiss on Jameson's lips. She stepped back and took a deep breath. She held out her hand to Jameson. "Ready?"

Jameson sensed this speech, this visit with their friends had marked a shift in more than the campaign. For the first time, Jameson understood the gravity of what Candace was stepping into. And, she knew that the hill they were climbing was about to get much steeper. The next six months would determine who would accept the nomination for the Democratic Party. The turmoil of the last six months would be nothing by comparison. Jameson had been preoccupied with the notion of unfair press coverage, constant travel, and the everyday realities of a campaign. She had known there were competing agendas and ideas. She understood now that those existed far beyond egos and ambition. The corporate world, the intelligence complex, foreign governments, social organizations—everyone had a stake in a presidential election. Was she ready? She looked at Candace's extended hand and smiled. As much as she needed Candace, she'd begun to realize how much the world did too. The reality scared her, but not nearly as much as it made her heart swell with pride and with love. Jameson found herself musing again, wondering how she had been so lucky to get to share her life with Candace.

"What are you thinking?" Candace asked.

"Just how much I am looking forward to watching you," Jameson said.

Candace's eyes sparkled. "Listening or watching?" she teased.

Jameson winked.

"That's what I thought."

"Where are we at?" Bradley Wolfe asked.

"Their first televised debate is January 31st," Klein replied.

"And, you think Keyes will challenge her?"

"I don't *think*. I know."

"And, what about Drury and his committee?" Wolfe questioned.

"It's not going anywhere of consequence," Ritchie answered.

Wolfe's displeasure was immediately evident.

"I didn't say it won't work," Ritchie continued.

"I want her out of commission," Wolfe said. "Not limping toward the finish line. I want her on the stretcher."

"You don't want to run against Keyes," Klein said.

"Excuse me?"

"You don't."

"Keyes is a weasel," Wolfe said.

"Exactly, *he's* a weasel."

Wolfe reclined in his chair. "Are you telling me that you think George Keyes will be harder to defeat because he's a man?"

"Yes," Klein answered.

Wolfe grinned. "What is it with you, Klein?" he asked. "Problems with women?" he goaded.

Lawson Klein bristled. "I don't have problems with women. I have a problem with women who don't know their place."

Wolfe laughed. "And, where would that be exactly? Your bedroom?"

Klein's face flushed with anger. Ritchie interceded. "The point is that we need Governor Reid to go down."

Wolfe chuckled. "I don't think we're her type."

Ritchie groaned. "Brad..."

"All right," Wolfe surrendered. "So, we want the good governor to make it to the general—fine. Seems risky to me."

"Maybe. She's an easy target in a general election," Ritchie said.

"Really?" Wolfe questioned.

"She's already compromised with this new investigation into her role in failing to safe guard the embassy in Moscow."

"That was years ago," Wolfe reminded him.

"True, but her entrance into this race has raised all kinds of discussion about her relationship to Merrow. We all know that there are skeletons there."

Wolfe let out a heavy sigh. "You're the strategists," he said. "I'd remind you that I now have a field of five candidates I need to best to secure the nomination."

"Not an issue," Klein said.

"Is that so?" Wolfe asked.

Klein grinned. "You just stay on message," he advised Wolfe.

"And, what message might that be?"

"Make them all look like the establishment lackeys they are," Ritchie replied.

"And, Reid?"

"For now, let us worry about Candace Reid. We'll pave the way for you. Keyes will chip away at her base, erode it a bit before she secures the nomination. By the time the conventions finish, she'll be amassed in a media blitz questioning her integrity the likes of which she's never seen."

Wolfe nodded. "And then?"

"You keep doing what you've been doing all along," Klein said.

"What might that be?" Wolfe asked.

"Follow the script."

"Are you feeling okay?" Jameson asked Cassidy. "Alex will kill me if you go into labor here."

Cassidy laughed. "I wonder if this one will be the one to follow in her Momma's footsteps."

"Why?" Jameson asked.

"She seems to find foreign policy interesting," Cassidy said. "No labor, JD. Although, I think she's trying to move herself around in there." Cassidy laughed when Jameson went pale. Jameson reminded her of Alex. This was Cassidy's fifth pregnancy. She'd miscarried once three years earlier. Alex was always a bundle of nerves when the time for delivery neared. Cassidy was confident she could deliver a healthy baby a hundred times over and Alex would still be a nervous wreck each time. She patted Jameson's arm. "I'm fine; I promise."

Jameson nodded. Candace came up between them and noted Jameson's nervousness. "Are you all right?" she asked Jameson.

"Yeah, why?"

Cassidy chuckled. "Fallon's been giving me fits," she explained, rubbing her belly.

Candace smiled. It was the perfect momentary distraction. "Bet you're glad you never had to go through that with me now," Candace winked at Jameson.

Jameson shrugged.

"Ready?" a voice came up behind them.

Candace turned to its owner. "As I'll ever be," she told Jane.

"Good," Jane replied. She offered the group a wink and headed for the stage.

Jameson watched as Candace took a deep breath and exhaled it slowly. "You'll be great."

Candace nodded her thanks. She listened as Jane's short speech wound its way to her introduction. One more deep breath and Candace made her way onto the auditorium stage.

"She's not usually nervous," Jameson commented.

Cassidy kept her gaze on Candace in the distance. "She's not nervous, JD."

"You don't think so?"

"No. She's just aware."

Jameson and Cassidy sat in the chairs placed for them off stage. Jameson took a nervous breath. "She's got this."

Candace looked out at the audience. The lights made it difficult to discern faces. Normally, that unsettled her. Today, she found herself feeling grateful. She was not looking to connect with individuals today. Today, she was looking to command an issue—to look, sound, and convince people she could act as Commander in Chief.

"Thank you all," she quieted the crowd. "I appreciate the opportunity to speak to you today about something I think we are often remiss in discussing. Campaigns can become emotional; not just for the candidates, but for our constituents. They're often laden with personal innuendo and the bravado of larger than life personalities. It's sometimes easy to forget that the presidency consists of far more than photo ops, speeches, and ceremonies. While those things may seem trivial; they are not. The President of the United States stands as a symbol to the world of what our country stands for, what we believe in, what so many before us have fought to defend, preserve, and protect. We've battled in this country; battled each other to form a more perfect union. This country stands as a shining beacon on a hill to so many around the world who are less fortunate; who are still fighting to achieve basic human rights, who suffer under oppressive regimes, struggle with abject poverty, and live in fear of war and genocide. As our world has become smaller, as we have become connected, the dangers to our more per-fect union have become more palpable. We've endured at-tacks by extremists who seek to undermine our way of life, who want to pit us against one another. We continue to struggle to find balance between fair trade and exploitation. Living in a global community is complex—at times, it's dan-gerous, but it is our future. If we hope to secure a peaceful, prosperous future for our children, we must navigate the path forward with care, never forgetting the role The United States plays as a leader in this new global community. We must be strong in our convictions, forthright about our inten-tions, deliberate in our communication, and compassionate when it comes to the welfare of our human community."

Cassidy smiled and shook her head. "She's amazing."

Jameson grinned. "Yeah. She said you wrote it, though."

"No one writes Candace's speeches. I just tailor them, help her find the words she seeks that help her stay on track." Cassidy chuckled. "Besides, she never sticks to the script."

Jameson laughed. She knew that was true. Candace always deviated, if only slightly. Jameson had heard Dana comment that Candace had an uncanny ability to read the emotion of a crowd. She knew when a message needed to be expounded upon and when it needed to be vacated. Can-dace had told Jameson that Cassidy was a master of setting the stage for what could be deemed Death by the Doldrums. Jameson had been confused. Candace had explained:

"She knows how to set the stage," Candace said. "How to hook people so that facts and figures sound more

like pie in the sky ideals. Facts and figures—thoughtful and decisive action are what makes great leaders, Jameson. That's not what wins an election. Cassidy understands that better than any speech writer I've ever worked with."

"Are you worried about this speech?"

"Worried isn't the word I would use."

"Aware," Jameson mumbled.

"What?" Cassidy asked.

Jameson shook her head. "Just realizing what you meant earlier," she said. She looked back out at Candace. "Did she?" Jameson asked Cassidy.

"What?"

"Go off script already?"

"Only a little." Cassidy winked. "And, it was better than what I'd written."

Jameson nodded. *Show them, Candace. Show them who belongs in that White House.*

———

"Great speech," Dana complimented Candace.

"It was; wasn't it?" Candace smiled. She walked side by side down a long corridor with Dana. "I can't take the credit for this one. Cassidy wrote most of it."

Dana nodded.

"Oh boy, I know that look," Candace said.

Dana sighed.

"What's wrong?" Candace asked.

"Glenn called."

Candace raised an eyebrow at her friend.

Dana sighed again. "Keyes gave an interview to *Talk on the Nation*. It airs tomorrow."

"And?" Candace asked.

"Glenn got a transcript."

"Go on."

"He's echoing the Republican claims."

"Which ones? Candace asked.

"That you have been at this so long you have no ability to think outside the box. You are the party's flunkey." Dana was surprised when Candace greeted her news with laughter. "You're amused?" she questioned.

"You're not?" Candace returned. "George has been in Democratic politics as long as I have."

"Yes, but..."

"It's nonsense. He's seldom broken with the party line on anything. You know that as well as anyone."

"Doesn't matter what I know. He's trying to knock you out of this race."

Candace smiled.

"Candy, he's gaining some momentum."

"Of course, he is."

"Glenn is..."

"It's Glenn's job to worry about that."

"You're not concerned?" Dana asked.

Candace took a deep breath and turned to Dana. "Concerned? Yes. Not surprised. What did you all think? That George Keyes was going to enter a presidential race and not try to win?"

"He's not the most popular figure in the party."

"And, *that* is what will benefit him." Candace started walking again.

"Candy, he might not cut into the most liberal part of the base; he will pull some of the centrists away from you."

"I would expect so."

"What are you going to do?" Dana asked. "Glenn and I will work the press, rework your schedule. I talked to Shell; she has some great ideas…"

"I've no doubt."

"But ultimately it's up to you."

"Yes, it is."

"The first debate is a values debate, Candy."

"And?"

"You know as well as I do that he is going to gently exploit who you are."

Candace shrugged.

"Candy? We need to plan your response. It's only four weeks away."

"I don't need to plan my response to him or to the moderator."

Dana shook her head. Candace was an adept orator. She was quick witted and possessed a command of nearly any issue a journalist or moderator could raise. This debate would be about the values that a president brings to the office. Dana fully expected that Candace's family would be raised and that her support of liberal social issues would factor. Candace might be able to secure the nomination solely on the excitement of progressives in her party. She would need the support of moderates to win the general. "Candy…"

Candace stopped again and turned to Dana. She smiled. "It's funny; isn't it?"

"What's that?"

"Well, Senator Keyes and the Republican field are all trying to paint me as the establishment candidate—the insider who votes according to what her party dictates, the career politician who puts the money of donors first in how she votes, in what legislation she puts forth."

"That's funny?"

Candace shrugged. "At the same time, you're worried about them attacking what sets me apart. I'm too progressive; right?" Candace laughed. "So, establishment is predictable and progressive is reprehensible?" She shook her head.

"I know that I should be following this..."

"It's their Achilles heel."

"Huh?"

"Playing both sides," Candace explained. "It's how I will win."

"I'm not following."

"They think they know who I am," Candace said. "They might even believe they know what I know. They don't. Let them paint with whatever colors they choose, Dana. Stick to what we've always done. I'll talk to Glenn."

"Candy, this election is not like anything..."

Candace nodded. "I know. You need to trust me, Dana. It's going to get much uglier."

"And, you are determined to stay out of the mud."

Candace chuckled. She'd already had heaps of mud thrown at her. "You mean that I'm determined not to fling any."

"I do."

Candace grinned.

"Candy?"

"Let's just say that if and when I do, it will be more than a handful. And, it won't just stick; it'll stain."

Dana was surprised. Candace did not like to fight dirty. "Candy?"

"This isn't just the biggest race of my life," Candace said. "A lot is at stake, Dana. What I talked about up on that stage? That's the tip of the iceberg. I'm hardly perfect. One thing I do know, a careless captain is likely to sink us all."

Dana noted the seriousness of Candace's voice.

"I'll do whatever I have to do to win this," Candace said.

Dana's eyes widened.

Candace smiled. "Within reason," Candace clarified. "I have to be able to look at my kids without guilt," she said. "I have to be able to face myself in the mirror. If I don't give this everything I have, I'm not sure I will be able to do either."

"You believe everything you said up there; don't you?" Dana guessed.

Candace nodded. "Every single word—yes."

Christmas Eve

"Momma?" Cooper jumped in front of Jameson.

Jameson smiled. Cooper was a bundle of excitement. "What's up, Coop?"

"Where's Jonah?"

"Oh, buddy, Laura isn't feeling so great," she explained. Laura was almost two weeks late delivering what would be the newest addition to the family. She was slated

to be induced the day after Christmas if she didn't go into labor by then. Jonah had called that morning and told Jameson
that Laura wasn't up to even a short drive. She was exhausted. Jameson was sure that Cooper was disappointed.

"Oh." Cooper hung his head.

"But, you know," Jameson said. "We can Facetime
Jonah and Laura after we eat if you want?"

"Really?"

"Sure."

"Jonah said he'd help me and Spence with Santa."

"What's this about Santa?" Candace came into the
room.

Cooper smiled at his mother. "Dylan told me to feed
the reindeer," he said. "He said they have... ummm.... Sway
with Santa."

Candace laughed. Cooper had spent the afternoon of
Candace's speech with Alex and Cassidy's son, Dylan. He
hadn't stopped talking about the teenager since. When Candace stopped to think about it, Cooper had been talking
about the trip to Connecticut incessantly. In fact, she'd heard
him telling Spencer that Dylan had the coolest planes and
that he was going to fly one someday. She wasn't surprised
to hear that Cooper had told his older brother about Dylan's
reindeer theory. She was even less surprised that Jonah had
offered to help. "Well, I will bet that if you ask Scott, he will
help you and Spencer feed the reindeer. There's a whole bag
of carrots in the refrigerator. Ask Marianne; she knows where
they are."

Cooper scampered off happily.

"What is that grin about?" Jameson asked Candace.

"When Jonah was little, I think he was about Cooper's age he fed the reindeer every year until he was ten." She shook her head. "He made me buy a whole bag of carrots every year just to feed the reindeer."

"Uh-huh."

"I've always kept a bag thinking Spencer would follow suit one day."

Jameson smiled. "Dylan made an impression on him."

"He did. They have a lot in common, those two."

"I guess they do," Jameson agreed.

Cooper and Spencer shared a special kinship. They had both lost a parent, and they both had found solace in the care of Candace and Jameson. Dylan, much like Cooper, had lost his father and ended up being raised by two mothers. Candace was certain that far beyond the fact that Dylan was John Merrow's biological son, Cassidy had recognized the similarities the two shared. Cassidy's public persona had diminished over the years, but it had never completely vanished. People remembered the affable school teacher who had charmed the masses. For years, the Democratic party had groomed Cassidy's ex-husband, Christopher O'Brien for higher office. He had ended up an embarrassment to the party. Cassidy had suffered some of the fallout as well. Overall, public perception of Cassidy Toles had remained positive. So positive, Candace knew that on more than one occasion Cassidy had been approached about entering political life. That was not Cassidy's passion nor her aspiration. Candace was grateful for her friendship with Cassidy. While she valued Cassidy as a professional resource, it was Cassidy's perspective that Candace cherished the most. Cassidy had become more than a friend, she'd become an adviser, and not just about speeches.

"Candace?" Jameson pulled Candace from her thoughts.

"I was just thinking how lucky Cooper is to have so many people supporting him."

Jameson nodded. "He is." She looked at Candace curiously. "You've been quiet all day. Is something bothering you?"

Candace smiled. "No."

Jameson was skeptical.

"No," Candace promised. "I was just thinking that in a week the world is going to start spinning in a million directions."

"Worried about the debate?"

"Not worried."

"Aware?" Jameson asked.

"That's a good way to describe it." Candace took Jameson's hand. "For the next two days, I don't want to think about the campaign. I don't want to watch the news or look at a paper," she said. "I just want to enjoy Christmas with the kids. I admit, I wish Jonah could be here."

"Me too," Jameson said.

"Mom!" Shell's voice rang through the house.

Candace shook her head.

"Do you think she'll still be doing that when she has two of her own?"

Candace raised an eyebrow.

"Never mind," Jameson said.

"Mom," Michelle peeked around the corner. "You have got to come out here and see this."

Candace looked at Jameson. Jameson shrugged. They followed Michelle to the back door.

"What are they doing?" Jameson asked.

"Apparently, Dylan said Coop should leave Rudolph a message," Marianne offered as she came in the door from outside.

"Do I want to know?" Candace asked.

Marianne laughed. "Let's just say your bag of carrots didn't cover it."

Candace and Jameson exchanged a confused glance and walked to the back door.

"Is that my asparagus?" Jameson asked.

Candace tried not to laugh; about the only green anything Jameson would eat was asparagus.

"They needed to spell all the words," Marianne said.

"Who gave them my asparagus?" Jameson asked.

Michelle looked away.

"Shell! You could've suggested sticks or something," Jameson complained.

Michelle turned to Jameson. "It's for the reindeer, JD. They don't eat sticks."

"What? They're four and five; they don't know that!"

"So, you wanted me to lie to your son and grandson?"

"Yes!"

"JD, that shit is nasty."

"It's my asparagus!"

"You mean your a *sprig of ass*?" Michelle teased.

Candace lost all hope of keeping it together and burst out laughing.

"Big help you are," Jameson groaned.

Candace tried to make herself be serious. She looked at Jameson and lost all hope again. "I'm sorry," she apologized through her laughter.

"Just what did they need to spell that was so important?" Jameson asked.

Marianne smiled. She pointed out the door.

"It's 4:30, Marianne. I have no idea what that says," Jameson pointed outside into the darkness.

"It says, *don't forget my mommies*," Scott said when he walked into the kitchen.

Jameson's jaw dropped at the same moment her heart stopped. "Who needs asparagus," she said, pushing back a wave of emotion.

Candace slipped her arm around Jameson. "He really is something," she said.

"Mommy!" Cooper burst in through the back door.

Candace smiled at him.

Cooper grabbed both his mothers' hands. "Look!"

"I see," Candace said.

"Dylan said he used to spell his name so Santa could find him," Cooper said.

"But you didn't spell your name?" Jameson questioned.

Cooper looked up at her and smiled. "Momma, Santa knows where I am."

Jameson was puzzled.

"He always finds me," Cooper explained.

Candace understood. Cooper might have had a rough beginning. It was clear to her that no matter what it might have been, Cooper's mother had always made sure Santa brought him something. "Of course, he does," Candace said.

Cooper beamed. "He knows where kids are," Cooper said. "But sometimes he might forget about the old people." Cooper grinned and skipped back out the door toward Spencer who was playing in the snow.

Michelle looked at her mother and Jameson and gloated. "Well, now we know how Santa finds all his grannies."

Jameson glared at Michelle. Candace burst out laughing again. Jameson finally gave up and laughed along. "Grannies?" she asked Michelle.

Michelle patted her stomach and winked. "Six times over before you know it," she said. "Come on, Mel."

"Where are we going?" Melanie asked.

"I think there's still a bunch of asparagus in the fridge. Maybe we should tell the boys to cover the front yard just to be safe."

"You wouldn't!" Jameson called after her.

Candace shook her head. *Lunatics.*

———————

"Momma?" Cooper pulled on Jameson's hand just as she was about to leave his bedroom.

"What is it, Coop?"

Cooper reached over the side of his bed and fumbled for something. Jameson was surprised when he handed her a picture he had drawn. Jameson looked at it. It was his rendition of the three of them. They were, of course, surrounded by what Jameson surmised to be dinosaurs.

"This is beautiful, Coop. What's it for?" she asked him.

"It's for you and Mommy," he told her. "Just in case Santa forgets."

Jameson sat down on the edge of Cooper's bed. "Cooper, Santa won't forget me or Mommy. Don't worry."

Cooper smiled, but Jameson sensed he was concerned.

"And, you know," Jameson looked at her son. "Mommy and I already got the best present anyone could ever give us. Not even Santa could deliver a better present," she said.

Candace hovered in the doorway and listened.

"The new car?" he asked innocently.

Jameson grinned. She and Candace had just purchased a new SUV, although Jameson doubted either of them would get to use it much for the next few years. "It is a cool car."

"Yep. It has TV!"

Jameson chuckled. "Yes, it does. But I didn't mean the car," she said.

Cooper tilted his head curiously.

"I meant you," she told him.

"I'm not a present," he giggled.

Candace stepped into the room. "Momma's right." She came up and sat beside Jameson. "You are the best present we could ever ask for."

Cooper grinned from ear to ear and then laughed. "I don't have a bow!"

"Do you want a bow?" Jameson teased, tickling him gently.

"No!" he laughed harder.

"Do you know what I want for Christmas?" Jameson asked Cooper.

"A new tool belt?"

Candace snickered. Jameson was always looking at tools. She caught the sparkle in Jameson's eyes. *Santa might have that one covered.*

Jameson nodded. "That'd be nice, but what I really want?"

"New pencils?" Cooper was enjoying the guessing game.

Candace listened, enjoying Cooper's innocence and the emotional light in Jameson's eyes.

"What I really want is to watch you open all your presents tomorrow," Jameson said. "That's all I want."

"But you need presents too," Cooper said.

Candace patted Cooper's leg. "Don't you worry," she said. "Santa won't forget Momma. Even if he did, your message would remind him."

"Yep. But, what if he doesn't have your presents on his sleigh?"

"He's magic," Candace explained. "How do you think he gets down chimneys?"

"Right!" Cooper bounced on his bed.

Candace pulled his blanket up around him. "Now, you'd better go to sleep so that Santa can do his job. You know, he waits until you are sleeping to visit."

"How will he know?" Cooper asked.

Candace winked. "Magic," she reminded him.

Cooper nestled into his bed and pulled the covers up to his chin. He closed his eyes tightly.

Candace smiled. "Goodnight, sweetheart." She kissed him on the head.

"Night, Coop," Jameson said. She kissed him. "We love you."

Cooper pried one eye open. "Love you too," he said. He shut his eyes tightly again.

Candace led Jameson from the room.

"Why is he so worried Santa will forget us?" Jameson wondered aloud.

"He's home, honey. I suspect that deep down, Cooper feels the same way we do."

"What do you mean?"

"I mean this is the greatest gift he's ever gotten. Sounded to me like no matter how bad things got, someone always made sure Santa found Cooper." Candace could tell Jameson was a bit lost. "I've been traveling. Lots has been happening these last few months," she said. "I think Santa is something he's always been able to count on. He wants that for us too."

Jameson shook her head. "Guess it was worth my asparagus."

Candace chuckled. "I'm sorry about your vegetables."

Jameson rolled her eyes. "Easy for you to say. You've got enough fortune cookies stashed away to survive Armageddon."

"Pick a food that reindeer don't eat," Candace suggested. She started heading toward the stairs.

"How do you know they don't like fortune cookies? You're the one who said Santa is magic! Maybe he tells fortunes too," Jameson called after her.

Candace laughed. *Lunatic.* "Maybe you should write a letter to Santa and ask," she called back.

"Who's writing a letter to Santa?" Marianne asked when her mother stepped into the living room.

"Jameson," Candace replied. "She wants to see if the reindeer will accept my fortune cookies as a substitute for her asparagus."

Marianne shook her head. Jameson appeared behind Candace.

"Laugh it up," Jameson said. "I can get a supersize bag of fortune cookies for less than a bundle of that asparagus."

"You really are hung up on that," Michelle commented. She spooned some ice cream into her mouth and flopped onto the couch. "Hey? Where is Grandma? I thought she was going to be here?"

Candace nodded. "Jeffrey surprised her this morning. She'll be over for dinner tomorrow."

"She could have brought Jeffrey over," Marianne said.

"I think he might have wanted a little time with her today," Candace's tone told everyone to drop the subject of Pearl's notable absence.

Scott was sitting halfway under the tree trying to put together a train track for Spencer and Cooper. He groaned and threw the instructions aside. "There are two architects here. Do you think one of you could help me?"

Jameson looked at Melanie and shrugged. "You bought it," she reminded him.

"So?"

Jameson shrugged again. She picked up the instructions and handed them to Melanie.

"Why do I have to do it?" Melanie asked.

"Practice," Jameson grinned evilly. "You're going to have to do it times two, so you might as well start now."

Melanie looked at Michelle for help. "Don't look at me. I'm still trying to figure out the birthing part."

"I thought this is what grandparents were for?" Melanie looked at Jameson.

"No," Candace said. "Grandparents provide the house, the meal, and the fresh produce to ensure Santa's arrival. Parents get to do Christmas construction."

"Hey!" Scott called out. "You have Coop!" he pointed at Jameson.

Jameson nodded. "Yep. But I bought things Coop has to construct himself like Legos." She accepted Candace's hand and followed her to the kitchen.

Marianne pulled herself from the couch and followed the path Candace and Jameson had just taken.

"Where are you going?" Scott called after her. "There's still Maddie's kitchen to put together."

Marianne shrugged. "You bought it, honey. I told you to get the Easy Bake oven."

"That's so lame," he said. "Shell? Help me out here?" Scott pleaded.

"Don't look at me," Michelle said. "I can't draw a straight line."

Melanie snickered.

"You know what I meant," Michelle threw her napkin at Melanie. "Mel will help you." Michelle got up and started toward the kitchen.

"Why me?"

"Like JD said, double duty next year."

"Why do you get off the hook?" Melanie asked.

Michelle turned around. "Hey, I have to figure out how to pump my breast. You get to play with toys." She turned and walked away.

Melanie and Scott looked at each other. Melanie threw up her hands. "Hand me the directions," she said.

"Giving in already?" Scott asked.

"Trust me; it's safer. She's been obsessing over this pump thing for weeks. She's not even due for six months. I'll finish the train. You start on Maddie's kitchen."

Scott laughed. "They're all a little nuts."

Melanie smiled. "Yeah," she agreed. "I think that's why we love them, though."

Scott sighed. He got up and pulled a giant box from the corner of the room. "Legos," he mumbled. "Why didn't I think of that?"

Christmas

Cooper rushed for the tree. He rushed past the train set and Maddie's kitchen.

"What are you looking for, Coop?" Marianne asked him. He whispered in her ear. Marianne nodded. "Oh." She took his hand and guided him through the mass of presents. She pointed to two boxes wrapped in red. "Right there," she whispered in his ear.

Cooper grabbed the boxes and turned to the family triumphantly. "He remembered!"

Candace was caught off guard when Cooper bounded into her.

"Here Mommy," he handed her the boxes. "Santa brought those for you and Momma."

"Thank you, Cooper."

"Open them!"

"Don't you want to open yours first?" she asked him. Cooper shook his head no. Candace handed Jameson her box and smiled at their son. "You want us to go first?" Cooper nodded again. "Okay."

"Should we do it together?" Jameson asked Cooper.

"Yep!"

Jameson nodded to Candace and the two began to unwrap their presents. Jameson lifted the top of the small box and held her breath. She could hear Spencer and Maddie's delighted giggles in the background, but it sounded far away to her. Inside the box was a silver heart necklace. It was simple. The only jewelry Jameson ever wore was her wedding ring. She lifted the pendant and looked at it. Engraved around its edge were the words *Cooper's Momma*. Jameson looked at Candace, silently asking if she was responsible for the gift.

Candace shook her head. She showed Jameson the contents of her box. Jameson looked at the gold bracelet Santa had left for Candace. A thin bar of gold was highlighted by two small diamonds. On the bar, the words *Cooper's Mommy* had been engraved. Candace took a deep breath and looked at Cooper. "Did you ask Santa for these?" she asked him.

"Yep," he answered proudly. "Dylan said he got his moms neckwaces."

"Necklaces," Candace gently corrected him.

"He has two moms like me."

Candace smiled at Cooper. "Thank you for asking Santa to bring us something so special," she said.

"Marianne helped," he told her.

Candace nodded. She leaned in and kissed Cooper on the cheek. "I will be sure to thank her too," she promised.

Jameson cleared her throat. "I can't believe Santa knew what to get me," she said. She fastened the necklace around her neck and smiled.

Cooper beamed.

"Now, you go on," Candace told Cooper. "And open the presents Santa left under the tree for you."

Cooper ran off to join Spencer and Maddie. Candace closed her eyes.

Jameson kissed Candace on the cheek. "He really is the coolest kid ever."

Candace nodded. "Yes, he is," she agreed. Spencer was playing with his train and Maddie and Cooper were exploring her kitchen. The wrapped presents sat nearly untouched. She laughed.

"They still have about a hundred things each to open," Jameson whispered.

"They will. Enjoy the peace while it lasts," Candace advised. "It'll last all of about ten minutes—if we're lucky." She captured Marianne's glance and squeezed Jameson's knee.

Jameson watched as Candace made her way over to Marianne. Her hand took hold of the charm resting on her chest. "Coolest kid ever," she muttered.

Candace looked at Marianne and shook her head. "You're too much," she said.

"Me?" Marianne questioned.

"Cooper said you helped him with Santa."

Marianne shrugged. "I guess he told Dylan he was worried that Santa wouldn't bring you anything because he didn't think old people wrote letters to Santa."

Candace chuckled. *Old people?* "I see."

"I helped him with his letter is all," Marianne said. "I saved it for you."

Candace squeezed Marianne's hand. "Thank you. You did too much."

"No," Marianne disagreed. "I told Shell about it. I wasn't sure what to get. Cooper just told Santa that his mommies needed something special like a necklace. Shell's the one who went and got the gifts."

Candace nodded. She leaned in and kissed Marianne on the cheek. Michelle and Melanie had headed home the previous night. They were due to arrive in time for dinner. "I'll be sure to thank her." She made her way back to Jameson.

"Legos!" Cooper screamed.

"Score one for Momma," Jameson grinned. She laughed watching the kids tear through one present after another. She felt Candace's hand on her knee. "What is it?" she asked Candace.

"The kids," Candace said. "Seems Marianne helped Cooper with his letter. Shell had our gifts made."

Jameson was not surprised. All of Candace's children had a heart of gold. All of them adored Cooper and worshiped their mother. "I take it back."

"What?" Candace asked.

"We have the coolest *kids* ever."

Candace took Jameson's hand. "Yes, we do."

"Coop!" Spencer's voice bellowed. "You got a walking dinosaur!"

Jameson looked at Candace. "Who..."

"Score one for Mommy," Candace said with a smirk.

"We are the coolest moms ever," Jameson said.

"I can't remember the last time anyone called me, 'cool.' Old, Nana—yes, cool..."

"You're totally cool," Jameson teased. "You're the hippest nana I know. And," she leaned into Candace's ear. "The sexiest one too."

Candace rolled her eyes. "You're nuts."

"Yeah, you've mentioned that. But am I a sexy momma?" Jameson wiggled her eyebrows.

Candace burst out laughing.

"What's up with your mom and JD?" Scott asked Marianne.

Marianne smiled. She was grateful to see her mother relaxed and happy. She patted his hand. Candace had mentioned the night before that she planned to pretend there was no campaign, no governorship, and no media for as long as she could get away with it on Christmas. "It's the calm before the chaos," she commented. She laughed when her mother was coaxed onto the floor to see Maddie's newest toy. Cooper's new remote controlled dinosaur was dueling with a remote controlled car that Spencer had gotten.

"This is what you call calm?" Scott asked.

"Want out?" Marianne asked him.

Scott squeezed her hand and pretended to think about it. "Not before I get my presents."

Marianne stared at him for a minute before cackling loudly.

"Momma!" Cooper called for Jameson.

Jameson waded through a wad of colorful wrapping paper and sat beside Candace. She leaned into Candace's ear. "You think I'm a lunatic? This is a regular asylum."

"I wouldn't have it any other way," Candace said just as Cooper's dinosaur crashed into her. She feigned terror which sent the kids into a fit of giggles.

"Come on, Coop. Let's take them in the kitchen where there's room!" Spencer and Cooper ran off with their new toys with Maddie hot on their heels pushing a toy shopping cart.

"That might get ugly," Jameson observed. She made her way to her feet and offered Candace a hand up. "I should pick this mess up."

Candace grabbed Jameson's hand and led her toward the kitchen. "It'll be there after coffee and Jurassic Park in the kitchen," she said.

Marianne watched Candace lead Jameson away. Scott tried to discern what she was thinking. "Are you okay?" he asked.

"Yeah," Marianne said. "Just realizing how much I'll miss them." She saw Scott's confusion. "This time next year she'll be getting ready to move into a new white house."

"If she wins," he said.

"She'll win."

"You sound sure. A lot could happen between now and then."

Marianne sighed. She was certain that a lot *would* happen in the next year. Some people might have called it a sixth sense; Marianne felt the future in her bones. "A lot will happen," she said. "That won't change the outcome."

"You don't want her to go," Scott observed.

"She's my mom," Marianne gave her answer. "She might be some people's great hope and some people's greatest fear; to me? She's just Mom."

Marianne got up and began the task of cleaning up the room.

"Marianne?" Scott took hold of her arm. "She'll still be your mom."

"I know. I just want to enjoy our chaos today before I need to deal with the whole world's tomorrow."

Marianne concentrated on the task at hand. She could hear her mother and Jameson laughing in the distance as their son and grandchildren playfully taunted them. She savored the sound. She'd grown to love having them all close. For some reason, reality seemed to hit her today. Washington DC was not a million miles away; it was not next door either. She took a deep breath. Within days, Candace's life would transform into a whirlwind of activity and travel. Nothing would ever be the same again for any of them. Marianne knew that. It's why her mother was determined to enjoy this holiday in the familiar, loving chaos their family always conjured. She closed her eyes and willed herself not to succumb to the melancholy creeping through her. *I'll miss you, Mom. I'll miss all of you.*

Chapter Sixteen

"Governor Reid," Jerry Barr looked at Candace. "Senator Keyes has said on the campaign trail that values can't be compromised. You have a long history of working with people on the other side of the aisle. Some would say to the detriment of your values. As president, how do you intend to move your agenda ahead without compromising your most strongly held beliefs?"

Candace smiled.

"Oh, boy," Michelle whispered to JD. She was positive the world was watching a collected, calm, affable Governor Reid. Michelle recognized her mother's smile as one that was laced by displeasure.

"She'll be fine," Jameson assured Michelle.

Candace nodded to the moderator. "That's an interesting question." She took a deep breath. "Politics isn't as complicated as some people make it out to be," she said. She looked out at the audience gathered. "Everything in life is created by and managed by people. Compromise is necessary if you hope to create meaningful change, whether that's in your personal life or for the world."

"But, what about your values?" Barr asked.

"I'm getting to that," Candace said politely. "First, I think it's important to understand what I value. What I value most in life is people. Life—all the aspects of our lives—are guided by and made meaningful by the people in it. That's what drove me to seek office years ago; the idea that someone like myself who has been given every opportunity has an obligation to help create those same opportunities for others." She looked back at the moderator. "When you say the word, 'values' you're referring to specific political issues that we've come to put in 'values' terms: marriage equality, for instance. A woman's right to choose, affirmative action, worker's rights, immigration reform, healthcare—these are the values that Senator Keyes is referring to. Those issues are deemed 'values' specifically through a religious lens in our country."

Barr nodded. "And, you have a history of compromise."

"I do," Candace agreed. "When I believe compromise is in the best interest of the people I was elected to serve. What I have never compromised is my commitment to fairness and equality."

"Senator Keyes?" Barr turned. "Your response."

"Governor Reid voted twice in the senate for bills that tightened restrictions on immigration and agreed to amendments that increased health care deductibles for middle-class Americans in order to get a piece of legislation she sponsored passed. There are two clear examples of compromising what she espouses as her value on people, even breaking with our party in the process. In my estimation, that is compromising one's values. On the hot button issues, the governor makes impassioned pleas. People look at her life rather than her voting record. It's her voting record that reflects her values and what she will do if elected. That is decidedly holding up the establishment's views, not her values."

"Governor Reid?"

Candace took a deep breath. She needed to banish the sarcastic response she heard taking shape in her head. She looked at Senator George Keyes and smiled. *Opportunistic son of a bitch.* "Senator Keyes is correct. I've often found myself in the difficult position of weighing whether to abandon my support for a piece of legislation. What I think is disingenuous about his assertion is that I have compromised my values to placate the establishment. Senator Keyes has offered two examples of instances when he believes my vote has betrayed my values. Let me address those specifically."

"Please do," Senator Keyes spoke.

Candace grinned. *Be careful, George.* "I will," she said. "The first you are referring to I believe is a bipartisan bill that sought to balance the issuance of certain types of work visas. As I recall, that piece of legislation sought to create more opportunities for foreign corporations investing in our job force. Claiming I abandoned my principles because I supported a bill with intricate and specific limitations is a gross over-simplification."

"Correct me if I am wrong, wasn't it you that just said politics is not complicated?"

Candace nodded. "I did say that. I didn't say that legislation was not intricate." She took a deep breath. "I'm not going to defend my decisions to vote for those bills."

Keyes gloated. "That bill resulted in less opportunity for middle-class immigrants."

"Arguably—it did," Candace conceded.

"And, yet you espouse that you believe this country was founded by hard working immigrants?"

"It was," Candace said calmly. "It also is not the 1800s," she said. "Or even the 1900s. In 1960, when my grandfather was first elected Governor of New York, the population of the United States was just over 180 million people. Today, it surpasses 325 million, and it continues to grow. By the year 2025, there will be more than 345 million people living here. There are over 40 million American citizens living beneath the poverty rate, Senator Keyes. I'm not opposed to immigration. In fact, immigration is a key component in sustaining and growing our economy. I *am* in support of creating as many opportunities for our citizens as we can through a variety of initiatives. Those initiatives include smart immigration laws. I don't want to deny honest, hard-working people from coming to America to pursue the American dream. I do want to make sure it is done sensibly."

Keyes bristled.

"And, on health care?" Barr inquired.

Candace sighed lightly. "I don't think there is any secret on where I stand on healthcare. In my view, we fail if we do not provide for the health of our nation."

"You say universal," Keyes interjected. "You vote differently."

"There's never been legislation presented to provide universal healthcare," Candace replied evenly. "If I had ever believed we *could* pass it, I would have introduced it myself when I was in the senate. It would not have passed, and you know that as well as I do."

"So, hiking prices is your alternative?" he asked.

"Not one I enjoy—no. Again, you boil down a two-thousand-page bill to the size of a pinhead," she said. "The amendment you're referring to was not an amendment that sought to increase deductibles; it did limit restrictions on carriers. As I said, there's a case to be made that could have led to an increase in deductibles for some middle-class families."

"Hardly reflecting your values," he muttered.

Candace smiled. "That bill helped insure millions of people who had no coverage prior to its inception. I wish there were no compromises to be made. There are. And, when I'm elected; I can assure you that refining and revising our healthcare system will be one of my administration's top priorities. Doing that, I believe, will dramatically impact the economic outlook for many of the families struggling today. By doing that, we will be able to revisit and retool our immigration laws. Everything impacts everything else," Candace explained. "Every decision I have made or will make in the future is steeped in that understanding. I'm blessed," she said. "I enjoy the rights I have as a woman and as a lesbian because people fought and risked, and yes, even compromised from time to time so that I might enjoy the same rights as others. I've had the opportunity to get an education, access to medical care, and even the privilege to serve because people were willing to sacrifice along the way; people who held to their convictions while understanding the need to listen and compromise to create change. Compromise is not at odds with conviction. A leader has to know when compromise undermines her conviction and when compromise compliments it. I've never voted for a piece of legislation that diminished a woman's right to choose, that placed undue hardship on poor communities, or that was laden with racial bias. I never will."

Barr nodded. He turned to Keyes. "Interesting exchange," he said. "As a follow-up, have you ever wished you could have a vote back? With hindsight, have you ever wished you'd voted against a bill you supported? Senator Keyes, you first."

George Keyes nodded. "Of course. I try to limit those regrets," he continued. "That's where I believe conviction, as the governor put it, is an asset."

"Governor Reid?" Barr directed Candace to answer.

"All the time," Candace chuckled. "Hindsight, as they say, is 20/20," she said. "No one can predict the next minute. There are a million variables that change outcomes. So, yes; there've been times when I have looked back and wished I'd forecasted the outcomes better. There've also been times I've withheld my support and been surprised at the success a piece of legislation has enjoyed. It goes both ways. Senator Keyes is correct." She saw George Keyes smug grin. "Conviction matters. You can't change the past. That includes your vote. I don't dwell on the decisions I've made. I learn from them."

"On that note, I want to thank both the candidates for their time this evening. The next debate is February 23rd at The University of Pennsylvania. Thank you, and good night."

Jameson shook her head. "Not going to be an easy battle; is it?"

"Nope," Michelle said. "I'd like to know who's holding his leash."

Jameson watched as Candace accepted Senator Keyes' hand. "I wonder what she's saying?"

"Not what she wants to," Michelle quipped.

Jameson laughed. She walked with Michelle toward the right side of the stage. "Safe bet. What do you think?"

"About Iowa and New Hampshire?"

Jameson nodded.

"We need one. Both would be better."

Jameson exchanged a smile with Candace who was shaking hands with the crowd along the front of the stage. Candace gestured for Jameson to join her. "I hope I don't have to talk to him."

Michelle snickered.

"Jameson," George Keyes extended his hand.

"Senator," Jameson offered him a contrived smile. "Nice to see you again."

"You must be very proud of her," he said.

Jameson glanced over at Candace. Candace was laughing with what appeared to be a few college students. *You have no idea.* "I'm always proud of her," she said.

Keyes winked. "You remember my wife, Dorothy."

Jameson shook Dorothy Keyes hand. *Maybe if she clicks her heels a few times, you'll both disappear.*

"How are you, Jameson?" Dorothy asked sincerely.

Jameson smiled. "Can't complain," she said. "No one listens anyway."

"Isn't that the truth," Dorothy agreed.

Jameson was relieved when she felt Candace's hand press into the small of her back. She turned and was surprised to receive a light kiss on the lips from Candace.

Candace kept her hand on Jameson's back, sensing that Jameson's protective streak had kicked into high gear. "Well," she looked directly at Keyes. "Thanks for the spirited conversation," she raised her brow.

"I thought it went well," he said.

"I guess we'll see how well it went for both of us on Tuesday," Candace offered with a wink. "Best of luck, George."

"And you, Candace."

"Dot," Candace addressed Keyes' wife. She took a step away from Jameson and embraced the woman. "Good to see you."

Dorothy smiled at Candace. She had fond memories of conversations with Candace Reid over the years. She preferred that scenario to the current one. "Good to see you, Candy. By the way," she said. "That little boy of yours is about the cutest thing I've ever seen."

Candace glowed at the compliment. "Thank you." She took Jameson's hand. "We think so too."

"See you soon," Keyes said.

"Soon enough," Candace quipped. She chuckled when Jameson's grip on her hand tightened. "You okay?" she whispered to Jameson.

"I used to like him," Jameson muttered.

Candace laughed. She led Jameson off the stage.

"I don't know how you do it," Jameson said.

"Do what?" Candace asked.

"Make nice with assholes."

Candace kissed Jameson on the cheek. "Years of practice."

"Governor Reid!" voices began to call for Candace's attention.

"Go on," Jameson said.

"Meet you at the car," Candace promised.

Jameson nodded.

"And, so it begins," Glenn came up beside Jameson.

"Begins?" Jameson asked.

"This is the beginning, JD," Candace's campaign manager said.

"How do you think she did?"

"Real-time polling looks good," he said. "Doug and Grant will meet us at the hotel. We'll have a better idea in a few hours."

Michelle caught up to Jameson. "Hitch a ride with you and mom?"

"Sure. Do you think that SUV has a stocked bar?" Jameson asked.

"Need a drink already?" Michelle teased.

"No."

Michelle was confused.

"More like several."

Michelle put her arm around Jameson. "Tell you what; when we get to the hotel, I'll buy you a stiff milk to share with me."

"You had to be pregnant now?"

"I'm kidding. I'll buy you a drink from the mini bar."

Jameson rolled her eyes. "Big spender."

"On your dime? You bet."

Jameson shook her head. Michelle's teasing lightened her mood. She searched for Candace in the distance. Candace was answering reporter's questions good-naturedly and stopping to sign autographs for volunteers as she went, occasionally posing for a picture—smiling along the way. Candace's good mood was genuine. Jameson continued to be amazed by Candace's strength. She was sure that the tenor of the debate had irritated Candace at points. There was no evidence of that frustration now.

"What are you thinking?" Michelle asked Jameson.

"How much I love her," Jameson said truthfully.

Michelle smiled. She waited a beat and whispered in Jameson's ear. "Just be careful how loudly you profess that during Bible Study later. Keyes is staying on the same floor." Michelle climbed into the car.

"Thanks for the tip." Jameson laughed. "Maybe Keyes will wake us up with his…"

"Gross!" Michelle smacked Jameson.

Jameson was pleased with herself. "Never know."

"JD," Michelle grimaced. "I'd rather hear you and Mom."

"That can be arranged."

Michelle groaned. "I give up."

Jameson shifted to make room for Candace in the back seat when the door opened again.

"What are you two up to?" Candace asked suspiciously.

"Nothing. Shell was just wondering if Senator and Mrs. Keyes might find the Bible in the bedside drawer."

"I was not!"

Candace chuckled. "Lunatics."

Tuesday, February 4th

Iowa Caucus Day

"Momma?" Cooper looked up at Jameson. Jameson offered him a smile. "Where's Mommy?"

"Mommy is upstairs with Shell."

Cooper played with the fries on his plate. "Is Spence coming?"

"No, buddy, not today. But, tomorrow we're all going home," she told him.

"Mommy too?"

"Mommy too," Jameson promised.

Cooper picked up a fry and ate it happily. Jameson had taken away from the hotel room for a swim at the indoor pool and then for some dinner in the hotel restaurant. The commotion upstairs was too much for Jameson. Cooper had seemed content coloring in the bedroom while watching a movie. Jameson could hear the voices in the common area as people milled about. Everyone was making calls trying to discern where Candace stood in the polling. It was making Jameson nervous. Candace had stepped into the room to check on the pair and immediately detected Jameson's discomfort.

"Why don't you two go down and take a swim; get out of here for a couple of hours," Candace suggested.

"I don't want to leave you when…"

"It will be hours before we know anything."

"You're so calm."

"Nothing I can do now," Candace said. "Except wait and hope what I have been doing were the right things."

"What do you think?" Jameson asked.

"I think," Candace said as she placed a kiss on Jameson's lips. "That you should take Cooper downstairs to the pool and get away from here for a while."

"Is that going to look like…"

"It will look like you are taking our son to do something fun because that's what it is. Jameson—go. Take a swim, get a bite to eat. Spend some time with Cooper out of this room for a bit. By the time you get back, he'll be ready for a nap."

Jameson laughed. "No offense, you probably could use one."

"Do I look that bad?"

"Just tired," Jameson replied.

"I'm okay."

"What do you think?" Jameson asked.

"I'm trying not to," Candace laughed. "I think the crew out there is doing enough thinking for all of us."

"What's the news say?"

"What they always say," Candace said. "You know how it is; it's hard to tell, Governor Reid has been leading in the polls, but Keyes has closed in—it's always the same. They have 24 hours to fill."

"Are you sure you're okay with me stepping out?"

Candace kissed Jameson softly in reply.

"Okay. Call me if you need me to come back."

"I will, but I won't. I'll see you in a couple of hours."

"Momma?"

"Yeah, Coop?"

Cooper pointed to an advertisement on the table for ice cream sundaes.

"You want a sundae?"

Cooper nodded. "Can we bring one to Mommy?"

Jameson smiled. She doubted Candace would be in the mood for ice cream. *Fortune cookies—definitely.* Cooper's hopeful expression made it impossible for her to say no. It gave her an idea. "I'm not sure ice cream will make it all the way upstairs," she said. "What about if we send her something she *really* likes."

"Chicken wings!" Cooper squealed.

Jameson laughed. "You've certainly got Mommy's number," she said. "I think chicken wings would be perfect."

———

Shell answered the door to the hotel suite. "Can I help you?"

"Sorry, to disturb the governor," the bellman apologized. "But, Ms. Reid asked us to deliver this." He handed Michelle two large brown paper bags and a card.

Michelle immediately recognized the smell wafting in the air. *JD, you are too much.* "Thank you," she said. She turned to the room. "Anyone have some cash?" Glenn scurried over and handed Michelle a twenty-dollar bill."

"That's not necessary," the bellman told Michelle.

"Trust me; it's more than worth it," she said. Michelle shut the door and went in search of her mother.

Candace was sitting in the small kitchen area sipping a cup of tea. "What's that?" she asked Michelle.

Michelle set the bags on the table. "Smells like Chinese take-out. Read the card," she suggested, handing it to her mother.

Candace opened the card.

Thought you could use an escape. In lieu of Genie's lamp or knowing where the back door to this place is, this is the best I could do.

Candace smiled.

Thanks for making me take a break with Coop. He wanted to bring you a sundae. I thought this might be better. I asked for extra cookies.

"Of course, you did," Candace chuckled.

We'll be up soon. Cooper wants to check out the bowling alley.

Candace shook her head. *I'm sure that is all about Cooper.*

And, the gift shop.
I know it's not much. I wish I could do more. I love you.

"Mom?"
Candace closed her eyes.
"You okay?" Michelle asked.
"Better than okay," Candace replied. "Care to share my poison?"
Michelle took a seat beside her mother. "I thought you'd never ask. One question, though."
"What?"

"Do we open the cookies now or wait 'til the results come in?"

Candace laughed. "If Jameson were here, she'd just add 'in bed' to all the fortunes anyway. I say we go for it."

Michelle rolled her eyes. "Chinese Bible Study? Twisted, Mom."

Candace retrieved the boxes from the bags. "Don't knock it, 'til you try it, Shell."

Michelle grimaced. "I don't want to know."

"And, here I thought you were our billboard."

"Ha-ha. Pass me the chicken wings."

Candace passed Shell the carton. As usual, Jameson knew exactly what Candace needed. *I don't know what I'd do without you, Jameson.*

"How close?" Michelle asked Grant.

Grant shrugged. "Waiting for Polk. Still only 23% in."

"What about Linn?" Michelle asked.

"She's up by 3% in Linn with 67% reporting. Johnson County, she's down by 1%. That's 99% in."

"She's going to win," Michelle said.

Grant nodded. "Based on the margins she has in the rural communities, I'd say that's a safe bet now. The question is by how much," he said. "The more wind in her sails heading to New Hampshire, the better."

Michelle took a deep breath and looked at the three dueling TV screens at the far side of the room. "Come on, Mom."

"Candace?" Grant poked his head into the kitchen.

Candace greeted him with a smile.

"Polk is coming in now," he said.

Candace nodded. "I'll be right there." She looked at Jameson. "Ready?"

"You know, you already won," Jameson said. "I don't know why they haven't called it yet."

"The media? I'd say caution, but drama is the reason. The truth is, I'll be relieved to hear them say it. And, when they do? The margin will become the story and that will mean more."

"Not exactly like baseball, huh?" Jameson said. She took Candace's hand.

"Not exactly, no."

Candace and Jameson entered the large common area and took a seat on the couch. Candace took a deep breath, let it out slowly and focused her attention on the news coverage.

"It looks like we are ready to call tonight's Iowa Caucuses for Governor Candace Reid. We've waited for the last county to come in. Let's turn to David Pierce at our map for the results."

"Governor Reid has held a slight lead all night in Iowa. Polk County has the largest population. We've expected her to do well there. In the last few minutes, the outstanding precincts have begun to pour in. So, let's look at the map." He moved to the virtual map and began to touch it. *"92% reporting and Governor Reid is leading Senator Keyes 58% to 42%, which is above our predictions. That*

might change slightly; not enough for Senator Keyes to gain any meaningful ground."

"How does that look for Governor Reid going forward?"

"We've predicted that Governor Reid would come out ahead in Iowa. Polling suggested a tighter race, however. With her margin in Polk, she's looking at a 6 to 7 percent victory over Senator Keyes."

"That, of course, means she will receive more delegates," the anchor interjected.

"Yes. Delegates are awarded proportionally, so she will not be miles ahead of the senator in delegate count. The result suggest that the governor has gained momentum early on. I'm sure that her team is hoping this gives her the wind at her back heading to New Hampshire. She and Senator Keyes have been polling neck and neck in the Granite State. Another victory, particularly another one as commanding as this, would put her squarely in the position her campaign has been hoping for as Super Tuesday approaches."

"Well done," Glenn told the team. His phone rang. He smiled at the staff, stuck a finger in his ear, and made his way from the room.

"Congratulations," Grant looked at Candace. Before he could continue, his phone rang.

"The congratulations go to all of you," Candace said. "I know this was not an easy battle. So, let's enjoy this one tonight and make sure we know what went right this time, and what we kept from going wrong before we hit the east coast next week," she told them. She smiled at the room.

"Now, it seems like we have a crowd to address downstairs."

"How long should we tell the press?" Michelle asked.

"Twenty minutes," Candace replied.

"I'll make it happen," Michelle promised. She placed a kiss on her mother's cheek.

Jameson kept her eyes on Candace as phones continued to ring and one by one, Candace's staff readied themselves for her speech and their on-camera appearances. Candace remained still, breathing slowly and steadily as she processed the situation and prepared herself for the next step. "I'll get Coop," Jameson offered.

"No," Candace said. "I asked Dana to stay up here. Let him sleep," Candace said.

"Are you sure?"

Candace nodded. "Positive. I'm going to get myself together," she said.

Jameson's brow furrowed as Candace left. She watched as Candace closed the door of the bedroom they were sharing. She sat on the couch for a few minutes, observing the controlled chaos in the room. Candace's reaction to her win surprised Jameson. She chuckled at the realization that Candace's victory had set off another flurry of activity. *It never ends.*

"You okay, JD?" Dana came up beside her friend.

"I thought she'd be happier," Jameson replied.

"She's pleased with the result."

Jameson looked at Dana skeptically.

Dana smiled. "It's a higher margin than we thought," she sought to explain.

"Isn't that a good thing?"

Dana nodded. "It is, but it puts more pressure on her to win decisively next week. The good news is she should get some momentum from this."

"Should?"

"You know the drill, JD. I suspect she'll add a few appearances between now and next week. And, I would bet she's in that room calling Cassidy right now."

"Cassidy?"

"Yep."

"Why?"

"She's retooling her speech."

"Her victory speech?" Jameson asked.

Dana smiled. "It will be a thank you," she said. "Less about the win, more about the work ahead and the hard work of the campaign volunteers and staff. If it had been closer, she would have claimed victory more forcefully."

"You know that makes no sense," Jameson chuckled.

"Not in a sensible world—no," Dana agreed. "Right now, it's all about humility and managing expectations." Dana squeezed Jameson's arm.

"Dana?"

"Yeah?"

"Think she'll get another day off?"

"Between now and New Hampshire?" Dana asked.

"Ever."

Dana's compassionate smile gave Jameson her answer.

"That's what I thought," Jameson said.

"She's going to need you more than she ever has," Dana said. "For the next nine years or so." She laughed.

"Nine?"

Dana winked. "Oh, I'm counting on two terms," she said. She headed off to speak with Grant.

"Nine years?" Jameson closed her eyes and chuckled. "Cooper will be 14. Jesus! I'll be over 50!"

"And, I will be ready to retire," Candace's voice offered.

Jameson opened her eyes. Candace smiled at her lovingly and held out her hand. Jameson sighed and accepted it. She let Candace gently pull her to her feet.

"Candace?" Grant called over. "Shell said it's the five-minute warning. We should head down now."

Candace held up a finger. "I'll meet you in the hall." She turned to Jameson. "I love you."

Jameson could see just a hint of insecurity in Candace's eyes. She understood its cause had nothing to do with campaigns or elections. She smiled. "You'll never retire," Jameson said affectionately.

"You don't think so?"

"No," Jameson laughed. "Step back? Maybe. Retire? Never."

"Think you have me pegged, huh?"

Jameson leaned in and kissed Candace gently. If Dana's expectations held true, the next decade would be spent living a life Jameson never dreamed of. She pulled back from the kiss and smiled at Candace. Jameson had been living a life that surpassed any dream for the last six years. It had been filled with unexpected potholes and unfathomable joy. Looking at Candace, Jameson was reminded that she wouldn't change one minute nor one thing about the woman looking at her. "You surprise me every day," Jameson said honestly. "I wouldn't change it."

Candace wiped some lipstick from the corner of Jameson's mouth.

Jameson winked. She took Candace's hand. "So? Let's get moving before Shell calls you herself." She started to walk toward the door.

"Jameson?" Candace tugged Jameson's hand to stop her. Jameson turned curiously. "Thank you."

Jameson smiled. "You're welcome. Now, come on before I get blamed for making you late to your own party."

Candace let Jameson lead her away. She smiled at the faces she passed along the way. The five-minute trek to the downstairs ballroom seemed endless. She could hear the fervor in the short distance. She stepped up to the stairs of the stage, stopped and took a deep breath.

Jameson squeezed her hand. "What are you thinking?" she whispered.

Candace whispered back. "I was trying to figure out how many more times I have to wear these heels before I can retire."

Jameson laughed, surprising the people around them. "How about we just get to election day first?" she suggested.

Candace shrugged and leaned into Jameson's ear. "Will you buy me new shoes if I win?"

Before Jameson could reply, Candace was leading her up onto the stage to the sound of raucous cheers and chants. Candace stepped up to the podium and Jameson had to suppress her laughter. *If only they all knew I married a lunatic.* Candace's voice pulled her from her musings.

"Thank you, Iowa! Here we come, New Hampshire!" Candace's voice rang out.

Jameson grinned when the crowd called back. "Here we come White House!"

Here we come.

To be continued in:

ELECTION DAY

COMING IN JANUARY 2018: Commander in Chief

Visit www.thebumblingbard.com for more information